Missing Skulls and a Flying Coffin:
a Pink and Wong mystery

R L Jones

Published by LeRoy Press

A Cataloguing-in-Publication entry is available from the National Library of Australia

ISBN 978-0-9756107-0-1 (paperback)
ISBN 978-0-9756107-1-8 (ebook)

For Susan

Now all of us our wives must take
For Health and Race improvement's sake
The mother's an anatomist
And Cupid's with an oculist.

—Edward Dyson, 'Scientific Selection',
Lone Hand, 1907

Prologue
Creating a Specimen

It was dark, but that was what he wanted. The freezing wind created goose bumps on her exposed skin; the ragged garments provided scant protection as she hurried down the bluestone pavement. The wet flagstones glistened on and off under the lone flickering streetlamp. Arriving at the only wooden door in the red brick wall—one half of the laneway—she tapped gently. The door swung open and she entered quickly, shivering.

'I did it. I sold it at Berry's again. 'Ere's the money.' She handed over some bank notes.

'You owe me again. No one else will do your dirty work,' she continued. 'Why are we meeting here and not at the museum tomorrow morning, like normal?'

She pulled a brown paper package about the length of her forearm from her coat pocket and handed it to her companion. 'I got this as well, as you asked.'

'At least you can do something right, Issy,' he snapped. He partially opened the paper parcel to reveal a long, curved animal tusk.

'What is it?' she asked. 'Creepy if you ask me.'

'Diprotodon tusk. Not that you'd understand. For our special client. I've been told you were drunk and mouthing off about certain secrets at The Champion in Gertrude Street again last night. Too pissed to remember? I warned you.'

The damp visitor looked sullenly at her feet. 'What do yer mean? I said nothing. Who's spyin' on me?'

'Keep quiet,' the man whispered urgently. 'Go ahead … down this passage.'

He pointed. The damp visitor obeyed, as she was accustomed to do, and began shuffling down the dark passage. She didn't see the club as it descended onto the back of her skull, cracking it open like an egg.

He quickly leant over and, after feeling the absence of a pulse in his victim, wrapped some cloth around the skull to contain the blood. After putting on a mask, he dragged the corpse a little further down the corridor, until he came to an open door. The acrid smell of formalin was overpowering. Grunting, he heaved the body through the door and across a large room full of long tables covered in white sheets. He struggled with the dead weight through the another set of open doors into a smaller room full of baths. They were also covered in white sheets, except for one. The exposed bathtub was half full of liquid. He undressed the body and stood back with a look of surprise.

'Pregnant,' he muttered under his breath.

After this brief pause, he grabbed the cadaver under its arms and lowered it into the liquid. He then took a canula, which was attached by a tube to a jeroboam of fluid hung from the wall above the bath, and he inserted it into the artery in the neck. Another canula was then inserted into the cadaver's carotid artery in the neck with a tube leading to a drain in the floor to allow the blood to drain as it was replaced with preserving liquid. He then walked to a shelf and carried back another large fluid-filled glass bottle, which he poured into the tub. After a few such trips, the bath was full. He covered the bath with a white sheet like the others. After washing up in one of the white laboratory basins along the wall, he left, securely locking the door behind him.

Chapter One
Blue Babies

One Blue Baby
Heliopolis, Egypt
Wednesday, 7 April 1915, Dawn

Ambrose's eyes opened to the sound of the call to prayer. Disorientated with sleep, he almost fell as he rolled off his camp bed in the darkness. After quickly dressing in the still unfamiliar uniform, he stepped out of his tent into the dim light of the courtyard. Beneath his boots were intricately designed tessellated tiles, partially covered by shallow drifts of desert sand that had been deposited by the high winds overnight. His eyes wandered to the far corner of the courtyard, where an Arab worker had already begun the endless task of sweeping the sand away. Still drowsy, Ambrose was hypnotised by the rhythmically swaying broom, until eventually he blinked the sleep from his eyes and focused on the cluster of pyramids materialising on the horizon. These monoliths were framed by an emerging orange dawn and dominated by the oldest and largest—celebrating the Pharaoh Cheops since time immemorial.

Ambrose and his fellow student volunteers had been consigned to a tent in the courtyard of the Grand Heliopolis Hotel. He marvelled at the transformation of a luxury hotel into a field hospital for the Australian Medical Corps. The expansive courtyard was now a forest of army tents, used to keep those with infectious diseases away from the injured housed in the main building. He ruminated on his accommodation. He had hoped to be bedded down in the luxurious building itself, with its exotic Persian-Moorish revival architectural style facades and interiors designed along European lines. But no such luck.

It was freezing cold at night in the courtyard but at least they had been provided with extra blankets. He shivered. Apart from the cold, he was in good spirits. He certainly wasn't worried about catching any diseases from the infected patients in the other tents—most of the current occupants were soldiers with bad cases of venereal disease gifted to them in the brothels of Cairo. The few non-syphilitic patients had measles, a disease he had suffered as a child and so gained immunity—one of the facts he had learnt in his brief nine months as a medical student.

It seemed like an age ago since he'd started on this adventure, even though it was less than six months since his arrival in Egypt. After he'd completed his end-of-year examinations in Melbourne, he had deferred his course and volunteered as a medical orderly and stretcher-bearer. Within a very short time, he found himself on a troop ship to Egypt.

I'll resume my medical degree as soon as this war is over, in a matter of months, according to the Melbourne newspapers.

His tent companions were fellow students from the Melbourne medical school, although he was not particularly friendly with any of them. It was the first time these boys had been away from home and, after the initial excitement, the long sea journey had deflated their enthusiasm for travel. Especially as the *Kyara* had been an ill-suited and overcrowded ship. Ambrose, on the other hand, had spent a good portion of his nineteen years living in Java with his adoptive parents. Unlike most of his fellow volunteers, he enjoyed the travel, the sense of foreignness; he had loved the Javan food and dreaded the drab fare he faced when he returned home to Melbourne for school.

I'm tired of the canned food in the camp, he thought, standing in the sand. *Where shall I go?*

He had ventured only a few times into the nearby streets to find the cafes that could relieve him of his gastronomic boredom. He wanted to see more and explore.

I'll find one of those little places with the men smoking hookahs outside and have coffee or peppermint tea and grilled chicken and eggs and the various anonymous but delicious pastes on offer, all with warm flat bread and pickled vegetables.

He knew his main problem was that many of the cafes nearby had recently converted their menus to suit the mundane tastes of the newly arrived soldiers—especially those of the Australians, the best paid of the Empire troops. As soon as he left the camp precincts, Ambrose attracted a small group of young boys. With his uniform marking him out as a soldier, he presumed he appeared a profitable and exotic sight. He gave out a few boiled sweets and attempted to shoo them off as he strode down the narrow streets in search of suitable sustenance. He hailed a cab and climbed into the back seat. The interior smelled of tobacco and hair cologne, and the upholstery was rather the worse for wear. At least he was rid of his followers.

'Where do you wish to go, sir?' the driver asked in excellent English. He wore a large fez on his head.

'Take me to your favourite café, please. I would like an Egyptian breakfast.'

'I will take you to the best café in Cairo, young doctor. Are you sure you don't want Australian food?'

'Definitely not,' Ambrose replied with a shudder. 'Egyptian, please. What is your name and how is it that you speak such good English?'

'My name is Youssef Fanous. Cairo is an international city, and many of us are multi-lingual.'

Ambrose had leave for twenty-four hours; he might as well do a little sight-seeing after he ate.

'After breakfast, will you drive me around to see the sights?' he asked.

'It will be my pleasure. And you are in luck. Today is not a fast day, so you can try the full menu at my favourite café.'

Youssef ordered an excellent breakfast for Ambrose, just as he had imagined he would enjoy, and sat companionably at an adjacent table, drinking peppermint tea and smoking a communal hookah. After the best meal Ambrose had enjoyed since his arrival here, they set off.

Very soon they were cruising along the grand palm-lined boulevard that separated the newly built suburb of Heliopolis from central Cairo, adjacent to the pyramid district.

With the window open to let in a cooling breeze as the day warmed up, Ambrose remarked to Youssef, 'I've been told that this is the gayest and most cosmopolitan city on the face of the Earth. From my early impressions, it is a most beautiful place and must be endlessly fascinating.'

'Yes. They say that this part of the city is a new edition of Paris—only more so!' replied Youssef.

Within a few hundred yards, they were amidst the medievalism of the Mâmalukes and, as they passed through, he was delighted to find himself in a suburb that dated from pre-Norman times and in which rose the magnificent citadel of Saladin. Palaces abounded everywhere, and the scenes on the Nile seemed just as they were in the picture encyclopaedias that had entranced him in his youth.

'Sir, I live nearby. May I stop there and speak to my wife, please?'

'Of course,' Ambrose answered. As far as he was concerned, the more he could see of how locals lived, the more fascinating his day off would be.

They drove up streets that gradually became narrower, surrounded on either side by two-storey mud-brick dwellings; children hung over the parapets that surrounded the rooftop bedrooms on each of the buildings. Before them, flocks of local children playing in the street scattered as his taxi appeared.

Youssef stopped and jumped out nimbly, leaving the engine running. He entered a nearby doorway, leaving Ambrose to entertain numerous children who gathered around him.

After a few minutes, a young man rushed up to Ambrose. '*Yumkinuk musaeadatay ya sayidi jayid*?'

Returning, Youssef intervened and an animated conversation ensued. Ambrose only picked up a single word that was repeated a number of times: '*kulira*'.

'Youssef, is he talking about cholera?' asked Ambrose.

'You know? Yes, young doctor. He is my cousin. His believes his little sister is sick with the cholera and he wants help.'

Ambrose had never encountered cholera, but medical students were taught of its horrible impact. Ambrose didn't have to think about it, remembering the heart-wrenching stories he had heard from his teachers and his oath to help heal.

He learned forward to instruct Youssef: 'Drive to the house. I will do what I can.'

Youssef and the young man jumped into the cab. The car screeched off and drove at speed around the labyrinth of streets until it pulled up in a cloud of dust outside another mud brick abode. Ambrose could hear crying through the front entrance. They disembarked and entered the cool dim interior. On a bed of sorts in a corner was a tiny child surrounded by a large group of women, who parted as he approached the bed. The child was very still but breathing, her complexion was bluish, and she was emaciated. Ambrose knew from his studies that she was exhibiting classic signs of cholera, and her emaciation meant she had already lost too much fluid. Faced with the tiny body in front of him, and under the expectant gazes of so many, he was suddenly lost.

'Youssef, I'm sorry. I'm just a medical student, but I can confirm she does have cholera—I've seen it in textbooks. That means there is nothing I can do here. All one is able to do for a cholera patient is take them to the nearest hospital as soon as possible.'

'It will cost too much money for this family,' he replied.

Ambrose stared at the little child, and then at the expectant women looking so terrified and impotent.

'I'll pay. Let's get going to the nearest European hospital.'

Youssef translated the message, and immediately the women surrounded Ambrose, offering him their effusive thanks.

Youssef scooped up the tiny body. 'We'll get her to the hospital. It's in Qasr El Eyni Street.'

Soon they were speeding through the streets. They arrived at the hospital and rushed with the child into the foyer. On enquiring at the desk, a young doctor came to see them.

He shook his head. 'We can't treat everyone, I am afraid.'

'I'm a medical student with the Australian Medical Corps at Heliopolis. This child is a relative of my cab driver, who has shown me great courtesy. I'm happy to pay for any possible treatment,' Ambrose replied.

'We will do our best, but there isn't much we can do other than hydrate her and hope the cholera disappears. It can happen, if she has a strong constitution. We will have to put a catheter in her to deal with the dehydration. A few days and she might survive,' said the doctor. 'Pay at the counter, and I'll get a nurse.'

Ambrose and Youseff accompanied the tiny child as she was taken into a huge ward full of cholera patients, many of them terribly emaciated, blue-skinned, and near death. Poor nutrition had weakened these poor souls and, along with polluted water supplies, made them an easy target for water-borne disease.

The young doctor pointed out the few that were near death. 'In this ward are the patients who could raise just enough money to gain some treatment. Mostly the sufferers die in their homes. It is arbitrary, but luckily it is usually very quick. Many die; some recover over time, and a few don't contract the disease at all. It's a great mystery.'

After the child had been admitted and the money paid, Youssef drove Ambrose back to camp. 'I can't thank you enough, Doctor Ambrose. I and my family are in your debt forever. You must join us for a celebration.'

'It was my pleasure, Youssef. Let us see how she is in the morning.'

As the cab disappeared, Ambrose was overcome with shock and nausea. He rushed to the nearest bush, vomiting behind it.

*****

The following morning, Ambrose woke to someone shaking him.

'Get up, Ambrose old man. We're moving out today. Lemnos first, and then to the Dardanelles to give the Turk a bloody nose. Some place called Galliopoli. Wake up, won't you? We're on our way.'

Another Blue Baby
Wednesday, 17 August 1921
Gertrude Street, Fitzroy, Melbourne, Australia

Ambrose stared vacantly out the window, raindrops dribbling down the grubby glass. His gaze settled on a few dead flies on the windowsill; appropriate props, he thought, for the net curtains that were grey rather than pristine white. He absentmindedly took a bite from a cheese and pickle sandwich and sipped his cup of tea. The tea was cold, and the sandwich was stale—curling up at the edges, having been left some hours ago by Caitlin, the receptionist. He'd been too rushed off his feet earlier to eat lunch.

Looking down into the street and feeling a little depressed, he watched two drab-looking women, battling wind and rain under a straining umbrella. One was carrying what looked to be a baby. Were they heading towards his clinic? They certainly needed a good reason to be out in this weather.

A pickle fell on his shirt and rebounded onto the windowsill. It was a mustard pickle. Yellow. He cursed and wiped the stain, just making it worse. He returned to his sandwich. The day had begun insignificantly enough, he thought, with a normal progression of coughs and sniffles, boils to be lanced, gout, and teething babies. It was looking like another bad influenza season—still nothing like 1919 ... so far.

It's late, and I'm weary. He sighed.

The Oddfellows clinic was a long way from the wealthy private eastern suburbs or Collins Street with all the specialists' rooms he had imagined in medical school, but he had neither the medical contacts in Melbourne nor the funds; he had lived abroad in Java for most of his schooling. But now, since his return to Melbourne, he was more at home here in Fitzroy, a suburb on the wrong side of Melbourne society. He had also gained a measure of respect for many of his patients. Meeting them had brought him to the realisation that they were, by and large, poor but hard working, and they paid what was for them quite a large sum of their weekly earnings so they could belong to the Oddfellows Friendly Society. Membership of one of these workers' cooperatives provided them with services from health care to funeral expenses.

Ambrose thought of the patients he'd seen so far today. Mostly good souls who valued what he had to offer: working class, many of them new migrants, all clinging to those markers of decency that make them the 'respectable' poor. Ambrose stared at his reflection in the glass, observing the well-cut suit, pressed cotton shirt, and paisley bowtie.

I am still dressing the part for those affluent environs from which I seem so far … well, mostly.

He stared down at the scruffy brogues on his feet. *At least I don't have to worry about them here, or indeed a pickle stain.*

*****

23 Faraday Street, Carlton
Twenty minutes earlier

'Mother, mother!' Ruby called frantically. 'Little Iris has come on all funny!'

Kathleen O'Donohue bustled into the room removing her apron, the smell of a cake in the oven wafting in from the kitchen. She stared at the baby in the cot as she stroked her tiny head.

'Oh dear, oh dear … she's odd looking, ain't she? I was hoping she'd pick up today. We'll 'ave to take 'er to the clinic. I pray they will see us. Hurry, wipe 'er down again and wrap 'er up. It's cold and rainin' outside. Get yer coat and brollie … Quick girl!'

After frantically rushing around, the two women and the baby, all wrapped up against the wind, braved the outside and slammed the door. Bracing themselves against a sudden gust of icy wind, they walked briskly along Faraday Street towards the Nicholson Street tram stop, just fifty yards away. After arriving at the tram stop, they were lucky and only had a short wait.

'God's will,' Kathleen whispered to Ruby.

A few minutes later they were decanted from the relative warmth of the tram onto the pavement outside the depot on the corner of Gertrude Street.

'Hurry now, girl, this is no place to dawdle,' Kathleen snapped.

Crossing Nicholson Street was like crossing the Rubicon—or as Kathleen thought, *a different world*. Respectability was replaced by disorder and decay. Some street urchins had followed them and so she urgently pointed to the Oddfellow's medical clinic further down Gertrude Street. The two women and the baby walked quickly under the umbrella in the rain the short distance from the depot up Gertrude Street to the clinic. Pleased to have arrived at their destination, Kathleen climbed the stairs and entered, followed by her daughter. They removed their coats, placing the umbrellas in the elephant foot holder provided, and approached the receptionist's desk, all the while Kathleen inwardly reciting her rosary, fiddling with her beads.

'Excuse me, miss, but we need to see the doc urgently. Little Iris 'ere is very sick and we don't know what to do. I'm Kathleen O'Donohue, and I'm on your books and up to date, I am.'

'If you don't have an appointment, you can't see Dr Pink. He's on his own today as the other doctor has called in sick. You'll have to make an appointment for tomorrow,' the receptionist replied.

'Miss Caitlin O'Shannessy, you may not recognise me, but I know your mother from St John the Baptist in Clifton Hill. We've taken the Mass together.' Tears welled up in Kathleen's eyes. 'Little Iris might die if she'd not seen today. Will you deny her a chance?'

Caitlin seemed surprised at first, but after a moment's thought she burst out, 'O'Donohue … I remember now. My mother has spoken of you. As for your baby, they all say that the babies will die, and lots do I'm afraid, Mrs O'Donohue, as you well know. I'll ask Dr Pink as a favour because you know my mother.'

*****

Ambrose's reverie over his late lunch had been interrupted by the hushed but intense conversation in the front office. He entered the waiting room to investigate.

'It's all right, Caitlin, I'll see them. Come in.' He gestured to the door.

Ambrose was unsurprised to recognise the two women as those he had just seen outside the window.

'How can I help? Why is it urgent?' he asked.

'Here, Doctor,' Kathleen burst forth. 'We can't afford too much, but we're desperate! My niece Florrie's baby here ... I can't do nothing with her!'

'Put the baby on the inspecting table,' he directed, at the same time clearing it of several bottles, jars, and other medical parapher-nalia that had found their way there from the overcrowded bench.

'Unwrap the infant please, Mrs O'Donohue,' he ordered. Looking at the younger woman, he asked, 'Are you Florrie? Is this your child?'

'Oh no, Doctor,' she replied, blushing.

'This baby is my little grand-niece, Iris,' Kathleen interrupted. Pointing at the younger woman, she added, as if an afterthought, 'And that's my girl, Ruby.'

She placed Iris on the examining table. Unwrapping the clothing around the child, Ambrose's next questions about the whereabouts of Florrie, her mother, faded from his mind. What was before him was truly disturbing. On the table lay a malnour-ished baby, the lower part of her body smeared with watery diar-rhoea, her skin almost shrivelled and bluish.

Heaven's above, she looks just like the child in Egypt ... the one with cholera. He still saw her at times in his dreams of the war. *Had she survived? Had the saline drip been able to save her?*

He'd never been able to return to Egypt to find out. Never knew her name or who to contact. After the horror of Gallipoli, higher command had realised their foolishness in wasting future doctors for short-term stretcher bearers, and those medical students who had survived, including Ambrose, had been put on a boat to return to Melbourne for medical school.

This child couldn't have the same disease as the little Egyptian girl. It's simply not possible … not here in Australia?

Ambrose shook himself out of his reverie, aware of the strained silence and the two women watching him. He went immediately to the wash basin and scrubbed his hands, the only noise being the faint clicks of Kathleen's rosary beads.

'Why haven't you brought her to someone before?' he exclaimed. 'You may well be too late! If it's cholera, it could well be too late.'

'Cholera!' Kathleen exclaimed. 'I've heard something about that … isn't it what the Chinese get? My beautiful Iris couldn't have cholera! I only took her from the asylum a few days ago—with the permission of the super, of course. She weren't too good, but she was improving, wasn't she, Ruby? At least that was 'til a couple of nights ago.' She choked back a sob. 'The nice gent from the asylum brought her some fresh milk. I thought it would fix her up good.'

Ambrose eyed her. 'The asylum? In Kew?'

'Her mum Florrie's sick … in the asylum.' She pointed at her head. 'She couldn't feed her natural like. *She* don't have cholera!'

'We'll need to get her to the hospital, as quickly as possible. Take her to the children's hospital near the exhibition buildings.'

'We don't have a ticket,' Kathleen replied, holding back her sobs with great difficulty.

'You don't have a ticket? I hadn't thought of that. How forgetful of me!' *Everyone needs a ticket to get a place in the hospital.* He struck his forehead with the palm of his hand.

'I haven't got one, but I can arrange it tonight. Where do you live? Leave the details with Miss O'Shannessy and I'll come around to pick her up for admission to hospital. In the meantime, get some more fresh milk—and Mellin's food.'

'What's that?' the older woman sobbed, raising her arms in despair. 'I can't afford much.'

'It's a powder that you mix with water and milk—it's a substitute for breast milk. Who brought you milk? Is more coming? If not, you'll need to get some from a reputable dairy. Jones's around the corner is fine. Tell them I sent you.'

He placed a shilling coin in her hand and scribbled out a script.

'Go and get this ointment made up and apply it liberally after you have washed her. You have been washing her?'

'Oh yes, Doctor, but her skin is so bad, and then she gets the runs all the time and we can't get enough milk into her. We've been using made up formula until we got the milk.'

Ambrose grabbed a jar as more faeces escaped from the baby and managed to collect some of it into the receptacle. He sealed it shut, walked across to a jug and basin, and washed his hands again. As he looked in the jar, he became even more alarmed. The diarrhoea was the colour of water that rice had been cooked in.

'A classic symptom,' he muttered to himself with a growing sense of dread, almost panic. But of course, that was impossible. *It could not be here.* He shook his head incredulously. He'd take the sample to the new bacteriology lab at the university.

Men more experienced in the new science of bacteriology—those manning the new lab that had been set up in the medical school—would help him find the correct explanation, because this baby in front of him showed every symptom of being struck by cholera, and everyone knew there was no cholera in Australia.

As the women left, thanking him profusely, Ambrose grabbed the telephone.

'Reggie, can you get a ticket? I'll bring in a child later this evening. She isn't poor enough to attend without one. I want you to look at her ... Three hours ... That'll have to do then.'

Pausing only to cut short Caitlin's apologies for bringing him an extra patient, Ambrose took her offered slip of paper with Mrs O'Donohue's address and headed to his car to deliver the specimen to the university laboratory. He was sure Dr Hugo, the doctor in charge, would want to examine it urgently.

Ambrose had only made it as far as the door when he was halted in his tracks. The door swung open violently towards him and a young man rushed in. Under his arm, he clutched a violin case.

'Hedley Leroy, what brings you to the clinic?'

'Brose, give us a lift to the uni, will you? I've got a rehearsal. Thought you might be leaving, and I was in the area.'

'Of course, my car's parked outside. You're a lucky chap. I'm going to the medical school. Late again?' Ambrose practically ran down the stairs.

'What's the rush?' Hedley inquired.

'I need to get to the lab urgently. You'd hardly believe it. I'm struggling to get my head around it myself, but I think I just had a patient with cholera.'

'You're joking, of course,' replied Hedley.

'I wish I was! I can't get her to the hospital immediately because they haven't got a ticket, but Reggie says he can meet us with one at the patients' address at seven. Then we'll take her in my car after football training.'

It was raining lightly, and evening was setting in as they drove through the streets filled with office workers journeying home from work. Ambrose hoped the lab would still be open. He turned into Elgin Street, with its veranda fronted shops and rows of bare-branched elm trees.

'Who runs this new bacteriology lab?' Hedley asked.

'Dr Pascal Hugo,' replied Ambrose.

He's good. He worked with Louis Pasteur in Paris before he came out here. He was in the French colonies in South-East Asia … he would have seen cholera there, surely. Will he be able to see me?

There were many cars on the road, and his thoughts ran fast and furious. Ambrose became quite agitated, first when delayed by a slow-moving horse and cart, and then by some bicycles.

'HEY! GET OFF THE ROAD! Dim-witted bicyclists … trying to get yourselves killed,' he muttered to no one in particular.

'I hope you have more patience with your patients … if you get my drift,' said Hedley. 'It's not like you to get so wound up over nothing.'

'This could be much more than nothing!' snapped Ambrose.

The car veered left a little too fast into Swanston Street and executed a particularly hair-raising U-turn opposite the medical school. Ambrose slammed on the brakes at the entrance to the school and, looking around, struggled to find a free place to park. He cursed aloud, as a luxury Studebaker Big Six had parked in a way that took up enough room for several cars. He finally parked illegally, and they both jumped out. Ambrose rushed through the doors, waving to Hedley as he headed off to the Conservatorium of Music nearby.

Glass cases full of pathology specimens and bones lined the corridor as Ambrose hurried down its familiar path. A small eighteenth-century skeleton came into sight, staged as if it was playing a recorder. Ambrose gave a mental salute. Sometime in his years of education here, the salute to the skeleton had become an unconscious custom. The label read: 'Anonymous Parisian Street musician and beggar'. Apparently, it had been preserved to demonstrate the rare spinal disorder 'mermaid's syndrome'—or

Sirenomelia. This Parisian's remains had been brought to Victoria sixty years ago with the state's first medical professor. Many medical students found the pathology specimens, especially this skeleton, macabre additions to the corridor, but for Ambrose, they had been a comforting reminder of his commitment to medical study, the importance of understanding the mysteries of the human body, and of the eccentric collecting habits his parents made during their missionary travels.

Ambrose spied a light in the office fronting a larger laboratory with the title 'Lecturer in Bacteriology' affixed. But on arrival, there was no sign of Dr Hugo. Ambrose entered and placed the jar containing the faeces specimen on the table. Taking a deep breath, he scribbled a note to accompany the specimen: 'Cholera?? A. Pink.'

Putting it in writing, the idea seemed absurd. Everyone knew that cholera had not reached Australia, and thanks to the nation's strict quarantine regime, it never could. Shaking his head at his surely outrageous fears, Ambrose rushed back out of the office.

'Watch where you're going!' exclaimed the man Ambrose almost knocked over. To Ambrose's horror, it happened to be Sir Richard Butterby. Above Butterby's tall, powerfully built frame was a large head crowned with a distinguished head of grey hair. Underneath were searing blue eyes, a large equine nose, and thick, almost lascivious lips. He wore a white lab coat over a tweed suit. He was one of Melbourne's leading surgeons, with an international reputation as an anatomist and anthropologist. He was particularly proud of his large head, presumably as he had written and lectured extensively on skull size as a sign of racial and intellectual superiority. Butterby had the demeanour of one used to being obeyed, and his reputation amongst nurses and junior doctors was generally one distinguished by dislike and fear.

If I am to become a surgeon, it's professional suicide to cross the professor. Having nearly knocked him over, I will need to be even more assiduous attending his anatomy lectures at the university and his operations at Melbourne Hospital on Saturday mornings, even though the crowd of students is often impassable.

At all other times, he did his best to avoid the man, and his cranial theories.

'My apologies, Sir Richard,' mumbled Ambrose.

'Pink, isn't it?' the great man queried as he paused to peer condescendingly at Ambrose.

'That is correct, sir.'

'What the hell are you doing in this lab? Thought you hoped to qualify to be a surgeon.'

'Just dropped off a specimen from a patient of mine in Fitzroy. Looks a bit like cholera.'

Sir Richard exploded. 'Cholera? Rubbish! Never been here. Stick to facts, young man.' He glared at Pink for a moment. 'Haven't seen you at my public talks recently. Important to keep up with the right politics if you are serious about being a professional man,' he said accusingly. 'I'll expect you at my lecture tomorrow night, shall I? Young medical men like you need to take an interest in politics. Important that the better people run the country. Important national issues a young man like you should care about. Need all the support we can get. Join us in the Australian Protective League! Eight o'clock sharp! Fitzroy Town Hall,' he barked as he strode past Ambrose down the corridor.

'Yes sir, I'll see you then, Sir Richard,' Ambrose called as he continued on his way, though conscious he had already been dismissed from the mind of his departing senior. *The things one did for one's career.* He certainly didn't want to spend what little free time he had attending political lectures just to get on the right side of a senior surgeon.

Ambrose ran out of the building, jumped into his illegally

parked car, and headed south at high speed towards the football ground and training, noting absently as he did that the space-hogging Studebaker Big Six was now gone. If it was Butterby's car, the motor surely matched the man.

The traffic was heavy and the roads were wet and slippery but, arriving in the gloom, Ambrose marvelled as always at the stadium that seemed to him to be proudly advertising the sporting prowess of the young men of the new nation. Why, then, did it always make him feel a little inferior? He parked in the surrounding parklands and dashed through the entrance to the clubrooms. His nose was assaulted by the overpowering smell of eucalyptus liniment, which, he thought, along with sweat and leather, was the smell of football. Wooden lockers lined the walls not taken over by benches.

'Early as usual, Brosie,' shouted a teammate rummaging in a locker further down the room.

'Evening, Paddy!' called Ambrose, ignoring the jibe. 'My boots studded?'

'Yes sir,' replied his favourite trainer, Patrick Murphy, a large, bald dock worker and a staunch union man. 'Why're you here tonight, Doc? Coach said tonight ain't compulsory. St Kilda is out early because there's work at their ground, so they borrowed our facilities. If you get out soon, you can watch McNamara place kicking. 'E started a few minutes ago.'

'Dave McNamara?'

'That's right,' said Paddy.

Kitted out in his gear, Ambrose ran out onto the turf oval just in time to see McNamara, one of St Kilda's leading players, hoist the ball from the centre into the goal square—about ninety yards. The group of onlookers, who had stopped to watch the best kick in Victoria, applauded. Ambrose was impressed; McNamara still had it. He wondered if he could interest him in helping Wally, one of the neighbourhood lads Ambrose had been training. Next to McNamara, Wally had one of the most impressive kicks he had ever seen. Any club should have snapped him up by now, but he was half Chinese. Ambrose filed this unpleasant thought next to his nagging concern for baby Iris and decided it was time to focus on his own training.

Ambrose never made it past the warmup. The fading light meant he missed seeing a mud patch when he accelerated to take a mark. Having twisted his ankle, he would be out of action for a week, at least according to Paddy. He found Hedley sitting on a bench in the club rooms, waiting for a lift home, and hobbled over to him.

'That was clever!' Hedley offered cheerfully, his grin making it clear he knew just how well the sentiment would be received by Ambrose.

Ambrose refused to take the bait. 'You can come with me, but we are going home via a patient's house and the hospital.'

'I got my dates mixed up. The rehearsal's tomorrow. That's why I came straight here, to get a lift. Please!' Hedley would rather take a circuitous route than risk himself, or more specifically his instrument, to the rigours of a wet and windy Melbourne evening. They were soon on their way, with Hedley in the driver's seat.

'Lucky we arranged to meet. It'll be quite a few days at least before you can drive with that ankle.'

'Putting your limited medical knowledge to use at last,' replied Ambrose, referring to their first year of studying medicine together.

'Very funny. I remember our days together around the dissection table well—the smell of rotting flesh and formaldehyde comes back whenever I'm in your presence. I'm delighted that I quit sawing bones early and started a music degree. I prefer fiddling and making music, if it pleases your majesty!' Hedley nodded, as it was too difficult to execute a full bow from the waist and drive as well. 'At least you have a friend who will tolerate your awful cello playing.'

HONK! HONK!

'Watch out, you idiot! You nearly hit that car!' Ambrose exclaimed.

* * * * *

Number 23 Faraday Street was one of the small Carlton terrace houses that surrounded the larger residences from which the rich had fled in the previous decades. The efforts the O'Donohues had gone to in order to demonstrate their respectability were obvious in the house he faced. Apart from the usual wrought iron lace veranda, fence, and decorative brickwork or stucco in the form of busts of unnamed goddesses that adorned the other small terrace houses, number 23 was well-kept and clean. It was decorated with pots of geraniums and proper curtains in the window, unlike many of its poorer neighbours who had attempted to guard their privacy with newspapers stuck on the glass.

The injury sustained at training may have momentarily allowed Ambrose a respite from his fears for the little girl he'd seen earlier that day, but they had been with him ever since he had seen her, and now they flooded back even more intensely. As he knocked on the door, he could hear wailing inside—but not the wailing of a baby.

The door was opened by a man with an olive complexion and a tightly clipped salt-and-pepper moustache and beard, appearing to be in his fifties.

'Say, what do you want, sir?' His Italian accent was sibilant from the low volume of his voice, almost a whisper.

'I am Dr Pink,' Ambrose answered. 'I am treating the sick child living here.'

'Well, you're not treating her anymore,' the stranger replied. 'The baby has died. She should be with her mother. We have come to return her. You can leave, Dr Pink.'

'Died?' Ambrose was shocked. 'In that case, I will most definitely need to examine the child.'

'Apply at the asylum!' the man snarled.

At that moment, two large figures dressed in orderly's clothing appeared at the door, one clutching the baby. As he followed them down the path, pushing Ambrose aside, the stranger hissed, 'And we will certainly be asking for an investigation of your involvement in this death. You seem to have given the O'Donohue woman advice—bad advice it appears. Mentioning cholera to her was a very dangerous idea.'

They climbed into a large car that had just pulled up outside.

Ambrose froze. Strangely, he was also sure he recognised that car. He couldn't quite make out who was sitting in the driver's seat. Even more perplexingly, he could have sworn that the bundled child moved slightly as it was passed into the car. It sped off.

Another car arrived, and out jumped Reggie Robinson, waving a piece of paper.

'I've got you the ticket. We can take the child to the hospital.'

Ambrose stared at him, speechless, and then rushed into the house, but the women were inconsolable. Kathleen was muttering, 'They said she's dead,' over and over.

Reggie joined him. 'More trouble old friend?' he remarked, clearly unaware of the events that had taken place. 'I think you need a hobby to cheer yourself up.'

Chapter Two

The White Race

Thursday, 18 August 1921, 8pm

The next evening, Ambrose gate-crashed Hedley's violin prac-tice. Listening to Hedley endlessly practising scales was some-times almost more than he could tolerate after a day at work. As Hedley boarded with him, it was a regular experience.

'Butterby suggested in no uncertain terms that I was to attend his lecture, and I want you to come as well. I need company!' said Ambrose.

'I will not be coerced into attendance against my will. I'm struggling with this C# minor scale and I have a lesson tomorrow,' his friend replied.

The argument continued and Hedley was voracious in his complaints, but to no avail.

They arrived early for the meeting and parked on Brunswick Street, the main street in Fitzroy. Pools of light poured onto the pave-ment from the lit windows of the few shops still open. Also punctu-ating the ink-black pavement were dim rays of yellow from the few regularly placed gas streetlights. This meagre street lighting attracted trouble as well as moths. Indeed, a few groups of indeterminate fig-ures were slinking around corners and in shadowy recesses. These conglomerations of drifting humanity consisted of young men dressed in ill-fitting trousers and nondescript coats with flat hats hanging at various angles, mostly puffing on fags or the occasional short pipe. A few girls were scattered amongst the larger groups.

'Why didn't you park outside the hall in Napier Street?' Hedley asked as they walked rather briskly down the dark confines of King William Street, descending into the stygian gloom that hung over the maze of back streets.

Ambrose grimaced. 'At this hour, as soon as you leave the main street, a parked car becomes the object of great interest to certain criminal types that inhabit this neighbourhood. I should know—I work here. Better parked in a main street. The real troublemakers call themselves the Fitzroy Roses. Their leader is Squizzy Taylor, and this is his patch. So keep your eyes open. I thought another pair of fists might deter the louts that hang around the back lanes here.'

'Wonderful! It gets even better. You didn't tell me I was the bodyguard. Outrageous, when you know I depend on my fingers!'

They continued further into the pitch-black maze.

'Why are we going to this talk anyway? Every time I've heard you talk about Butterby's stuff, it hasn't exactly been complimentary. All that ranting about the "New Imperialism" in those long opinion pieces in the newspapers, and going on and on about reducing democracy and giving more control to the elites like him. It's enough to make me a Bolshevik!'

'I know, I know, but it's hard to get on in the surgical world, and well-nigh impossible without a patron. At the moment I have none. He asked me to come—it was practically an order really, and I can't afford to antagonise him.'

Hedley continued unabated. 'And then there's all his stirring up fear of foreign powers, especially communist Russia … and how the bloody Ruskis will bring revolution here with the help of the trade unions.' It seemed Hedley wasn't ready to give up.

'Yes, yes, let it go, Hedley. I agree with you: you should be grateful you don't have to listen to him prattle on about the white man's superior skull during lectures! Let's just listen, clap politely, and get out of here, and I'll treat you dinner,' Ambrose replied as they mounted the steps to the hall, the cold night propelling them forward into the light and warmth.

The large hall had a high wooden ceiling with a stage at one end. Hanging on the walls were the banners of the Girls' Friendly Society and other such worthy groups, and an honour board for those fallen in the last war had just been erected beside the one memorialising the Boer conflict.

The space was crowded. Ambrose recognised many faces, both medical professionals and students, at the front of the hall. A far more motley crowd lingered at the back. As Ambrose and Hedley tentatively sat down in the middle seats, both of them felt the tangible tension hovering in the air.

'Remind me again why we are here?' whispered Hedley.

Ambrose kept his response to an eye roll and continued to scan the hall for familiar faces.

Hell! thought Ambrose. *There in the front row is the man from the asylum with the Italian accent. Beside him looks like one of the large orderlies who had taken the child, along with some other large looking heavies. It looks like Gus McBride, the surgeon, is in the front row as well.*

The Italian looked back at Ambrose and seemed to recognise him, as he immediately leant across and spoke to the men, who turned and stared. Ambrose felt very exposed. The atmosphere was bizarre, he thought.

The introduction for Butterby was short. Then Butterby came to the podium and prepared to speak. As soon as he opened his mouth, the storm broke, emanating from the crowd at the back of the hall:

'*Stand up, damned of the Earth*
Stand up, prisoners of starvation
Reason thunders in its volcano
This is the eruption of the end.'

The rousing sound of the international socialist anthem, the 'Internationale', was deafening. Someone had clearly smuggled in an instrument, as a trumpet began accompanying the singing, while a group of men and women bashed the corrugated iron walls at the rear of the hall in time to the tune. To add to the chaos, another group at the rear counted out Butterby at the same time, as if he was a boxer who had been knocked out in the ring.

'ONE ... TWO ... THREE ... FOUR ... FIVE ... SIX ... SEVEN ... EIGHT ... NINE ... OUT!'

At the conclusion of the counting, cheers broke out from all the noisemakers at the rear of the hall.

Butterby had returned to his seat on the stage during the cacophony, glowering furiously at the rowdy audience at the rear who had forced him to silence. As the cheers began to die down, the chairman of the public meeting, Herbert Brookes, engineer and well-known public figure, moved quickly back to the podium and raised his arms.

'Gentlemen, ladies, I implore you to let the speaker have his say! What would you do if Lenin and his Bolshevik hordes came to Melbourne?'

'Teach 'em to kick a footy,' a wag at the back shouted.

'Smash the capitalists!' cried another voice.

The meeting descended into chaos again, and raucous laughter and handclapping filled the hall. The trumpeter began on another of his revolutionary repertoire, this time accompanied by a fife, voices, and corrugated iron percussion. The forces of socialism had come well prepared to this meeting.

Ambrose noticed Hedley starting to tap his feet to the rhythm, the musician in him coming to the fore. 'Not the time,' he hissed, hoping that Hedley wouldn't break into song.

They were unfortunately positioned, sandwiched between the furious Butterby supporters in the front and the wildly demonstrating crowd in the back rows of seats. Many heads had turned and were frowning in their direction. Many rose to their feet, scowling with contempt.

Ambrose stirred uncomfortably and turned to Hedley. 'Let's get out of here before you decide to join the Bolshevik choir. I'm doing myself no favours in Butterby's eyes witnessing this debacle. If he sees me now, it will probably only annoy him. This will teach me to follow the great and good!'

'Hey! Did you see that?' Hedley yelped as a shoe whistled past his ear.

Turning, Ambrose instinctively ducked as another object flew at speed, just missing his head on its way to the stage. The few police present ran onto the stage and began escorting the dignitaries off. Ambrose took his chance and elbowed Hedley. They rose and walked as briskly as possible to one of the back doors. Ambrose noticed an elegantly dressed woman wearing a red hat with some shadowy companions in the dark recesses of the foyer at the back. He certainly turned his gaze in that direction.

They exited into the cold, dark night to find themselves in a back alley. Suddenly the side doors at the other end of the building burst open, and a group of men almost fell out into the lane. The orderly who had taken the baby from the O'Donohues' house was in the lead. They looked around and, on seeing Ambrose and Hedley, one shouted. They began to move towards them.

Ambrose tugged on Hedley's sleeve, urging him to a run. 'Ooh … my ankle!' In all the commotion, he had forgotten his sprain.

'Grab my arm,' Hedley whispered loudly. 'Have I thanked you again for inviting me?'

Ambrose's twisted ankle was well bandaged, but a quick hobbling limp was all he could physically manage. Behind them, the sound of running leather on bluestone seemed to rapidly get closer. Ambrose accelerated as best he could while Hedley took some of his weight. They had reached the corner of Moor and Young Streets. If they ran down Moor, Brunswick Street beckoned with its shops and streetlights and foot and vehicle traffic. But sinister figures stood under the light on the corner. The alternative—along Young, parallel to Brunswick—was darker and offered some concealment and so, in the split second they had in which to choose, they instinctively crossed the junction under the lights and darted into the sea of darkness. It was difficult to move quietly or quickly while hobbling. They had managed to get about halfway down the block when Hedley pulled Ambrose up against a recessed wooden gate in a brick fence. The clouds cleared momentarily, and thin moonlight illuminated the scene.

'I can't hear running,' he whispered in gasps.

They looked back. The figures pursuing them seemed disconcerted now they had reached the intersection, their heads turning to look down the four exits from the crossroads, trying to catch a glimpse or a sound of the escaping pair. At the same time, a number of cars roared up into the intersection, and a group of men jumped out and began talking to the pursuers. They were pointing away from Hedley and Ambrose towards the town hall. After a brief conference. most of them headed towards the hall.

The smashing of glass shattered the silence. Men were running and shouting. It sounded as if a fight was breaking out.

'Psst. Hey, mister!'

Completely engrossed with the events at the intersection, Hedley and Ambrose almost jumped out of their skins. Then the gate opened, and a small boy partially poked his head out.

'What yer doing? Come on in, why don't yer?'

Without a moment's thought, they both slipped through the gate. On the inside, they discovered themselves in the backyard of a house. They were both still panting and alert for footsteps, so it was a little while before they focused on the young boy in front of them. In the dark they could just make out that he was barefoot and raggedly dressed and not too clean by the look of it. They couldn't attribute the bad smell to him, but only because of what looked like a pile of rotting refuse in one corner of the yard. The wooden back door of the house opened a little, and giggling emerged from the gloom.

'I know you, mister,' the boy addressed Ambrose. 'You're the doc from Gertrude Street. You helped me sister when she was up the duff the first time. Is Squizzy's mob after ya?'

'I have no idea who was chasing us, young fellow, but thank you for saving us. What is your name?'

'William McGregor … Will to yer, mister. You can come through the house and into the lane, if you like. That'll get yer into Kent and then St David. You'll lose 'em for sure!'

They nodded, thankful for their spot of luck, and followed young Will into the kitchen at the rear of the house. It was a tiny room with an iron stove and no fire lit. The walls were of cheap plaster and newspapers partially covering large gaps. A rat scurried into a hole in the wooden floor. The boards creaked and bowed as they walked past the few bedrooms containing a number of unconscious and semi-conscious people. The sweet smell of opium was everywhere. They reached the front door.

'I'd like you to come to the Oddfellows clinic next week, William, in Gertrude Street. Do you know it?'

Young Will nodded.

'I have no cash on me, but I would like to reward you. You've done us a great service. See you then.'

'Ok, Doc. I'll catch yer soon.'

They quietly exited the house and worked their way back to the corner where the car was parked. They were approaching the vehicle when a shout rang out, and behind them appeared a group of men running. It was the asylum orderly and friends again.

They must have been searching for us. What bad luck, thought Ambrose.

Ambrose threw his keys to Hedley after he opened the passenger door and climbed in. Hedley accelerated off just as Ambrose struggled to shut his door. At that moment, the group of men ran around the corner. They rushed forward in an attempt to grab Ambrose's car door handle, but Hedley pushed the accelerator flat to the floor and the wheels screeched. They heard rocks strike the back as he looked in the rear vision mirror.

'Follow my directions,' Ambrose said as he pointed for Hedley to turn right down Greeves Street, followed by a right turn into Napier.

They slowed down once they reached Napier Street, as a flotilla of vehicles arrived outside the town hall. The crowd were exiting, and many were milling around. They stopped the Riley halfway down, engine idling. Rocks were being thrown, and fighting broke out between the demonstrators in the hall and the new arrivals, who had clearly been called as reinforcements by the Australian Protective League. The figures were strangely silhouetted against the streetlights and the full moon—a puppet show of soldiers.

Ambrose's mind flashed back to the trenches. *No!* He banished the image from his mind … or at least he tried to. This was Melbourne and all would be well. Police cars passed them, and the crowd began to disperse. Relief and the sudden flashback had made Ambrose agitated as they drove home through the darkness.

'Who were after us?' asked Hedley.

'I'm not sure what made us targets, unless they thought we looked and sounded like "toffs",' replied Ambrose.

'Speak for yourself,' replied Hedley.

'I don't think it was the communists at the back of the hall,' Ambrose said. 'If that man from the asylum was involved, they must have been some of the hoodlums connected to the Australian Protective League. There are rumours they are forming a secret militia.'

'Who are they exactly?' said Hedley.

'Didn't I say? They were the group who set up the meeting tonight. You know, that new right-wing group set up to fight Bolsheviks and trade unions. Obviously, Brookes, McBride, and Butterby are involved. Also, the Italian doctor from the asylum. Is young Iris and cholera involved in this somehow?'

'Maybe, but perhaps they were just street roughs out for some money and fun? You said yourself this is a tough neighbourhood,' answered Hedley. 'Now I've kept my end of the bargain. How what about that dinner you mentioned?'

*****

They arrived home late, fed but not at peace after the night of action. Ambrose felt the need to return to the only place in the world that gave him any peace: the home he had bought with his parents' inheritance. Would he sleep tonight?

Even a good dinner had not restored his mood. The adrenalin of the chase in the back laneways of Fitzroy had worn off, his ankle ached, and he knew he needed to face the despair of the O'Donohues again, as soon as he could find any more information for them.

'I'm not feeling great, Hed. I think I'll go to bed.'

'Fine,' replied Hedley. 'I'll hold off on any late-night practice and get some sleep myself. Need a hand getting up the stairs?'

Ambrose shook him off and retired, with well wished goodnights exchanged. He limped up the stairway to his bedroom, then opened the door onto the veranda and stared out into the dark gardens. He hoped he had managed to hide it from Hedley during their dinner, but the events of the evening had been deeply unnerving. It was unlikely he would sleep well tonight. Rather than make the attempt immediately, he opened a bottle of scotch and poured himself a large drink.

*****

It was always the same dream, but with variations. It seemed like an old companion when it came. He was staggering through a labyrinth of trenches. Acrid smoke filled the sky as occasional explosions shook the ground. Bloodied body parts lay around as if carelessly misplaced by their owners. Music he vaguely recognised played in the distance—what was it? Desperate faces begged for help, but he could do nothing. 'I failed my exams,' he cried out to the disembodied voices that came from just outside his line of vision. He turned sharply, but they were never there. He walked on and on until he turned a corner. A number of coated mysterious figures, including one with a red hat, were coming for him with knuckle-dusters.

He woke in a sweat. It was still dark, and he thrashed about in his bed, regularly disturbing Molly, his Australian terrier, at his feet.

I wish Mum and Dad were still alive.

His studies in medicine had introduced Ambrose to ideas about heredity. He knew his own background would make him suspect to many. Only last semester, Butterby had delivered a scathing lecture on Sigmund Freud and his new ideas about psychoanalysis. He had argued that Freud's theories were a product of all that was deranged and perverted in modern thinking, and, far from a legitimate reaction to trauma, shellshock was a sign of a small head and mental deficiency. What would Butterby think of his dreams? Would he think his trauma was a sign of hereditary weakness? Would being adopted be linked to this?

All he knew about his natural mother was that she was related to his adoptive mother and had died in childbirth. His biological father had never been spoken of. He was told very little about him, and felt unable to force the issue as it clearly gave his adoptive mother such distress. Despite being devout Methodists, his parents had never given him any indication that he came from a less than normal background. Instead, they had welcomed him into their lives and their extended travels as missionaries in South-East Asia. Even when they decided he needed to return to boarding school in Australia, he knew it wasn't because they viewed him as a burden, only that it was what they thought was best for him.

These unproductive thoughts circled endlessly through his mind as he lay in his bed. In this state, even his choice of home struck Ambrose as a sign of a potential degeneracy. He knew eyebrows had been raised amongst his peers, medical and Methodist alike, when he chose to buy a house in Fitzroy, even though it was in the most salubrious part of the suburb.

He knew that 'Fitzroy' was also an English name that indicated the original holder was a bastard of a king. His circumstances were not so different. An orphan—although with no suggestion of royalty, of course.

Perhaps, deep down, he empathised with the insecurity of the inhabitants of this rundown suburb. The extreme juxtaposition of past wealth and current squalor that characterised Fitzroy certainly seemed to somehow mirror his own sense of growing internal disjunction—feelings he disguised with a respectable veneer of smart clothing and education. But that seemed more and more like window dressing to him.

He rolled off his bed, pulled on a dressing gown, filled his glass with whisky, and walked out of the room to the landing and up the ladder to the tower room. He stared out the southern window to the dark sky and the distant lights of the city. The atmosphere was brooding—a bat fluttered suddenly in front of the window, causing him to flinch. *Was that an omen?*

Home was 44 Alfred Crescent, a once-fashionable, elevated double-storey Victorian terrace house in North Fitzroy, purchased with the legacy his parents left for him. With a large ornate art nouveau veranda but without the stucco ladies who kept watch from every other veranda in the grand crescent, it had been modernised just before the Great War by a dentist. On either side of the grand front door were ruby glass panels with stylised etchings of fuchsias. The 'Fuchsias' was the nickname for his club, the Melbourne Football Club, a reference to the blue and red guernsey worn by the players, imitating the red and blue colouring of the common fuchsia flower. Understandably, the alternative nickname of 'red legs' was preferred in the heat of the battle. It also had a rather impressive tower from which Ambrose could see for miles into the central city and surrounding suburbs. He particularly loved the Edinburgh Gardens opposite, and walking through groves of elms and other majestic trees. In the summer, bands played in the rotunda at the weekend. He and friends would take some beer and wine and light a fire and cook lamb chops over a campfire for dinner if the evening was fine.

Ambrose often spent time with the local boys practising kicking for goal in the small sports oval amongst the trees and shrubs. This is where he had met Wally, the oldest son of his neighbour, Billy Koochew, a Chinese tailor who, with his Norwegian wife, had filled their small terrace with five children, many of them fanatical footballers. A few Chinese footballers managed to overcome the general mood of prejudice and play in football competitions, but only very few, and they were often given a bad time. Wally was particularly gifted at seventeen years old, and following his father in the tailoring trade when he could be wrenched from the field, he had become Ambrose's special protégé. Ambrose had even got him a tryout with the Melbourne football club, after considerable nagging. He had been accepted and was to play in the reserve team the following week, although a member had returned his membership when he discovered a Chinese name on the team lists.

It was the unfairness of it all that made him feel more and more part of Fitzroy. He had discovered that he could help people here—and he was changing himself. There was, however, the small matter of the dead baby Iris and the threat of action by the Italian doctor to deal with. But perhaps that was best tackled after a decent sleep.

Chapter Three
Debutante Blues

It was daylight, and Molly was barking in the backyard. Ambrose had slept well and long on Friday and had the day off yesterday as his wonky ankle meant he couldn't play football. He woke up ravenous, aware that he hadn't eaten very much yesterday and was unlikely to do so today unless he got himself out of bed, and went in search of food.

Ambrose descended the stairs and entered the kitchen to find the iron stove fully stoked, lit, and a kettle boiling on top. Hedley and Reggie were sitting at the table. He hadn't seen Reggie since the night the baby was taken from Canning Street.

Reggie was generally quieter than the rambunctious Hedley, appearing to view the world with slightly detached amusement. He was elegantly dressed, courtesy of Henry Bucks gentlemen's-wear store, an attribute he had passed on to Ambrose. Even more scrupulous than Ambrose about his appearance, he was currently sporting a pale linen suit, mauve shirt, and brilliant yellow cravat. The effect bordered on dandyish. Tall with narrow, slightly stooped shoulders, he had a thin, mobile face with a well-cut head of brown curls slightly receding. He was training at the children's hospital in Carlton as well as working in his father's practice in the city.

Ambrose's housekeeper, Mrs Simpson, was busily discussing the newspapers with the two young men. She looked up and redirected her attention to Ambrose, tutting and fussing as usual.

'I know you, and I knew you'd forget to buy food for the weekend. Mr Simpson went and got your usual order from King and Godfrey's yesterday. You can pay them next week—he put it on your account. Oh, and a delivery from Rathdowne Cellars arrived. More drink, I'd imagine!' Mrs Simpson looked unimpressed.

'Thank you so much, Mrs S. You're my guardian angel. You're only supposed to do for me three days a week. We'll need to discuss payment later.'

The neat little woman in her fifties started setting the table. She had grey streaks in her brown hair that was tied in a bun at the back. Her cheerful print dress and her quick smile could light up even the gloomiest day.

'Thank you for coming today, Mrs Simpson,' said Ambrose. 'You're a life saver.'

'No, I am not,' she replied briskly, 'but I wish you'd take more care of yours. You drink too much. We all want you to do well, you know.' She rummaged about in the meat safe. 'You have some cold cooked potatoes here. I'll fry those in some butter as well as some bacon and eggs. Then I'll be off—after I clean up.' The restorative scent of frying potatoes and bacon filled the kitchen. 'You sit down now, and relax. You're in the newspaper again. Here!' She thrust forward a copy of *Table Talk*. 'Look on page ten.'

As always, his friends were delighted as his diminutive housekeeper ruled over Ambrose. Hedley jumped up and intercepted the paper before Mrs Simpson could hand it to him.

Unlike the other two, Hedley clearly had little interest in his dress, which regularly verged on slovenly. Today it consisted of brown corduroy trousers, a loose shirt, and a Harris tweed jacket with brogues on his large feet. On the bridge of his nose perched a pair of thick-rimmed tortoiseshell glasses.

'Let me, Mrs S. "Society pages", he read with the best posh accent he could muster. "'Dr Ambrose Augustine Pink MBBS was as dashing as ever at the afternoon tea last Sunday to raise money for the missions in the Pacific, dressed in a well-tailored cream linen suit, pink shirt, with a paisley bow tie." He cocked his head, attempting to mask his grin as he improvised the final sentence. "'All somewhat compromised by a pair of brogues that could have done with a polish.""

'True, true,' Reggie laughingly exclaimed. 'Never polishes his shoes.'

"'Tall, broad-shouldered, and an excellent sportsman, Dr Pink has his curly auburn hair shaved short at the sides in a style favoured by athletes and it frames a pleasing and open face. For the many debutantes who would love to learn more, we can reveal that the Ambrose and Augustine came about, as he told us, because his adoptive father, a Methodist minister, had been rather keen on the early Christian church fathers..." Without looking up, he adlibbed once again. "'However, anyone with a facility for reading character from faces would have noted the occasionally worried, almost apologetic expression underneath his sporty cut. One can only speculate that this insecurity stems from his experiences spent as a stretcher bearer. Those who know him well, however, are allowed to see his soft side. Most of them comment at some time or other on his 'kind brown eyes', eyes that more than one young lady would love to have turned towards her.""

'Shut up and give it to me,' Ambrose said as he unsuccessfully lunged for the paper, while Reggie slapped his thighs in gales of laughter. 'They didn't write all that. Kind brown eyes ... what bullshit!'

Mrs Simpson refrained from further comment and sailed from the room. Hedley threw the paper to him.

'Sorry, my friend, but someone has to call out the pompous streak in you, have a bit of a laugh at you. If we're not doing the job of pricking your ego, and if you're too important to ask one of the debutantes to soothe your brow, perhaps you need something stronger. What do you think of this new therapy—Freudism?'

Wonderful, even his friends thought he needed analysis.

They sat finishing off the toast with eggs, bacon, mushrooms, chipolatas, tomatoes, black pudding, and the fried potatoes that constituted what Mrs Simpson considered a decent breakfast for young men. Ambrose mused on his position, as he tended to do after such troubled few nights. Hedley had opened a few raw nerves.

Surely life is, at worst, half-full, he thought. *There is really nothing to complain of, except perhaps a lack of any romantic attachment*—not that he would be foolish enough to bring that idea up to his friends.

'No lapsing back into your old habits—not good enough, Brose,' Hedley interrupted ruthlessly, determined not to let him sink back into silence. 'Reggie, you're a doctor. What's your diagnosis?'

'Yes, you definitely need more distractions,' he concurred. 'If it's not the debutantes you fancy, why don't you take up some more protégés at football, or some lost causes at the clinic? You could re-join the Methodists, finish cataloguing your father's collection, or start an art collection of your own ...'

His list of ideas was extensive, and Hedley and Ambrose let him prattle on. It was his way, and they found it diverting and comforting.

The three men had become friends at university, and their mutual friendship was characterised by a veneer of lazy tolerance and good-humoured teasing that belied their shared underlying loyalty and attachment. Less wealthy than his friends, Hedley's only caveat was that he would only share Ambrose's house if he paid rent. Reggie, on the other hand, lived outside Melbourne in the country at Westvale, an elegant country house surrounded by a magnificent garden and full of his own collections of eighteenth-century paintings and porcelain (hence his insistence on the psychological benefits of art). When in town, which was often, Reggie either stayed in his father's new apartment in South Yarra or, on occasions, with Ambrose in the North Fitzroy house. Having visited Fitzroy once, Reggie's father declared the accommodation and suburb as 'rather beyond the pale'.

'Another matter,' said Ambrose. 'I think I'll hunt out my service revolver after last Thursday. I don't know if it's this cholera business, but I feel that I'm being watched, perhaps even targeted. I didn't tell Mrs Simpson, but I'm almost certain that someone tried to run me over yesterday when I crossed Brunswick Street.'

The two friends looked at each other.

'We weren't going to mention it, but Hedley was concerned about Thursday night too. We've decided to stay with you until things get sorted out,' said Reggie.

'Hear, hear,' Hedley agreed.

'There's a young larrikin hanging about,' said Reggie, staring out the window. 'Might be casing the place. I'll shoo him off.'

Hedley moved towards the window. 'Isn't that the boy who saved our necks that night? What was his name?'

'William,' Ambrose said as he marched to the door, down the stairs, and into the street.

William was by now running down the street at speed.

'William … Will, come here! I'm not after you to hurt you.'

Will stopped and stared back without saying anything.

'Why are you running?'

'Got cold feet when I saw yer mansion, Doc.'

'Why didn't you come to see me at Gertrude Street as I asked?'

'I came on Friday, Doc, as I had plucked up me courage, but the lady threw me out. She didn't believe that yer wanted to see me. I ran now because I saw yer with those other gents and thought yer wouldn't want to see me.'

'Sorry, I was unavoidably detained on Friday and didn't get to work until late, so I was unable to tell Caitlin that you might come,' said Ambrose. 'Now, come inside with me. The gents are my friends. You've met Hedley. I have a reward for you—as I promised.'

Will uncharacteristically paused to think this time, then clearly decided to return rather than run ... or so Ambrose thought. He entered the house with Ambrose, clearly wide-eyed with wonder at the size and splendour of such a residence. Hedley and Reggie retreated into the various commodious chairs and observed with amusement the dialogue between Ambrose and his young visitor.

'Here's your reward,' Ambrose said as he handed over a shilling. 'Do you live in the house we met you in?'

'Sort of. Issy is me sister—or what I call me sister. I'm not sure who my mum and dad are, so I sleep there mostly and keep a lookout for her. That's how I found yer the other night. Issy's gone missing.'

'Where do you go to school?'

If it was possible, Will looked sheepish and defiant at the same time. 'I don't really go now.'

'How old are you?'

'Ten, I think,' he replied as his eyes wandered around the room.

At this point, Mrs Simpson arrived with a plate of biscuits and tea. 'Who are you then, young man?'

'William, lady.'

'Would you like a biscuit? A glass of lemonade?'

William's expression said it all, and Mrs Simpson placed the tray on the table and withdrew to get the drink.

Ambrose passed the plate of biscuits to Will, who nervously took two.

'Would you come back to Gertrude Street tomorrow? I might have some work for you—for payment, of course!'

'Ok, Doc. I'll come.'

As Mrs Simpson had returned, William was occupied for a short time emptying the very large glass of drink, after which he pocketed two more biscuits from the plate and headed for the exit.

'See yer tomorrow, Doc,' was his parting shot as he left.

'It seems that attending to the waifs of Fitzroy will be your hobby,' said Reggie. 'And by his appearance, you have much work to do.'

'Reggie's right,' Hedley interrupted. 'But haven't you taken on enough already? Football, work, the coroner?'

'I agree,' said Reggie. 'And *au contraire* to the opinion of all the gents and ladies of taste in South Yarra, I think this suburb and house may even be respectable one day.'

Ambrose and Hedley began throwing cushions at Reggie, and in the ensuing mayhem to which Molly enthusiastically contributed, the moment for any more soul searching passed.

Chapter Four

Yet Another Baby and a False Friend

Monday, 22 August 1921

On Monday morning, Ambrose woke early. By the time Monday morning came around, he was glad to feel that Thursday night's lecture and the chaotic aftermath was beginning to feel less like a real occurrence and more like an unpleasant dream. And Ambrose had been having a number of bad dreams lately. On Sunday night he had once again been tormented by dreams of war.

Some good news had come via a letter from a close friend of his parents and someone he remembered very fondly when living in Java, Pieter van Haandel, the coffee grower. He mentioned visiting Melbourne for work. It would be great fun to have him stay. It was a beautiful clear late winter's day and, after a brief breakfast at his favourite café on Lygon Street in Carlton—it being one of the days Mrs Simpson didn't housekeep for him—Ambrose drove down to the Coroner's Court on the Yarra River. He worked there part time, far more for the experience than the very small stipend. The combination of medical knowledge and solving mysteries appealed to him. It was more than a court, being the morgue as well and, befitting its role, it had been built in the grand legal architectural style of the late nineteenth century, with a cavernous foyer and courthouse behind a high brick fence with large ornate wrought iron gates.

Ambrose entered through the gates, bypassing the public entrance. He walked down the side of the building, past some early butter yellow jonquils that had naturalised in the space between the path and the fence. He went through the back office, which led to the mortuary and viewing gallery with a large window. No one was present. It was too early for the thrill-seekers and ghouls posing as concerned relatives of lost family members, an ongoing problem that needed to be addressed. The office was empty, so he went through the foyer to the post-mortem room. There was a strong smell of formaldehyde. He knocked at the door.

'Enter,' a man's voice boomed.

Ambrose stepped into the room to see the coroner, Dr Cole, in a white coat, opening up a cadaver of an old man.

'Have a look at this, Pink,' Cole said, with no further greeting.

Ambrose slipped on an apron and a pair of surgical gloves. He approached the body and fingered the enlarged liver inside the opening before running his hand along the wasted muscles of the arms and legs.

'About sixty years old. Looks like severe malnourishment caused by alcoholism. Another from the Benevolent Asylum, I suppose?' Ambrose remarked.

'Too true, but you missed the contusion on the back of the neck. Hit from behind by another inmate. We need to send a report to the police today. Can you get onto it?'

Ambrose wandered to another bench to begin the paperwork when he noticed a tiny body under a cloth. *Probably another abandoned baby found in the vegetable and flower market in Victoria Street,* he thought. *A popular dumping spot for unwanted babies.* He glanced at the label attached to the partially uncovered tiny leg. It said, 'Iris O'Donohue, Kew Asylum, age yet to be ascertained'. Ambrose stopped in his tracks and lifted the cloth.

'This isn't Iris,' he exclaimed.

'What was that?' Cole remarked, distracted by Ambrose's comment.

Ambrose stared at his boss, too startled for a moment to speak. Cole lifted his eyebrows in query, as it was clear despite his current state that Ambrose had something to say.

'I said, this isn't Iris O'Donohue, Dr Cole. I saw Iris O'Donohue on Wednesday afternoon at the Fitzroy clinic. And even though it can be difficult to tell little babies apart, I don't think this is Iris. It simply doesn't make any sense. I went to the O'Donohues' home on Wednesday night, and some men who claimed to be officials from the Kew Asylum took the child, claiming it had died. Iris was very sick when I examined her, but her great aunt had only had her for a few days at most. She struck me as a good woman, desperately trying her best for the child. I wasn't allowed by the asylum officials to ascertain her condition when I visited the house in the evening, which I found strange in itself.'

Cole was a thoughtful man and didn't interrupt Ambrose, although his expression indicated he did not seem convinced of the claim.

'That's interesting, Pink; however, it is not the story I have been told. Dr Silvio Negrone, the medical director of the asylum, called the constable on Saturday evening and informed him that the child had just died. Obviously that was some days after being retrieved from the O'Donohue residence. He told the police that they had been given information that the child was in danger—that Mrs O'Donohue had removed the child from the asylum through deceit and had neglected the baby in her care to the point of criminality. When they returned the child to its mother at the asylum, it was very ill and later died. The mother is a mental defective. The baby's great aunt is the one the police want to charge—for neglect.'

Ambrose was stunned. What could he say?

'The man who took the baby—Dr Negrone, I presume—told me she had died at the O'Donohue residence and that I would be reported for neglect. The baby I observed on Wednesday morning had skin blistering on the buttocks and was shrunken and blue. I know you'll think I'm inexperienced, but it looked like cholera to me. I examined a similar case in Egypt with the army in 1915.'

Cole was momentarily silenced but clearly shocked.

'Rubbish, Pink!' said Cole. 'There is not, and has never been, cholera in Australia, as you should know well. I don't think creating mysteries out of nothing is useful in this situation. And I didn't realise that you were involved as the baby's GP. You will be a witness now, so you'd better stay off this case.'

Frustrated and worried, Ambrose replied, 'I sent some samples of the faeces to the bacteriology lab at the university. I'll go up today and see what they found.'

'Nothing will be found,' Cole said in a most disapproving tone. 'Your work has been good in the short time you have been here. Do not spoil it with fantasy now, Pink.'

Ambrose had always found Cole a gentle man and had the impression that he liked him and thought he had potential. But he also knew that Cole had no time for anything other than cold, hard facts and reasoning at the coroners' court. If Cole thought he was making major mistakes or indulging in unwarranted speculation, then Ambrose would have no future within the Coroner's Court.

'I will hold a hearing this week. You will be required as a witness as you treated the child, so I shall see you there. And Pink, just a word of advice: your reputation is your most important asset as a medical practitioner. Going around talking about cholera is a very quick way to destroy it.'

His future at the Coroner's Court was fading before him.

Coroner's Court
Thursday, 25 August 1921

'All stand!' the clerk of courts called as he smashed his gavel three times.

The small crowd rose to their feet as Dr Cole entered the large wood-panelled courtroom. Ambrose sat off to the side in the box reserved for witnesses.

'I shall hear the representative of the asylum first,' Dr Cole said from the bench.

The barrister representing the Kew Asylum, Sir Digby Bent, stood with a florid face and resplendent in his attire, a horse-hair wig perched on his head. His voluminous body, developed assiduously over many gargantuan feasts in the gentlemen's clubs and restaurants of Melbourne, was amply covered in pleated black robes. The rosette affixed squarely in the middle of the back of his gown confirmed him as a King's Counsel.

How odd that they would brief a KC for such a case, thought Ambrose.

'Mad or bad, Your Honour, it matters not which she is. Kathleen O'Donohue must pay for the untimely death of the poor baby Iris, daughter of her niece. We will argue that she is mad rather than bad, but the case should be decided before the Supreme Court. Clearly Your Honour, mental deficiency and madness run through the whole family.'

'Can we hear from the mother Flora O'Donohue?' asked Dr Cole.

'I'm afraid that won't be possible, Your Honour,' answered Sir Digby. 'The superintendent of Kew Asylum, Dr Negrone, has declared her unable to give evidence on the grounds of mental incompetence. Not only is she mentally deficient, but she also suffers from melancholia and hysteria. She has hardly spoken for months.'

Ambrose observed the proceedings with growing horror and gave a wan smile to the tearful Ruby in the crowd.

'In that case, I will hear from Dr Negrone. Take the stand, please,' said Cole.

Negrone entered the witness box and took the oath.

'Did you identify the baby?' asked the coroner.

'Yes, Your Honour. The baby was identified by me and a junior doctor as the child Iris O'Donohue.'

'What was the condition of the child when she was abducted by the aunt?'

'The child had been a little poorly, but nowhere near death when Mrs Kathleen O'Donohue claimed to be her grandmother and took her from the asylum. Our knowledge of the family suggests that Mrs O'Donohue in fact may be mentally tainted herself, Your Honour. Any suggestion that it was another child is nonsense.'

'I'm not sure what you mean by that statement,' said Cole. 'The issue of identity has not been raised here, as the body has been formally and legally identified.'

The coroner then questioned the superintendent about the condition of the body and the known circumstances of her demise.

'You may be excused.'

Ruby sobbed, and Ambrose half rose from his chair.

'Do you have anything to add, Dr Pink?' asked Cole. 'I believe that you were the treating medical practitioner?'

Ambrose stood to his feet. 'I'm sorry, Your Honour. As assistant to Coroner's Court and treating doctor to the accused, and briefly the deceased, I ask leave to add some extra information that I believe to be relevant.' Taking a deep breath as he contemplated the possible end of his career, Ambrose ploughed on. 'Coroner, I must place on the record the fact that I do not believe that the child I had in Fitzroy in my clinic at Oddfellows two weeks ago was the same I witnessed at the examination in this institution. Furthermore, I believe the child in Fitzroy was suffering from … cholera.'

A collective gasp filled the courtroom, followed by a ripple of subdued conversation. Ambrose noticed from the corner of his eye that the reporters for the *Argus* and *Age* newspapers—day-dreaming in the first case and doodling in the second—had awoken from their torpor and now sat bolt upright, scribbling madly.

Negrone jumped to his feet. 'This is nonsense, Your Honour, criminal nonsense. Order Pink to be quiet. He needs to be investigated himself for irresponsibility unfitting of a medical man. He's causing public panic talking about cholera.'

Sir Digby Bent also rose abruptly. 'I object, Your Honour. There is no precedent for evidence such as this to be introduced at this point. All the evidence needs to be supplied to us before the hearing. I will contest this to the highest court. Many have been advocating the sterilisation of such families. We need to put this woman before the legal system of this state so that more can realise that the great national problem of the mentally deficient is in need of an urgent solution. She must be incarcerated, at the very least!'

Dr Cole indicated to Sir Digby that he should sit down. Digby stared at Ambrose.

'Dr Pink, I would caution you against the wild surmises of the inexperienced. You have not been asked as a witness to identify the body. That has been done by competent authorities from the asylum, and you were not brought in to make wild assumptions about any disease that afflicted the child, except if you have evidence. Do you have any new evidence to support your claim?'

'Your Honour, I left a sample taken from Iris Donohue with

Dr Hugo at the bacteriology laboratory at the university. I have been trying to contact Dr Hugo, both through the telephone and in person without success. I will continue to try to find out what the sample disclosed. I also respectfully make the point that I spent time in Egypt with the army in 1915, and I observed those afflicted with cholera. The child at my clinic had strikingly similar symptoms.'

'Pink, without a test result, this is nothing but speculation. Dangerous speculation at that, which I can't take into consideration in my judgement. This is merely a hearing to decide if there is sufficient evidence for a trial. I'm not going over everything here. The fine detail can be examined in the trial in the Supreme Court. I find that there is sufficient evidence of neglect causing death that Kathleen O'Donohue be taken into custody until she can appear for trial in the Supreme Court. I have heard enough to satisfy myself that there is enough evidence for a trial. Take Kathleen O'Donohue away.'

Mrs O'Donohue was led sobbing from the courtroom as her daughter and supporters rushed out into the foyer, likewise in floods of tears.

Ambrose found himself shaking with anger. He jumped into the Riley and drove up to the medical school. He had to find Hugo—where was he? If he wasn't in his office, he'd search for him. He pulled up in Swanston Street, only to find that damn Studebaker was taking all the parking again.

Ambrose headed into the depths of the labyrinthine medical school. Marching past dissecting classes and lecture rooms full of medical students, he couldn't see Hugo anywhere, and none of the students he asked had seen Hugo either. Just when he given up any hope of luck and was heading back to the entrance of the building, he heard raised voices, one with a French accent. The voices seemed to come from Hugo's locked office and were muffled by the door. He strode up and banged loudly. No one had been in the office when he had passed earlier. The door swung open slightly.

'Pink, vhat do you want?' Hugo, a tall, balding, cadaverous man with a goatee beard in his early fifties had blocked the door so that Ambrose couldn't see who was in the room.

'Did you get my jar, Dr Hugo?'

'Vhat jar?'

'The jar I left on your desk on Wednesday night with faeces in it—and a note saying that I suspected cholera.'

'You must be mistaken.' Hugo was pale, and Pink noticed a slight tremor in his hand as if he involuntarily held it up to block an expected imaginary outburst.

Then he slammed the door shut.

Ambrose pounded again. 'Dr Hugo, we need to speak about the specimen. How could the jar have gone missing?'

No answer was forthcoming, and no noise emanated from behind the door.

When it became clear that there would be no response from Dr Hugo, Ambrose left the building and retreated to a place on the pavement where, if he positioned himself beside the glass door, he could just see the section of the corridor outside Hugo's office. He didn't have to wait long. The door opened and he saw Butterby leave, heading towards the rear of the building.

What had Butterby to do with the new bacteriology programme at the university? Were the men friends or acquaintances? It had certainly sounded like an argument earlier. What could he do now? He neither had a body nor any other evidence of cholera, and yet he had claimed the child was a victim of a disease that brought fear into any society that suffered an outbreak. He certainly needed to back up his claims if his reputation, and possibly career, was going to survive this episode.

As Ambrose considered his options, he saw another figure leave the office. Angus McBride, a surgical honorary at the Melbourne Hospital about five years older than him, and one of Butterby's favoured acolytes. He'd seen him at the lecture. McBride burst through the door and stopped as he saw Ambrose. He looked startled for the merest moment, but quickly regained his composure.

'Brosie, old fella! Where have you been! Saw you at the Prof's talk in Fitzroy last Thursday. Disgraceful business. What did you think of it? And why weren't you sitting in the front with the rest of us? I've missed our drinking nights together. Fancy catching up?'

Typical, Ambrose thought. McBride generally asked a lot of questions, but rarely paused to draw breath and listen to the answers. Unless the speaker was a person of some importance, of course. But Ambrose was curious enough about McBride's connections to two of the main players in the case of baby Iris to reply in the affirmative. He was beginning to think of this as his own personal mystery.

'I'm around, Gus, just busy. I'd certainly love to hear all the hospital gossip. It would be good to catch up, thanks.'

'Let's say Café Denat for a meal, shall we? How about tonight? I'm free.'

How unusual, thought Ambrose. *I would have expected a drink perhaps, but not dinner at one of Melbourne's finest restaurants.*

'Sounds good, I'll see you there around seven then, shall I?'

McBride departed.

Ambrose had been tossing up whether to ask McBride about his presence in Hugo's office but decided he could probably find out more by pretending he didn't know that he'd been there. And he was curious about McBride's sudden friendliness.

The 'drinking nights' McBride alluded to had hardly been a personal affair, but rather the Medical Students Society meetings, of which McBride was a noisy and prominent member. In 1919, McBride had led the push to ban from the Society those who hadn't enlisted during the war and had instead stayed back and studied medicine. *He had only seemed happy to converse with me because he knew I had served as a stretcher bearer and had returned because I'd been ordered to do so.* Shaking his head in confusion, but determined to find out more, Ambrose jumped into the car and headed home.

Ambrose arrived in Alfred Crescent, parked his car, and walked to his front gate. About to mount the stairs to the front door, he was distracted momentarily as he could hear Molly barking frantically. He opened the gate and looked up at the front door. A severed pig's head stared down at him from the welcome mat. Someone was clearly warning him off—but off what? For the first time, he felt real fear.

Entering the house after his gruesome find, and rather rattled, Mrs Simpson excitedly ran from the kitchen waving the evening's newspaper at him. 'You're in the news! It's the main story!'

Ambrose grabbed it from her and groaned as he saw the full horror before him.

Sensational hearing at the Coroner's Court!

Doctor claims cholera has arrived in Melbourne!

Dr Ambrose Pink says thousands could die!

Government spokesman denies claim … says Dr Pink is being investigated. Dr Hugo of the new Bacteriology laboratory at the university claimed no specimens of cholera had been submitted to him, and that it was foolishness to claim cholera was in Melbourne, or anywhere else in Australia.

'Heaven help me, Mrs Simpson! I didn't say anything about thousands of deaths. My reputation may well have just been ruined. Hugo is lying!'

The telephone rang.

'What are you trying this time? I said find a hobby to get out of yourself. I didn't say spread wild rumours in the papers about pandemics. You know how dangerous that is. Do I have to stop you from committing professional suicide?'

It was Reggie.

CHAPTER FIVE

BACCHUS BIFFS BROSIE

Café Denat, 215 Exhibition Street
Friday, 26 August 1921

I t was raining. He'd dressed in camel-hued slacks, sky blue shirt with a grey, white, and black Macclesfield print bowtie, and his best sports jacket. He didn't want to overdress, but neither would he 'slum it', as he knew McBride was both rich and a snob. McBride, he surmised, rarely did anything without a purpose, and Ambrose wondered yet again why he had been chosen as a suitable dinner companion. Would there be anyone else? At least the food was good at the Café Denat.

After parking his car in Exhibition Street, he strolled towards his destination, smoking a cigarette. The restaurant was in the theatre district, which this evening was full of people milling around the pavement or having a meal. The pubs nearby had disgorged their drinkers after the 6 o'clock swill, as the new temperance laws demanded, so quite a few drunks staggered around outside as well.

'Hey mate, watch where you're going,' muttered a belligerent drunk he bumped into.

Ambrose stiffened and stepped back quickly—his nerves were certainly on edge. He found the anonymous-looking front entrance. After ascending the staircase, he was met as he loitered at the small table just inside the main dining room.

'Dottore Pink!' the waiter in evening dress exclaimed, waving his arms excitedly. 'You are most welcome.'

It was Giuseppe Favaloro, one of Ambrose's patients. His wife Maria was a member of the cloth-workers union and, as such, of the Oddfellows' Friendly Society he worked for. Giuseppe had a generous moustache, combed-back black hair, and a permanently worried expression, which often gave the wrong impression as he was essentially a cheerful man at heart, a kind husband and father, and a generous host. They lived near Ambrose and, as their doctor, he had been invited to festivities on a number of occasions—baptisms and the like.

'Giuseppe, lovely to see you here. How is the family?'

'Benissimo, Dottore, benissimo. Please come with me. 'ow many are dining?'

'Don't know, Giuseppe. I was invited by Dr McBride.'

'Ah yes, in the corner booth there. Just the two. 'e said it was a private dinner.'

He took Ambrose across the dimly lit room, polished black shoes sliding silently on the lush pile carpet, to the far corner, where he lit the candles at the table. It was impossible for Ambrose not to see himself, as the walls were lined with large antique gilt-framed mirrors. It was all white linen, silver cutlery, and crystal glassware. A late winter posy of flowers adorned the centre of the table: pure white snowdrops and pink camellias.

'A treat tonight—a treat. We 'ave a new chef via England. 'ee's French ... 'ee worked with Chef Escoffier at the Ritz in Londra. 'ee won't stay with us long, I think. Just arrived and full of stories and ambition.'

Giuseppe left and then quickly returned with the menu and a glass of champagne, golden with a very fine bead.

'Dottore McBride ordered one of the best bottles from the cellar. Told us to pour you a glass 'eef you came before 'im. This is the special menu—not à la carte.'

Ambrose sipped the nectar. *More than I could afford,* he

mused. *I'll enjoy this. Gus is certainly pulling out all stops tonight. I wonder why?* He studied the menu. *I'll enjoy the food and drink even if I need to stay wary about the company.*

The menu was extensive, with some of his favourites:

Consommé Poule-au-Pot au Madère

– o –

Huitres Favourite

– o –

Cailles Pochées a la Richelieu

– o –

Noisettes d'Agneau Fines Herbes
Pommes de Terre Parmentier

– o –

Supréme de Volaille Jeaneatte

– o –

Parfait de Foie-Gras
Salade Mignonne

– o –

Timbale d'Ecrevisses Américaine
Asperges Nouvelles

– o –

Pêche Melba liqueurs

'I say, you've been missing in action for the Redlegs on Saturdays, Brose. Injured I hear.'

Without warning, McBride had plonked down opposite him, puffing hard.

'Out of condition myself, but honoured to shout dinner to one of our team—even if he mostly plays in the second eighteen! Ha ha!'

Ambrose bridled.

'Good menu—new chef, I hear. I've ordered some excellent Chablis on ice and a red Burgundy. Montrechet, both from '19. Excellent vintage. Grande Cru you know. Damn expensive! My shout.'

He poured himself some champagne. McBride also always liked to tell people the price of everything, Ambrose recalled. It would be a long night. Why had he agreed to come?

'Won't the restaurant get into strife serving alcohol after six?' Ambrose asked.

'Don't worry—friend of the proprietor. Some of us pay his fines or pay off the police. Only fined occasionally. The authorities turn a blind eye. Also, keeping it up here above the street and the anonymous entry mean it's not flaunting itself. Appearances are everything, don't yer think?' He winked theatrically as he spoke. 'I say, Brosie, let's get started, I'm starving. We'll have the special menu, waiter.'

He waved off Giuseppe who had come to take their orders.

'Bloody dagos!' he muttered. 'How they produced all that great art nobody knows. I suppose we got the rubbish, like lots of recent migrants. At least we've stopped the yellow hordes! Ha ha!'

He was obviously cheered at this thought, and so he raised his glass and swallowed a good draft of fizz.

McBride is a young fogey, thought Ambrose, *by manner and appearance*. He could have been any age between twenty-five and forty, depending on the light, and his opinions certainly tended strongly towards the conservative. He had short blond hair and a florid complexion, large waist, and a flamboyant waistcoat and jacket. The remains of a handsome youth were still visible, but over-all, his red silk cravat only drew attention to the size of his ample jowls. *I bet he can't speak Italian as well as Giuseppe speaks English.*

The soup arrived quickly. 'Delicious,' they both agreed.

After the soup was a dozen oysters, followed by quail deboned and poached in stock served 'a la Richelieu', on a bed of piped creamed potatoes surrounded by stuffed tomatoes, mushrooms, and braised lettuce.

We are worshipping at the shrine of Bacchus this night, thought Ambrose.

'This Chablis is top notch,' McBride remarked in between mouthfuls.

Ambrose agreed. He found himself doing a lot of agreeing through the evening. As he had recalled, McBride's conversation tended towards the rhetorical, a nod or murmur of agreement was all he required or, it seemed, expected. The conversation, such as it was, progressed from discussions about surgery and the importance of charging large fees to Ambrose's medical practice at the Oddfellows clinic in Fitzroy.

'You'll be giving that up when you've qualified as a surgeon, no doubt!' Angus opined. 'Off to London to do the fellowship at the college soon, am I right? I was a medical officer in the war—rank of major, don't you know. Stayed on in London for a year or two after to complete the surgical fellowship at the Royal College of Surgeons. Lincoln's Inn Fields—lots of fellas did. Top notch experience.'

Well, this is easy, thought Ambrose, *with people like Gus, you don't need to say anything controversial. He tells you what he thinks and assumes it's what you think too.*

McBride then leant across the table and whispered loudly, 'I assume all that nonsense about you and cholera in the *Argus* was a mistake. Good idea to make a short statement saying you were mistaken, new to the profession, inexperienced, don't you think? Bad for your career if you don't. What about your patients in Fitzroy, Pink? Any Commies amongst them?'

Ambrose froze, taken aback by the swift turn in conversation. And this time, he noted, McBride was waiting for his response. His coughing fit in response was only partly feigned. He felt like one of his own anatomical specimens, pinned under McBride's suddenly focused gaze.

'I'm sure many are the salt of the earth,' Gus added. He sounded insincere. 'But I'm sure you are in a position to hear a lot of things. I know you're a patriot—don't suppose you hear any whisper of treason?'

'Of course, I'm a patriot!' Ambrose replied.

To this question, at least Ambrose could respond sincerely. But he didn't like the way the conversation had veered.

'I had a mixed lot of privates in my company during the war. Some were loyal fellas, others needed disciplining,' McBride continued. 'Had to have one or two of them shot for desertion to calm the others down.'

He can't remember how many?

The lamb was served, and Giuseppe offered the gratin of potatoes silver service style by Luigi, who then poured the red burgundy into large glasses.

'Oh my,' McBride exclaimed. 'The scent of this Burgundy is metaphorically as well as literally intoxicating.'

He hooted at his own joke. Ambrose smiled weakly and murmured his agreement. It was good.

'Only the best for one of the red legs.' McBride winked as Giuseppe poured his wine. He was clearly getting very drunk. Luigi departed and McBride leant closer.

'It was good to see you there at the Prof's talk. Questions had been raised about your ... well, some of your choices, personal and professional. Especially the slumming it in Fitzroy, you understand. But glad they've been put to rest, old chum. Have you heard of the Australian Protective League?'

Ambrose nodded.

'Well, whatever you've heard, know this. It's a group of patriots, first and foremost, professionals and businessmen dedicated to protecting our democracy. Care to come to a meeting? We're having one soon and I have been asked to sound you out. You'll meet some very important people—good for your career. You could be valuable where you are. There are some who doubt your suitability, but I'm sure you're our man.'

Ambrose stared and raised the glass to his lips to give himself some time to think of his response. *Gus is drunk and talking too much, and I'm being asked to be a spy in Fitzroy. What a lark! I'll go along with it and see what is going on. If I don't say too much, no one will suspect my sympathies. But what are sympathies exactly? I'll have to think about that. Perhaps sitting on the fence is a bad idea.*

'Fitzroy, Carlton, and Collingwood certainly contain a large population of potential recruits for the Bolsheviks,' Ambrose said carefully. 'Am I right in thinking that the Australian Protective League thinks of the area as a hotbed for revolution?'

'Absolutely! Great to see you have a sensible view about all this politics business. Just going to the loo,' Angus slurred. He departed the table and headed across the room, manoeuvring between the tables as if in a slow-motion ski slalom race.

Left to himself with his extremely expensive wine, Ambrose meditated on his strange attraction to Fitzroy and its inhabitants, Bolshevik or not. Just recently he'd wandered off Brunswick Street into the maze of back streets, laneways, and laneways-off-laneways looking for a sick woman he had been asked to visit. He had avoided the human excrement in the gutters that ran down the middle of the bluestone paved footpaths. All of this lay behind the façades of the large food and provision stores and crumbling grand Victorian terrace houses that lined the main streets of the suburb. He thought of people like Iris, Kathleen, and Ruby; all the sick women and children he encountered living in the tenements of Fitzroy; four in a tiny bedroom with a single bed, bathroom in a squalid backyard without a fence or tap for water. No, even if he still wasn't sure exactly where his political sympathies lay, he knew for certain that it wouldn't be with the Australian Protective League if McBride and Butterby were characteristic of its adherents.

'Hey Brosie, wake up.' Angus had returned, completing the second run of the slalom. The rest of the meal was just as indulgent a culinary experience as the beginning. Cold breast of chicken coated first in mayonnaise and then in chicken jelly, followed by unctuous liver pâté and salad accompanied with yabbies poached in stock and piled up robed in tomato sauce—asparagus as well. More champagne with *Pêche Melba*—that most international of Australian desserts (or Australian of international desserts), although the season dictated canned peaches—all concluded with liqueurs. As Ambrose staggered out into the cold air, he was determined tomorrow would allow a sleep in.

Back on the pavement outside Café Denat, McBride slung his arm around Ambrose's shoulder.

'I know a place where we can continue our night, Brosie,' he said, slurring slightly and moving around as if on a boat. 'Come on!'

He sailed north along Exhibition Street in the dark, the moon in the starry night looking down quizzically—even disapprovingly, or so Ambrose thought, as he was dragged along, not quite sure why he hadn't taken the opportunity to flee.

'Let's sing a song,' McBride announced, and he immediately burst into one of the medical school students' ditties, 'The Anatomists Song', set to the tune of 'A more humane Mikado' from the operetta *The Mikado* by Gilbert and Sullivan.

A more humane anatomist did never before exist
To nobody second, I'm certainly reckoned, a modern materialist.
It is my very humane endeavour to make, to some extent
The medical masses of students' classes to mine subservient.
My object all sublime, I shall achieve in time
To make anatomy up to date, anatomy up to date!

'Hiccup!'

Ambrose was still suspicious of McBride's sudden intimacy, even after being offered membership of the League, but in his semi-coherent alcoholic haze it seemed to him that it would be harmless to tag along. So, he gave up thoughts of escape and up and joined in.

I'll make each student gaze
In twentieth century ways
On the bones of his lecturer's skeleton
By means of the Roentgen rays.
The fellow who faints when he sees a corpse,
or thinks it a trifle ripe …

They continued on their way, singing until they reached the upper end of Little Lonsdale Street, or Little Lon, as it was colloquially known. They had only covered about half a mile in the last thirty minutes. Their progress had been hindered, first by a curious constable who stopped and questioned them, and then by a forced detour around a suspicious group of men lounging in the shadows. At one point, McBride vomited discretely into a bush. They finally turned left into Little Lon, and after fifty yards or so of staggering downhill they reached a dead-end lane running off to the left. At this point, Ambrose's inebriated companion-in-arms indicated their destination as a door just down this side lane. They tripped and stumbled along the bluestone flagstones in the darkness, and McBride hammered on the door, rather too enthusiastically for Ambrose's delicate head.

Ambrose began to feel claustrophobic, trapped in the narrow lane lit only by a single lamppost, with the extremely high brick wall of the grounds of a private men's club behind. Finally, the door swung open and before them was a very large man of dubious appearance, holding open the door and gesturing up a narrow flight of wooden stairs. The doorman said nothing, but clearly recognised McBride.

This is very stupid, thought Ambrose, but after one too many drinks, another one is never enough. He followed McBride.

Ascending the stairs, Ambrose could hear piano music slowly crescendo until it burst forth *fortissimo* as they opened a door and entered the first floor. They had arrived in a dimly lit room whose far reaches disappeared into the gloom. All around him, as his eyes grew accustomed to the light, his sight was assaulted by the spectacle of emu feathers, red and purple velvet materials, deep pile carpet, multiple chaises longues, and a bar with an infinite glistening array of bottles lining the whole wall behind. He thought it was probably meant to signify sybaritic opulence, but it all seemed a little cheap and garish. It all had the effect of inducing nausea in Ambrose—the excessive amount of alcohol he had consumed also contributed. On the walls were exotic paintings of nudes in the style of the fashionable artist Norman Lindsay, cavorting so outrageously that, to the medically trained eye, would have been anatomically difficult at best. In the deep gloom, on the various chaise longues heavily mascaraed creatures reclined—dressed—or partially undressed, in a variety of exotic clothing. Angus beckoned to one and then headed out to the rear door.

'Sorry, Brosie, be back soon. Want to check if it's all right to bring you to our headquarters.'

He disappeared behind a curtain hanging over a corridor. The realisation suddenly materialised through the fog of overindulgence that, for the first time ever, he had entered a bordello ... and what did McBride mean about headquarters?

The gorgeous and gloriously technicolour plumaged figure McBride had summoned approached, took Ambrose by the hand, and led him to the bar where she ordered two drinks. She raised her glass and purred, 'Drink, darling,' in a deep German accent. The touch of her somewhat masculine hand on his instantly produced a reaction in Ambrose not unlike being dropped in cold water. He began to regain some element of composure and sobriety. Nausea was still in attendance, but guilt had also stepped in.

What would Mother think ... and Father? You can take the boy out of Methodism, but not Methodism out of the boy ... completely, he thought. *I know what happens to those girls when the flush of youth wears off. I see them in the slums. What am I doing here? Why has McBride brought me? I surely could be compromised for being here. And it hardly fits the picture of the upstanding patriot protecting the vigour of the nation that I tried to project earlier this evening. Why are those seedy-looking men eyeing me off?* All these thoughts triggered his flight response.

'Sorry, miss,' he replied. 'I think I've had too much to drink. I'll be off home.'

'No! Drink!' she said firmly, and pressed the glass towards him again.

Now he was panicking, and the claustrophobia that had threatened in the lane welled up again. He knew he needed to get out. Ambrose turned to the way they had arrived, only to find the insalubrious man who had let them into the bordello blocking his way and scowling, while slowly drawing a pistol from his jacket.

I'm not going that way, he thought.

Only the rear corridor taken by McBride offered hope. He decided to take McBride's route, wherever he was. He gasped, 'Bathroom,' and moved quickly toward the corridor McBride had taken. His companion wasn't to be seen in the corridor, but there was a window slightly ajar. Fully in the hold of his panic and struggling to breath, all Ambrose could think was that he needed to get out, immediately. He lifted the window with as much effort as he could muster and looked out. He was one floor up and it was too far to jump to the street. Suddenly, a car pulled up below. He might just be able to land on the roof without serious injury—if his ankle held. A hand grabbed his jacket just as he threw himself onto the roof, rolling first onto the engine bonnet and then onto the flagstones. He waited for pain, but not much came—he was all right, or the alcohol had anaesthetised him. Unfortunately, the crash on the roof of the car had had the effect of decanting four figures from the vehicle, all dressed in black and armed with what seemed to be an assortment of exotic weapons. It was diffi-cult to accurately see anything, as the scene was poorly lit by the streetlamp.

'You!' one exclaimed, face covered in a black balaclava.

At that moment, a few ruffians armed with cudgels and knuckle dusters poured out of the door leading to the upstairs brothel.

'Give him to us,' one of them grunted to the black clad new arrivals next to Ambrose.

'Not today,' replied the obvious leader in black.

The ruffians from the bordello advanced. Briefly, the two opposing groups eyed each other off, with Ambrose caught in between.

What followed was all a bit of a daze as Ambrose attempted to retreat and slipped on the cobblestones, thus breaking the impasse. Figures leapt over him, and a frenzied battle began. In what seemed like seconds to Ambrose, but must have been a minute or two at least, the larrikins from the bordello were retreating at great pace. He stood with his mouth open, amazed.

'I apologise for the car,' Ambrose exclaimed. 'Thank you for your assistance. I'll pay for the damage to the roof.'

'We are only here because we have business further down the lane. Why were you in that place?' came the muffled reply. 'Can you find your way home?'

'I think so,' replied Ambrose. *Why is this person concerned for my wellbeing?* 'It would take some time to explain my presence upstairs, but it was only for a few minutes and I feared for my life. Once I get out of this dark cul-de -sac, I should find a cab … or my car.'

He continued, 'You just said "you" when we just met—have we met somewhere before?'

Ambrose was dismissed with a wave of a hand, and the four dark figures headed down the lane into the dark cul-de-sac. *What are they doing?*

Ambrose arrived home thirty minutes later, overflowing with questions that could not be answered—the dominant one being deep concern about whether he was being targeted, along with a promise to himself that he wouldn't do anything so foolish again.

CHAPTER SIX

NINETEENTH MAN ... AND A WOMAN

Gertrude Street Oddfellows Medical Clinic
Thursday, 1 September 1921

It was a week before Ruby O'Donohue plucked up the courage to visit the clinic again. Caitlin brought her in to Ambrose, as she was too shy to enter on her own.

'It's Ruby?' said Ambrose.

'That's right, Doctor. I've come about me mother. I dunno how long she'll last in prison.'

A storm was gathering outside, and the curtains started beating about. Ambrose shut the window.

'You have been on my mind. Can I help with the trial? That is, I'm not a lawyer, but do you need help in finding one?'

'That's what I come for. Me and 'er friends and the priest at St John the Baptist church have raised some money for the trial, but we don't know 'ow to find a lawyer even if we have enough money for one. You were so kind that day, what with the milk and the ticket for the hospital an all, even if we didn't need it in the end.' She paused, clearly fighting tears. 'And I wondered if you would manage it and get some 'elp for 'er?'

'Of course,' said Ambrose, wishing he had thought of their possible dilemma before. 'Leave it to me, I'll see what I can do. I don't imagine that you have enough for leading silk, but we need a good cheap barrister.'

Ruby nodded, although she looked as though she didn't quite understand what he was talking about exactly.

Ambrose explained: 'You won't be able to afford a well-known lawyer, a KC also called "a silk", but someone more junior could take the case and be just as good.' He paused. 'How much money have you raised?'

The amount wasn't encouraging, but Ambrose had worked around enough people like the O'Donohues to know that any offer from him to help would be soundly rejected. Small charities, he had discovered, were just about palatable to his proud but poor patients, but anything else would only offend. Still, at least she had come to him, and there were other ways he could help.

'I'll ring around some friends and see if we can get someone trustworthy who will do it for a reasonable fee. Wait, don't move. I'll try a friend from school right now.'

Ambrose slipped out to the front office and called a barrister who was building a respectable practice focused on property law. Ambrose knew he'd be too busy to help, even had he any experience in criminal law, but could always be relied on to know all the latest law gossip. He was answered after just a moment.

'Bill, it's Ambrose here. Sorry to bother you on a work matter, but I need an excellent solicitor or barrister to represent one of my patients. She's had a finding of negligence causing the fatality of a six-month-old baby in the Coroner's Court and will be going to the Supreme Court this month. I know you don't do crime—any ideas?'

'The best will cost you a bit. Does the client have money?'

'Bill, she's one of my patients, an elderly Fitzroy woman. Of course not!'

'Ever the quixotic, Brosie.'

Ambrose ignored his friend, well aware that Bill could be said to be a bit of a soft touch himself, hence being the first person he had thought to call.

'Well, in that case, your options are limited. Though, actually… if you're game, you can get excellent representation, at least from the legal point of view.'

'Of course, I'm game, but what do you mean from the legal point of view? What other is there?'

'Well, first up, she's a "she". Inexperienced, but very clever and hardworking. Just missed out on the Supreme Court Prize, unlike her uncle, who won it in his year. William Wong. So, as well as being disadvantaged by her gender, she's also Chinese. For some judges and juries, that's two obstacles already. Many clients are just not willing to risk it.'

'Well, I'm not sure we have that many options. And William Wong—I've heard of him,' replied Ambrose. 'Leading barrister in the civil courts, right?'

'That's him, a rarity in every way. His niece is a chip off the old block.'

Wong. Suddenly the name clicked into place. *Please, not Charlotte Wong*, he thought, and inwardly groaned, because of course, it was not as if Melbourne was teeming with female Chinese lawyers. Even as Bill said her name, he knew it had to be her. He considered asking Bill if he had any other suggestions, but knew his reluctance would only raise more questions and quite possibly be misconstrued.

Charlotte Wong—he knew her slightly from college, a few university social functions, and her reputation: determined, razor smart, beautiful, and always elegantly dressed. She had defences as thick as a crusader castle and was known to suffer from biblical doses of pride. She was slightly older than him, the niece of a trail-blazing and highly respected barrister. She had taken advantage of the Victorian government's Act outlawing the prohibition on women practising in the legal profession to follow in her uncle's footsteps. The family was known to be wealthy;

they made their money importing and selling bananas from Fiji, amongst other produce. There was no financial need for her to work.

Charlotte was not as famous as her uncle—yet—but Ambrose knew she had been an object of fascination to many at university. At one point he had rather thought it might be a good idea to try and get to know her better himself. Then had come the night of the college ball. She had been invited as the guest of a friend of his, and somehow in building up the courage to approach her, Ambrose had become drunk as never before or since.

After one loud, and probably incoherent, attempt to speak with her, she had snubbed him, and he had retreated to drink his sorrows away. Unfortunately, he saw her again once more that night, when she opened a window of a friend's college room to investigate a disruption and found him vomiting into the hydrangeas outside. Their eyes had met for one startled moment before she retreated without saying a word and he returned haplessly to his retching. He assiduously avoided her ever since. Anyway, she was Chinese and arrogant to boot. Most professional men wanting to excel in society through the traditional path would not consider being attached to her in any permanent way. He was different, of course. It was years ago, Ambrose told himself sternly. She had probably forgotten who he was. In any case, a temporary embarrassment should mean nothing to someone who had lived through the war. And really, it wasn't so much his fault as her priggishness that was the problem, he assured himself. He would just have to bite the bullet. Promises needed to be kept. Pausing only to gain Ruby's approval, he used the number Bill had given him, to be answered by the clerk of chambers, who arranged an appointment for them following day.

*****

Ambrose trained well that evening, and as he warmed down in the changing rooms afterwards, he was both excited and a little apprehensive when Percy Wilson, the captain-coach, approached him from across the room.

Paddy Murphy was rubbing down his leg and recovering ankle with liniment and winked at Ambrose. 'You'll be in, I reckon, Doc.'

Wilson slapped him on the rump.

'You're in—nineteenth man, Brosie. We're playing the Roys at their home ground next week. Make sure you get to the ground early. Two o'clock at the latest. We want an hour to warm up and discuss tactics. Also, we have very few players, what with niggling injuries and the flu doing the rounds. You might be promoted to the starting line-up, so don't damage that ankle again! Oh, and by the way, your Chinese boy, Wally, will be sitting next to you on the reserves' bench.'

Ambrose knew that as nineteenth and twentieth men, they would only get a chance to play if someone had to come off the field with an injury. But given Fitzroy's reputation as a tough playing team, he thought there was every chance at least one of them would get a chance to pull on a guernsey for the Fuschias. He grinned as he left the change rooms and walked towards his car. He couldn't wait to see the Koochews' reaction to the news of Wally's selection.

Selbourne Chambers, William St
Friday, 2 September 1921

Ambrose picked Ruby up from her home, worried she would be overwhelmed if she arrived at the barristers' chambers alone. She told him Kathleen had been profuse in her thanks, but remained deeply depressed, the loss of Iris weighing heavier on her now that she had been accused of having a hand in it. Ambrose tried to be reassuring, but was cautious not to say anything to Ruby that would give her false hope.

When they entered the arched entrance to Selbourne Chambers in the Supreme Court enclave, he could feel her withdrawing into herself at his side. Sharp on 10am, they arrived at the second-floor room and knocked. A slim woman, quite tall, with black hair cut into a bob complete with bangs, opened the door. Her skin was pale, her magenta lipstick made the green of her cat's eyes look even deeper. Her make-up could not completely disguise a thin scar diagonally dissecting the right side of her brow. She wore a charcoal grey suit over a white blouse with semi-sheer stockings and mid heel oxford two-tone shoes. Hanging on the hat stand inside the door was a black coat and a red cloche hat. She was just as put together, beautiful, and dauntingly unapproachable as Ambrose had remembered her to be. She thrust her hand forward. Her handshake was strong, and her greeting businesslike, although Ambrose thought he detected a slight softening in her appearance when she spoke to Ruby.

'Come in, Doctor Pink and Miss O'Donohue. Take a seat.'

The room was comfortably furnished with wall-to-wall bookshelves and heavy leather furniture. She sat behind the desk.

This doesn't look inexpensive, thought Ambrose.

Ruby sat on the edge of her seat, clutching her hands and staring at the floor.

'I think we've met … the college ball?' Charlotte inquired, arching her brows.

She remembered.

'Youthful exuberance, poisoned chalice, never repeated.' Ambrose blushed.

Charlotte laughed. Was she laughing with or at him?

'Of course, understood. I've heard of you via Billy Koochew. He says you are a footballer and have taken his son under your wing. You must come to the Chinese Association football match. It's on in two weeks.'

'I would be delighted,' replied Ambrose, smiling.

Maybe I was wrong about her, not much priggishness in evidence at all. Does that make things better or worse? And is it a good sign that she'd apparently thought to ask around about my reputation? Or is it unfortunate?

Dragging his attention back to the matter at hand, he outlined the main facts raised at the hearing at the Coroner's Court.

When he had finished, Charlotte paused for a moment.

'I think the best defence is her reputation. It wasn't emphasised enough at the coroner's hearing, and I'm intrigued about the disparity in the times. Was the child at the O'Donohue residence long enough for such a quick decline and death? It smells fishy to me. I have heard stories about the asylum…' She tapered off, obviously not wanting to discuss her thoughts further in front of the still visibly worried Ruby.

'The baby Iris I examined in the clinic clearly had the signs of cholera—the blue skin and diarrhoea was distinctly like that of a cholera sufferer. The baby in the morgue was completely different,' said Ambrose.

'Not worth following,' she said briskly.

Ambrose felt somewhat insulted. He must have looked it, because immediately Charlotte interjected.

'It's not that I don't believe you, but how is it possible to prove the switch unless the child was identified as not being Iris? Ruby, do you know how the baby was identified? Was it by your mother?'

Ruby sniffed into her handkerchief. 'I was there too. We stood outside the glass but she was a long way from us and … well, I dunno if I could tell the difference 'tween little babies at that kinda distance. We only had poor wee Iris with us a few days.

There were a lot of larrikins and their girls, laughing and pushing! Also, they asked the asylum people, and they said it was her.'

Ambrose frowned. 'They really should not open that viewing room for the public, it's a disgrace.'

'Still, I don't think we can follow that lead. As we have a jury for the trial, if we can simply show your mother is of good character and had no reason to harm Iris, we may well have a chance at winning the case.'

'I'm so happy,' sobbed Ruby.

'Don't count your eggs before they're hatched. It won't be easy.'

As they departed, Ambrose commented, 'I like your chambers.' He wondered whether Bill had got his facts about her career wrong after all.

'I'm afraid they are not mine, Dr Pink. I am trying to establish myself at the bar and have just started reading with a friend of my uncle's. He was in court today and offered me the use of his chambers.'

I've insulted her again, thought Ambrose.

He drove back to Gertrude Street after dropping Ruby home, ruminating on his first meeting with the enigmatic Charlotte Wong. *I don't think I made a good impression. She still seems rather proud and priggish. Lots of money and prickly about being a female barrister and Chinese, I suppose.*

He arrived only to discover young Will sitting in the waiting room, his receptionist Caitlin eyeing him with more than a little suspicion.

'Come into my surgery, Will. I've got a plan.'

After sitting down, Ambrose stared hard at the young lad. 'How would you like a proper home, Will?'

Will looked both confused and surprised. 'er ... er, how can yer do that, Doc? I couldn't leave Issy! Anyway, she's not back yet.'

'I have found someone around here who is happy to offer you a room to sleep in and who will give you meals at night, sometimes at my place. She's my housekeeper Mrs Simpson. You met her—remember the lemonade? And Mr Simpson, of course. I'll be paying, so you'll have to answer to me as well. You can help Mrs Simpson and run errands for me, but you must go to school—at the North Fitzroy public school just around from where I live. Issy's not far away, so you could keep an eye out for her also. I have been making enquiries for her as well, but I have nothing to tell now. I think we had better go to the police. She has been missing for too long. What do you think?'

Will looked somewhat startled and hesitated for a few seconds. 'Ok, Doc, I'll give it a go.'

'Now I want you to come with me and I'll introduce you to Mrs Simpson. Have you got any possessions we need to collect?'

'Not at the mo, Doc.'

After decanting young Will into the care of Mrs Simpson, he returned home where Molly met him with joyous barks and a fair bit of spectacular leaping. He gave into her entreaties and headed out with her to the park.

Round 16: Melbourne vs Fitzroy
Brunswick Oval, attendance: 8,000
Saturday, 3 September 1921

Ambrose sometimes filled in at the clinic on Saturday if a doctor was sick or wanted some leave. This was one of those days. After returning home and eating a pie for lunch, he grabbed his bag with all his gear and walked through the park to the football oval, picking up Wally for his first game with the first team. The Brunswick Street Oval that was home to Fitzroy, or the Roy Boys, was just on the southern edge of the park. They were both very nervous today. Normally playing football helped him to relax after long hours in the practice. The exercise, excitement, and camaraderie took him out of himself. He needed it. Complications of baby Iris's death and all the unusual events that had followed had been really getting to him.

It was a fine early spring day, and the world was out and about. Saveloy stands had been set up by hawkers every hundred yards or so with their steaming red sausages and snowy white buns, all lubricated with mustard or tomato sauce. In between these, although fewer in number, were ice-cream vendors, almost all of which had Italian heritage. The paper boys were calling out their invitation to 'Come and gedit … read all about it … all the latest … Heralds right 'ere!' Ambrose could see that Wally took none of this in, eyes fixed ahead at the stands surrounding the oval.

'I'm nervous, coach.' Wally looked ashen.

'Good, you'll play well when you get on,' Ambrose replied. 'I know there are only a few Chinese players in the various football leagues, but you're not alone and you have been trained by me, so you have a friend in the club. As well as Paddy, of course. You won't be needed for any heroics.'

It was difficult for Ambrose today as well. Over the last few days, he had received more telephone calls than normal: pestering calls from journalists wanting him to back up his claims about cholera, and others more sinister—either silent or, on two occasions, whispered threats. A cloud of dread anticipation hung over him as he walked through the park. He was thinking of telephoning the newspapers to say he had probably been mistaken about the cholera.

They entered the ground and Ambrose pushed his way through the gathering crowd, Wally tailing behind. A group of young girls fluttered their eyelids as he passed.

"Ees posh or sumfin."

"Ees a fuckin' Fuchsia, I reckin,' said one of the young men in the group, clearly unimpressed. 'Who's the chink with him?'

Rather nervously, Ambrose and Wally finally found their way through the crowd to the visitors' rooms.

'Brosie!'

It was Cam McLeish, Detective Inspector with the Victorian Police and fellow second team player with the Fuschias.

'Cam. How are you? Not kitted up?' replied Ambrose.

'No. A niggling injury kept me out, but I thought I'd come along and watch you make a fool of yourself in the firsts.'

'So kind of you! This is Wally, my protégé and fellow reserve. We hope to get a run.'

'What were you doing coming out of Selbourne Chambers a few days ago with that young woman? I had given evidence in court and was heading back to Russell Street when I noticed you. I didn't shout because you were too far away.'

'Organising the defence of an innocent patient of mine,' replied Ambrose.

'Who's your brief?'

'Charlotte Wong. Just beginning at the bar.'

Cam looked thoughtful for a moment. 'I'd be careful if I were you, Brosie. She doesn't always keep the most salubrious company. Come and see me after the match if you want to know more.'

Ambrose was about to reply when the siren sounded. The team was called together for a last-minute talk. At 3pm sharp, the siren sounded again, and the sides clashed. It was clear from the crowd that the majority were working-class Fitzroy supporters who had no sympathy for the toffs of the Melbourne Football Club.

The barracking of the Fitzroy poor that rose above the general roar was rich in colloquialisms. 'FUCKING FUCHSIAS' had the benefit of convenience, meaning it and its derivatives were the most widely shouted. The umpire also copped a lot of abuse with frequent comparisons between the umpire and blow fly larvae—'WHITE MAGGOT'.

Much was at stake as both teams were just out of the top four that would play finals beginning in a few weeks. Melbourne's captain-coach, Percy Wilson, was magnificent, following the ball as a ruckman and in the forward line, but it was a tough, bruising match that went neck and neck right into the last quarter. Ambrose and Wally sat on the fence at the wing position on a bench in the tiny wooden enclosure for the coach, reserve players, and runners (who were constantly running onto the ground with messages to the players and bottles of water) and anxiously watched as the score see-sawed through the match. He also struggled to ignore the abuse and jibes—and an occasional expectoration—directed at them by the Fitzroy spectators behind the shed.

The match was near its conclusion with only a few minutes left, and Melbourne was down by five points when the Melbourne centre-half forward and leading goal kicker, Harry Harker, was hit from behind in a pack of players and crashed to the ground. The cheers from the home supporters drowned out the groans of the Melbourne fans, who also cried out 'free kick, free kick!' but to no avail. The umpire clearly wanted to get out of the ground and home safely that night. In the ensuing melee, a Melbourne player punched the jaw of the offending Roy Boy and immediately start wringing his hand. The trainers ran out to Harker and immediately signalled for the stretcher. As they carried him off, Smith, the player with the broken hand, accompanied them to the bench.

'Brosie, Wally, you're both on!' snapped the coach, Wilson, who had run over to the sideline. 'Centre-half forward and half forward flank.'

Ambrose jumped up, threw his gown to the ground, and ran

onto the field as the stretcher crossed the boundary line. Realising Wally was not with him, he turned and there he was, still sitting, frozen with fear. He rushed back and escorted his young protégé to his position and slapped him on the back, which seemed to have some positive effect. Wally gulped. Ambrose was welcomed by the Fitzroy centre-half back, O'Brien, with a less than gentle shoulder shoved into his chest.

'You're a dead fucking Fuchsia!' The giant laughed. Ambrose gulped.

The umpire bounced the ball on the spot where the Melbourne star had fallen. The ruckmen leapt into the air and a general scrum ensured. The ball bounced and rolled around inside a great moving mass of players. Ambrose stood out on the side of the pack waiting for the ball to appear.

Suddenly, it shot out in his direction. He grabbed it and ran—in the wrong direction! The crowd roared in surprise, but it was a ruse. He quickly baulked his opponent and headed left for a bit of space on the far flank, bouncing the ball every ten yards. He was quick but Sullivan, the Fitzroy rover, had won a number of Sprint Gifts around the country, and he was gaining. Ambrose began to panic as he knew it was too far to the goals for him to kick and the angle was too acute. Added to which all his teammates were covered by Fitzroy defenders … except … except Wally. He instinctively dropped the ball to his boot, passing it to Wally, who now was the centre of much attention as the ball was heading his way. Just a mere moment after Ambrose kicked, Sullivan dived. He fell just short of his target and grabbed Ambrose by the ankles, forcing him to crash to earth.

The siren ending the match sounded amidst the wild screams of the crowd. But the tackle was blatantly below the waist; not even a fearful umpire who wanted to get home could question the decision. He immediately signalled for a free kick down field …

to Wally! The outcome of the match was now in his hands, or rather boot.

Oh my God, thought Ambrose—as much as rational thought was possible on such occasions. *Will he cope? It's a long way out … maybe sixty yards or more. The angle is bad … forty-five degrees at best. What do I tell him whenever he is kicking?*

'Calm, calm, calm,' he shouted somewhat counter-productively as he ran to Wally.

Free kicks awarded after the siren would only score if no player touched the ball. A point either side of the central goal posts would mean they lost by four points. Through the middle untouched, and they won by the narrowest of margins—one point.

The biggest Fitzroy players crowded into the goal square to reach up and touch the ball if it fell short. All the others, apart from the giant ruckman standing on his mark, stood in a corridor a few yards away either side of Wally's run up yelling abuse and whistling. Ambrose stood back and watched.

'Chewie on your boot, you fucking fuchsia chink!'

Wally carefully dug a divot out of the turf and carefully placed the ball in it. From his careful preparation Ambrose thought it looked like Wally was 'in the zone'. The crowd heckled and the booing grew louder and louder. Wally counted back his steps and paused. He moved forward, eyes firmly on the target ahead, and he threw everything into the kick.

It soared ... and soared … and soared.

Ambrose closed his eyes, he could hear the few cheers and the many groans. He opened them and, as if in a dream, the goal umpire was holding both his arms forward—a goal! Melbourne had defeated Fitzroy by one point, on their own turf no less. Ambrose could not remember a time he was so euphoric than at the sight of Wally being chaired off the ground on the shoulders of his teammates. So great was the crush of joyous supporters in the rooms after the game that it was some time before he could even get to Wally to congratulate him.

'Fantastic, Wally—you've made it!' exclaimed Ambrose.

'Thanks, coach, but I think I just got lucky.'

'Rubbish,' replied Ambrose. 'It takes real footballer's nerves to do something like that. I'm very proud … of myself for coaching you so well.'

They both laughed. The captain, Percy Wilson, appeared beside them.

'Well done, both of you. Thanks to you two, we're still in with a chance of making the finals. I didn't bring you a beer because I also wanted to tell you that one of our members just came in. He told me that there are a few men out in the crowd trying to whip up violence against the two of you. He asked around and they're not regular Fitzroy supporters. Instead of hanging around for a drink, I suggest you both leave now by the back door. How did you get here? We'll keep an eye out.'

'Thanks for the warning. We walked, coach. I'll take Wally back to my place now. Don't worry about us—it's not far.'

It was still just light when they opened the back door of the clubhouse and peered out into the parkland and across to Ambrose's house, obscured by trees. It was only about eight hundred yards, so they thought that discretion was the best part of valour. They were still in their football gear, and they decided to move as quietly and quickly as possible. Ambrose noticed a few distinctly suspicious-looking men standing together at the side of the clubhouse with all their attention focused on the front entrance.

'Let's go,' he whispered to Wally, and they both quickly strode, as quietly as possible, out onto the grass. They had gone about ten strides when one of the men observing the clubhouse turned to throw away his cigarette stub.

'Hey!'

They'd been seen. Ambrose bolted like a frightened gazelle and Wally almost immediately followed at full speed, four or five men following in pursuit. Gasping for breath but moving fast, Ambrose suddenly noticed another group coming from the other side of the oval towards them. *I should have got the boys to escort us home*, he thought with horror. Suddenly, the second group ran into their pursuers, but instead of joining them, a fight broke out. Ambrose and Wally stopped and looked back in amazement.

'It's my dad and his mates,' exclaimed Wally. 'He said I needed to be careful today. They must have been at the match.'

By the time Ambrose and Wally made it back to the scene of the battle, their vastly outnumbered pursuers had been routed and fled. Their rescuers suffered a few bruises, but were essentially unhurt. Wally hugged his dad and Billy, then introduced Ambrose to the others.

'I'm glad you intervened,' said Ambrose.

'I'm not really happy with my son playing if this is the result,' remarked a grim-looking Billy.

'It's not really about Wally. He isn't the target; I think I am. Come back to the house and I'll get you all a drink.'

'They might not have left permanently. I think we'll reject your kind offer, and we can take it in turn to keep guard secretly for a few hours at least. Wally can go with you.'

Sitting opposite each other in the sitting room—Wally with a lemonade because his dad wouldn't let him drink, and Ambrose with a beer—they took in all the excitement of the day.

'It's a start,' said Ambrose. 'But it's not going to a bed of roses having a Chinese footballer in the mainstream.'

'I'm up to it,' replied Wally. 'Especially with your support and that of all the good people out there.'

Crash!

A stone bounced along the floor, surrounded by shards of glass. Ambrose ran out and met Billy running from the corner.

'It was that black car.' He pointed to a speck disappearing in the distance. 'They covered the number plates.'

Chapter Seven
The Warning

Lecture Theatre, Anatomy Museum
University of Melbourne, Parkville
Monday, 5 September 1921, 7pm

Ambrose eased himself into the wooden desk and surveyed the scene before him. The lecture was about to start, and he and Reggie had managed to get the last two seats, way up high in the back row. Butterby's public lectures were certainly popular with some. Tonight was on the theme of the skull of Ned Kelly, the bushranger, and its relevance to the health of the white race. Lots of bigwigs were present, especially politicians. The programme indicated that the Minister for Education was to introduce Butterby.

Both Ambrose and Reggie—who was sitting next to him—were unsettled as they had just had rather a shock. Prior to the lecture, the attendees had been encouraged to peruse the anatomy museum attached to the theatre with all its rather macabre treasures. Pride of place was Butterby's newest teaching aide, a sagittal section of a pregnant woman, which had been unveiled specially for the event. It was confronting even for Reggie and Ambrose, who had done their stint in the dissecting room, but they had become particularly disturbed by its possible provenance. The large slide was the size of a small body, perhaps five feet tall. It had been made by using the very best fine-tooth bench saw to slice through the very small dead body of a young pregnant woman, thus producing thin slices of her body, which were preserved and mounted between two glass sheets held together by a sealed frame. Inside the outline of her figure, it was possible to see cross sections of all her organs and the unborn foetus.

According to Cornelius Hamon, Butterby's surgical dresser and assistant in the dissecting room, he had sourced the cadaver of a young woman from the Benevolent Asylum in Melbourne six months previously. This was written on a card attached to the slide.

Cornelius Hamon was a character that did not altogether inspire confidence, when confidence was a characteristic that should have been front and centre in someone who dealt with such delicate matters. Acts of Parliament had been passed to stop the sort of funny business that went on in medical school dissecting rooms in the past. Hamon was well known to many of the medical graduates as he had been a fixture at the school and Melbourne Hospital for some time. He invariably dressed in a black suit, which complemented his thin, brushed back black hair, short wiry frame, and pale complexion. He was known to be Butterby's man, and to have the uncanny knack of producing cadavers or body parts seemingly on demand.

'What did she die of, Mr Hamon?' asked Reggie.

'Consumption in the lungs, Dr Robinson.' Hamon immediately turned on his heels and retired into his back office, right behind the large jars filled with arthritic knees.

'Can't see much evidence of tuberculosis in those lungs,' remarked Ambrose, pointing. 'Could be any number of conditions.'

'Too true, too true,' replied Reggie.

Ambrose stared at the specimen, because that is what the young woman had been turned into.

'I just had an awful thought, Reggie. The locals around the clinic are wondering what happened to the little pregnant vagrant that had been on the streets of Fitzroy these last few months. She seems to have disappeared.'

Preferring not to despond into dark thoughts, he lightened his tone and changed the subject.

'It's funny that we are here today, as I'm going to visit my aunt in Bendigo on Wednesday as I have to see the family solicitor. Would you like to come? It's something about Dad's collection, and I think it involves skulls.'

Reggie looked pale after his experience in the museum. 'I think I'm free. Let's go into the lecture. It's feeling decidedly creepy in here.'

*****

After a rather long introduction, the lights were lowered and Butterby moved to the lectern. All around him, stretched up in a great semicircle of seats were the crème de la crème of Melbourne scientific society, eagerly waiting to hear the great man's pronouncements. He signalled to Hamon, who was sitting next to him beside a large glass slide projector. Hamon leant down and turned on a lantern, and immediately a photo of what looked like a working-class man appeared on the screen behind Butterby.

'Today, our new nation is facing a great crisis. As we need to fill this great southern land, it is imperative that we stock it with the best of humanity. This criminal whose image I have on the screen is currently in Pentridge prison and, if allowed to breed, along with all the other degenerates, would bring about the end of our race. By allowing criminals, prostitutes, the dregs living in the slums, aboriginals, drunkards, and sexual perverts of the homosexual kind to continue to share the full benefits of citizenship, we are committing race suicide,' Butterby intoned.

'Here, here,' murmured voices in the audience.

'It's all right for him,' whispered Reggie, 'but who's going to check what's going on in every bedroom every evening? No one's getting into mine.'

Hamon placed a skull on the desk.

'Here we have the skull of Ned Kelly, the criminal bushranger,' Butterby continued. 'I have measured its cubic capacity and have discovered that it is equal to the normal size of a fourteen-year-old boy. What I am saying is that the degenerate groups in society can be discovered by measuring their heads. I have measured thousands of heads in Victoria and around the world, as you can see from this next slide.'

At that moment a new slide with a table of measurements appeared on the screen. Butterby stood and stepped towards the slide with a long pointer in his hand.

'These are measurements that have been collected by me and my colleague, Professor Berry. As you can see, those with the largest heads are the educated classes, particularly university professors and professional men. Below them are middle-class respectable white women, then boys from the best schools in the state, followed by boys educated in the state schools. Under them are the socially inefficient groups that I argue should have limited representation in voting for government and should not be given the wasted opportunity of education. These are the slum dwellers, criminals, mentally deficient, deaf and dumb, and of course, many foreigners and almost all Australian Aboriginals.'

A ripple of applause went around the theatre.

'I reckon he hasn't measured the heads of the rich old fellows who fall asleep after lunch in the Melbourne Club! They'd be down the bottom,' whispered Reggie.

Some heads turned disapprovingly towards Reggie. 'Shssh!'

Butterby continued. 'The danger with this form of mental defect, which can only be diagnosed by measuring heads, is that if you passed one of these people in the street, they would pass for normal in the normal course of events. It requires very special diagnosis to tell that they have small heads and brains.'

A new slide came up with a photograph of two skulls next to each other.

'This question of breeding a superior white race in this great land of ours is the most important question of our age. What is this white race of which I talk, of which naturally enough includes all sitting here tonight? As the great Henry Mayhew pointed out in Britain last century, the white race is a separate and pure expression of the best of mankind and appeared very early in the history of evolution. I am currently conducting ground-breaking research that will prove that the white race is superior to all other races and effectively unrelated to the coloured races.'

He pointed at the larger skull.

'Thanks to my good friend the amateur archaeologist, Charles Dawson—sadly now departed this life—I have in my position a replica of the famous Piltdown skull, discovered in a quarry in Kent in 1912. The soil and other items in the same layer as the skull, including animal teeth, have dated the skull to the Pleistocene epoch, the age at which humanity began its inexorable rise over 10,000 years ago. You can see the large brain size and gracile features with the slightly recessed forehead which make so much like a modern white man's skull. If we now compare it with this other Aboriginal skull from the northeast of Victoria along the Murray River, we can see how the brain case is much smaller and the enlarged bony brows above the eyes make this a "robust" skull. From the excavated remains, including animal bones, we can date this skull also to the Pleistocene epoch. Thus, the comparison is clear. White men had superior brains to Australian Aboriginals from the very earliest times in our evolution.'

A round of applause interrupted him.

'I cannot go into this important story as I am yet to finalise my research. I hope to present irrefutable proof of the superiority of the white race in the not-too-distant future and hopefully in London. Thank you.'

Butterby sat down to tumultuous applause. This meant that Ambrose and Reggie could sneak out the back door unnoticed.

'With all the dodgy stuff Hamon seems to get up to in the body acquisition department, you really wonder whether those two skulls at the end were stolen,' Ambrose remarked as they left the building, shivering in the chill air.

'What a load of bollocks that lecture that was. See you early on Wednesday for the trip to Bendigo then,' answered Reggie.

Bendigo, Victoria, 100 miles north of Melbourne
Wednesday, 7 September 1921

'Let's go to the *Grande* in town and Aunt Mabel will feed us,' Ambrose said to his two friends as they entered the outskirts of Bendigo after a few hours bumping up and down on the dirt surface of the Calder highway. Hedley had also decided that he wanted a trip to the country—as did Molly.

'Mabel is Mother's sister, the entrepreneur in the family and one of the first in town with an automobile. Since the deaths of Mum and Dad, she has managed a number of cafes in town, but she has recently managed to get a loan—no small feat for a woman in a small provincial city—and has opened her own café, the Grande.'

The Grande was pretty well summed up by its moniker as it could be found not only on the top floor of a grand double-storey building fronted with a huge veranda, but also it was situated along Pall Mall—the grandest boulevard in the gold mining town of Bendigo. Aunt Mabel was important to Ambrose now he was without parents, as she was his closest relative, and he was exceptionally fond of her. He admired as well as loved her.

'Aunt Mabel,' he called as they entered the large bustling dining room on the first floor. The room was full of tables covered in white starched tablecloths with silver-plate cutlery and vases full of flowers from Mabel's garden in the centre of each table, as well as on side tables around the room. As it was summer, roses predominated … red, pink, yellow, white, and striped. Mabel turned from serving a customer and blew Ambrose a kiss.

'Be with you in a minute, Brosie. Sit there!' She pointed.

She soon approached the young men with obvious delight. She was a woman in her late forties dressed in a long black skirt, white blouse, and black jacket. She was unafraid to flaunt convention and she lived with her German lover, Eric Bach, whom she had acquired on an overseas trip. Being German, Eric had been interned during the war, but he was an excellent violinist and he had become the music teacher at the newly founded Bendigo High School.

'Nice to meet you on a less sad and formal occasion, Reggie.'

'You too, Mrs Bach. The funeral was a wonderful event, however,' he replied.

'What would you like for breakfast, gentlemen?'

'We'll leave it to you—the full works as usual, I hope!'

Shortly after, the waiter arrived with three servings of newly cured ham fried in butter, soft scrambled eggs with chives, and two large field mushrooms. All this on freshly toasted bread and accompanied by many pots of the Grande's best Darjeeling tea.

After breakfast they strolled out onto Pall Mall and headed north, passing, on the opposite side of the boulevard, the domed memorial for the returned soldiers, framed by Rosalind Park. After a short stroll, they reached the corner of Williamson Street on which the famed Shamrock Hotel stood. Hedley pointed out that the famous Australian diva, Nellie Melba, had stayed there on a concert tour and that she was returning and he hoped to play in the orchestra. Diagonally opposite stood the great Victorian wedding cake structure that was the post office, and next to it the Supreme Court, similarly ornate. They turned the corner and walked up Williamson Street to the solicitors' office just diagonally opposite yet another ostentatious Victorian edifice, the splendid town hall—further evidence of civic pride and the riches of the gold that ran beneath the streets. Directly facing the town hall some two hundred yards away and dominating the entrance to Rosalind Park was the emblem of the private wealth of the gold rushes, a giant bronze statue of George Lansell—the 'Quartz King', unveiled in 1906.

They entered an impressive Victorian building and Ambrose shivered slightly in the cool of the high ceilings and thick brick walls. They introduced themselves to a man behind a desk and were shown into an office with a large cedar desk and leather-bound chairs. Lowell Lindsay, solicitor and distant relative of the 'Quartz King', rose from behind his desk and pointed to their seats. Bearded in the old fashion and buttoned up in a dark suit, Lindsay represented the respectability often found in those removed by a generation from pioneer's forbears. Inherited money helped. Being an old friend of his parents meant he had a personal interest. Reggie and Hedley were introduced.

'Welcome, Ambrose. Your father and mother were much respected and loved, as I am sure you know. I have asked you here to discuss some extra matters relating to your bequest. Although we have settled the financial aspects, I didn't want to post these to you, and felt that you needed to come and collect them personally.' He pointed to several objects arranged on a side table. 'You now have the bulk of what your parents left you, which is an endowment rich in exotic artefacts.'

He stood and walked to a side table on which was a wooden box.

'You know, of course, that your father was a collector of … how shall I say it … native artefacts. The last of these items are what I have to give you today. I was left with this locked wooden box. He told me this was particularly unusual and would be most valuable. There were supposed to be two others, but I don't know what happened to them. I hand this over to you, key included, as part of the estate.'

Ambrose took the box and key. He opened the lid. Inside was a human skull and sheets of paper covered with his father's writing. The skull had no mandible, as was often the case with what was an obviously ancient skull. He took it out and examined it. The skull was unusual as it was somewhat small with a heavy bony brow.

'I wonder if this could be a skull of an early hominid inhabitant of Australia?' Ambrose remarked. 'I've heard Butterby lecture about such things.'

'Butterby?' the solicitor enquired.

'The Professor of Anatomy and a leading surgeon at the medical school,' Hedley answered.

Reggie interjected. 'It certainly would be of great academic interest if it hasn't been reported before. We should examine it properly later, Brose.'

Ambrose rifled through his father's notes until something caught his eye. He paused and read for a moment. 'This one is Javanese, not Australian.'

'Thank you, Mr Lindsay, you have been most kind and professional,' said Ambrose. 'I hope to see you on occasions in the future—as you know, my Aunt Mabel lives here.'

He, Hedley, and Reggie left the office and headed back to the car.

'I would like to see Aunt Mabel again if you don't mind. We'll get back to Melbourne by tonight. I believe she will be at home now—do you mind?'

'Of course not,' answered Reggie. 'I'd love to see the garden. You have spoken so much about it.' Reggie also had a beautiful garden. 'What was it that caught your eye in your father's notes? You seemed distracted for a moment.'

'It was a warning. I'll tell you when I know more. It's quite disturbing. We'll talk about it at length later.'

They drove the car down Pall Mall to the south, then turned right up View Street, past all the gold rush buildings, including the Temperance Hall, with all its memories of demon drink and Methodist reformers, and the Bendigo Art Gallery with all its treasures. The car then climbed a hill, this time passing on both sides the elegant homes of the rich. Upon reaching the summit, they arrived outside one of two mansions diagonally opposite each other. They parked outside one of them—the double-storied, double-fronted red brick house with an elegant veranda standing in extensive gardens. They got out of the car and surveyed the town beneath them. Bright sunlight heightened the glaring brilliance of the blue sky of central Victoria, while an extensive array of slate and corrugated iron roofs on red-brick Victorian buildings baked in the light. The olive hue of the eucalypts was the only other colour that could compete in this this intense light far from the sea.

They entered the cool and shade of the path to Mabel's house—guarded on each side by budding oak trees and hydrangeas—and knocked on the door. Mabel greeted them with hugs. The corridor had a large grandfather clock, which chimed twelve as they entered.

'Come into the sitting room, Brosie … Reggie. I'll get you some tea.'

'Don't worry, Aunt. We've been well fed and watered today, thanks to you. I wanted to ask you about something before we made our way homeward.'

'Can I wander in your garden please, Mrs Bach?' asked Reggie. 'I noticed a particularly fine *hydrangea petiolaris* climbing your brick fence. I've wanted one for ages.'

'Of course, Reggie! Let's all go quickly. You can have flowers, cuttings, and seeds to take back to Melbourne as well.'

* * * * *

They returned to the sitting room to discover a young woman in a tweed suit, her auburn hair bobbed, approximately Ambrose's age.

'Louisa!' exclaimed Ambrose, 'I didn't know you were home from Oxford. How wonderful.'

They moved to each other and embraced as did Reggie and Hedley, who had met her on numerous occasions.

'What are you doing here? I thought you were going straight back to Somerville College after the funeral,' Ambrose enquired.

'I've just delayed the inevitable, Ambrose. It is good to spend more time with Mother and Father.'

'What a bonus! It will be just perfect to get your opinion on this material too.'

Ambrose took the freshly acquired box to the card table in the middle of the room and opened it.

'Louisa, as you have just graduated with a degree majoring in anthropology, I think you might be just the person we need today,' said Ambrose.

Louisa looked at the notes on the table that Ambrose had taken from the box. 'One of the reasons I studied anthropology was because of your father—Uncle Gus. He showed me through his collection often, and I know all about this material. Let me explain.

'These are the notes of your father concerning his exploration and research into early humankind. The skull in the case is one of three very significant skulls he obtained. One of them—the one you have been entrusted with—was a skull he found with two extraordinary men in Java: Eugène Dubois and Pieter Valdemar Stein van Haandel. Dubois had come from Europe looking for skeletal remains of what he believed were early ancestors of modern humans, and van Haandel had a great interest in such matters and was living in Java. Your father went digging with them. Missionaries had abundant time to pursue hobbies.'

Mabel interrupted. 'This was around the early 1890s, before either of you were born.'

Louisa nodded and continued. 'You know, of course, about the international sensation Java Man, or more correctly *Pithecanthropus erectus*, caused when discovered by Dubois? So, the one you have in the box is your father's discovery from Java. The other two skulls—which you don't have, and which Mum and I believe were stolen from his house recently—were found near Cohuna northwest of here.'

'Stolen! When were my father's Cohuna skulls stolen, and by whom?' asked Ambrose.

They all stared in shock at this news.

'None of you will mention this outside these four walls, will you?' replied Mabel. 'I'm sure it was Professor Butterby, but I have no proof. You know him—did he teach you?'

They all nodded.

Mabel continued, nervously looking at Louisa. 'I feel we should keep this quiet.'

'Butterby often comes to Bendigo to give lectures for the Adult Education Society. He knew of your father's interests, so he would often come to the house and ask to see what your father had in his collection and to talk with him about it. A day or two after your father died, I was driving past the house and there was a large Studebaker outside with someone in it. Butterby drove a car just like it, but I can't be absolutely sure it was him. Later that day, I went to the house and it was open. Nothing seemed to be missing, so I wasn't concerned until I realised later that the two boxes with the skulls from Cohuna were not in the list of possessions. I informed the police, but they could do little. Your father kept the boxes on his desk and all of them were there before he died. I saw them. He told me he had decided to take them to the solicitors for safekeeping, but it seems that he only took one. This confirms to me that the others were most certainly stolen.'

'Why would he steal them?' asked Hedley.

'I don't know exactly, but Gus told me that Butterby was an extremist who was driven in two contradictory directions. He was an academic who had a profound interest in human anatomy and deep history, and so he was fascinated with the origins of humanity. On the other hand, he was a fanatic who believed in the supremacy of the white race and was concerned in case his theory could be disproved. His theory was that the white race was unique, separate, and among the earliest of the races. Any new discoveries had the potential to disrupt current knowledge and upset his theories—he wanted to control the whole story.' She turned back to Ambrose. 'Butterby had offered your father large sums of money for the skulls before, but your father always refused him. He always thought it a shame that such a skilled academic was also such an unsettling fanatic.'

Ambrose hugged his aunt and then Louisa, and headed for the door. 'Sorry to rush, but I'll come back soon.'

'Come and visit me in Oxford soon, Ambrose,' Louisa called as they walked through the garden.

The conversation slipped into introspective thoughts for all of them. Such things were not polite to divulge as guests. But they had received the information they had come for and had a long journey back. They drove Ambrose's Riley out of Bendigo, through Kangaroo Flat and over Big Hill on the Calder Highway. The land was parched, and the gums looked forlorn as the spring rains had neglected the region. Silence reigned. After an hour or so driving, they then eventually crossed the Macedon Ranges with its grand country retreats for the wealthy, stopping in Woodend for a late lunch.

Searching for somewhere to stop, they came across a café decorated in the German style: lace curtains, red and white cheque tablecloths, and Baltic pine everywhere. The umbrella stand and hat stand consisted of two giant carved wooden bears.

'Those bears,' said Reggie, pointing, 'Bavarian … nineteenth century … amusing and rustic.' He was always the one to appraise anything of possible value. 'You can drop me at Westvale, it's only a few miles from here. I'm staying in the country for a few days. I'll be back in Melbourne next week,' he continued, sipping on his tea.

'I haven't visited you in the country for some time. Invite me for dinner at Westvale soon. I'd love to wander in the garden,' said Ambrose.

'What are you going to do with your inheritance, Brosie?' asked Reggie, finishing the last of the black forest cake. 'Are you going to move to South Yarra?'

'Stop nagging me. You know I like where I live and I can't afford South Yarra. In fact, I've been thinking of buying another house in the crescent—the house next door has come up for sale. It is a good price and rather grand, if derelict. You even said you liked my house.'

'Even so, it's all a bit bohemian, and why two? Why North Fitzroy? Everyone who is anyone moved out of the inner-city suburbs years ago,' quizzed Reggie.

'I feel as if I have very little family now that Dad has died. I'd like to have children, and they could live next to me when they became older. I'm feeling rather lonely—I need to create my own family and group of close friends. I can afford two in North Fitzroy, and it's rare for two together to come up for sale anywhere.'

Reggie slapped his forehead. 'I'd forgotten—what was in your father's notes in the box that was of such interest?'

'Apart from the anthropological notes, there was a warning about Butterby.'

CHAPTER EIGHT
THE TRIAL

Supreme Court, William St
Friday, 23 September 1921

Despite the acclamation of his teammates and the many drinks pressed on Ambrose by the Fuchsia's loyal fanbase, Ambrose and Wally's heroics against Fitzroy had little long-term significant effect. With other players returned from injury, Ambrose spent the last two rounds of the season on the bench, Wally went back to the second team. Melbourne had to win both their matches to have any chance of making the finals, but although they beat Geelong, who were in the top four, the top team, Carlton, made mincemeat of them, and so Ambrose's season began and finished with his hand in Wally's spectacular goal.

Still, the end of the season had not been without its highlights. Somewhat to his surprise, Charlotte Wong had forwarded him the details of the Chinese Association match that she had mentioned when they met in her borrowed chambers. Ambrose attended with his neighbour Billy Koochew and young Will. They had been delighted to see that Paddy, the trainer and wharfie, and Wally formed a connection over the game. He had only managed to exchange a few words with Charlotte herself, who was seated elsewhere with her uncle and other dignitaries and surrounded by young Chinese men and women during the break, but she had seemed much more approachable. He hadn't had an opportunity to find Cam McLeish after the match against Fitzroy, so what he had been told about Charlotte played on his mind. What on earth could her unsavoury connections be? Regardless, Ambrose was confident she would provide the O'Donohues with the best possible representation when their case came to trial. Further speculations he tried to keep to a minimum, not wanting to set himself up for disappointment.

The day of the trial was a wet and windy Friday. A bad omen, Ambrose thought as he dressed in a conservative suit fitting for a day in the Supreme Court. While Reggie drove him into the city, his mind constantly wandered through a landscape of different topics, but always returned again to the matter of baby Iris. They parked on William Street outside the entrance to the Christopher Wren-styled magnificently domed Supreme Court of Victoria. Gathered outside the building was Ruby, the priest from John the Baptist Church, and other supporters standing with Charlotte, who was dressed in her gown and wig. Ambrose and Reggie walked up to the group, the wind lashing wildly around them.

'Let's get out of this weather,' was the first thing Charlotte said, leading the group up the stairway and through the impressive wooden doors. Ambrose introduced Reggie, who was uncharacteristically demur in his response.

'Dr Pink, I don't have an instructing solicitor. Could you sit next to me at the bar table and hand me any papers if I need them? I'll show you what they are when we are seated. We're in luck I hope—we've got Justice Cussen, a Catholic and a reasonable judge by reputation.'

As he greeted the others in the group, Ambrose felt relieved that he'd chosen his most conservative suit, now that he would be sitting right in the front.

After some time wandering through the labyrinth of the venerable building, they found the court assigned to the case. The main party took their seats in the public gallery and Charlotte took hers at the bar table, with Ambrose at her side. Shortly after, a great *whoosh* filled the room as the door was pushed open, signalling the entry of Sir Digby Bent. He was followed by a junior barrister and two solicitors; behind them the party from the Kew Asylum entered, including the Superintendent, Dr Negrone, and a junior doctor.

Sir Digby's junior barrister wandered over to Charlotte and stared at her. With a sneer, he spat out, 'Sir Digby asked me to point out to you that this is no place for a woman.' Before either Charlotte or Ambrose could reply, he turned his back and returned to his seat.

'Bastards,' whispered Ambrose. 'Let that be encouragement. They have already under-estimated you.'

Charlotte looked ahead, pale and tight-lipped.

The jury shuffled into the jury box on the side, and Ambrose anxiously scanned their faces to try to guess which way they would vote. Shortly after 10am, the tipstaff and associate of the judge entered from behind the seat on the judge's bench. The tipstaff immediately banged the gavel a number of times.

'All stand!'

The judge appeared from the same door and sat. The court followed suit. Cussen was a man whose appearance seemed designed to inspire confidence. He had had strong hands, rugged features on an open face with a pronounced brow, a mane of receding white hair, and a large moustache.

'Welcome to my court, Miss Wong. I have had the pleasure of your uncle appearing before me.'

'Thank you, your honour,' answered Charlotte.

'The prosecution may commence,' said the judge.

Sir Digby rose to his feet. 'Your honour, members of the jury, this case, although it only concerns a baby—baby Iris O'Donohue—this case represents a matter of enormous importance to the very foundations of our society and our race. Why, that great surgeon and anatomist, Sir Richard Butterby, wrote about matters relating to this very case in the *Argus* newspaper this morning. Should we allow the inferior members of our race to breed, then melancholy events such as we have witnessed with baby Iris will be all too common ...'

'Perhaps you could get to the point, Sir Digby?' Justice Cussen interjected just as Charlotte jumped to her feet to object.

'Of course, your honour,' replied Sir Digby. 'We will show that the poor idiot child, born to a hysteric feeble-minded girl of feeble-minded stock ...'

Charlotte jumped to her feet again. 'I object your honour. No evidence has been led to support such assumptions about the character of the child and her mother.'

'I agree, Miss Wong. Please lay out your case without the histrionics, Sir Digby.'

'Very well, your honour. Mrs Kathleen O'Donohue, the accused, attended the Kew Asylum on Friday 12 August of this year and, masquerading as the child's grandmother, gained access to the child. She then returned with it to 23 Faraday Street, Carlton. On realising the error, Superintendent Negrone went to the address on Wednesday, 17 August, only to find the child almost dead due to malnutrition and neglect. This heinous act was under the supervision of Dr Ambrose Pink. Dr Negrone then reclaimed the child and returned it to the asylum.'

'I imagine the medical board are investigating the role of Dr Pink?' asked the judge.

'The process has begun I believe, your honour,' replied Sir Digby.

Ambrose went pale. He had not known of this.

'I would like to call the first witness for the prosecution, Dr Silvio Negrone, Superintendent of the Kew Insane Asylum.'

Most of the morning was taken up by the prosecution out-lining the case against Kathleen. It all sounded very straightfor-ward, and Ambrose became more and more depressed about their chances of success.

'It seems that we are approaching lunch,' announced the judge. 'We will adjourn until 2pm.'

Lunch was a sombre event.

'What do you think, Miss Wong? How are we going?' Ambrose asked in a sombre tone.

'Don't worry,' she replied, to the obvious relief of Ruby, who was sitting quietly to the side. 'We haven't started yet, and I have some good arguments to put to his honour. There is a long way to go yet.'

Ambrose wasn't sure if this was designed to encourage him or for the benefit of the anxious looking Ruby, sitting quietly just within earshot to their side.

A bell rang, and they quickly re-entered the court room.

'Miss Wong, would you like to question the witnesses?' the judge asked once they were all settled and court had been declared in session.

'Yes, your honour. I have questions for Dr Negrone.'

Charlotte sprang to her feet, looking every inch as though she belonged here. Ambrose noticed that the hand holding her notes was shaking ever so slightly. He hoped no one else was observing her that closely. Negrone re-entered the witness box after having been sworn in.

Charlotte cleared her throat and began. 'Dr Negrone, you said that when you discovered that Mrs O'Donohue had taken the baby, you *immediately* went to retrieve her. Does that mean you were unaware that the baby was missing for five days and, if so, why?'

'I was absent from Melbourne and returned on the Wednes-day.'

'How do you know Mrs O'Donohue claimed that she was the grandmother if you were not involved in the decision to allow the baby to leave?'

'I was informed of the matter by my deputy, Dr Smith.'

'Is there any written record in the register?'

'No. His details are correct, as I spoke to him personally—'

'But, if there are no written records, all your evidence on this matter is hearsay.'

'I object, your honour!' Sir Digby exclaimed, rising to his feet, groaning and harrumphing.

'Objection overruled,' said the judge.

Sir Digby flopped back down.

'Where is Dr Smith?' asked Charlotte.

'I dismissed him for incompetence over the incident. I have no idea where he is.'

'Would counsel please come to the bench?' ordered the judge.

Justice Cussin spent some time talking to the two of them, and Sir Digby was obviously not happy. The phrase 'hearsay evidence' and 'not admissible' could be heard coming from the judge.

On returning, Charlotte resumed her questioning.

'Dr Negrone, I believe that your specialty is psychiatry?'

'That is correct. That is why I am in charge of the asylum,' he answered, smirking at his team.

'Do you, or rather, does the institution have any records of baby Iris's health other than a birth certificate?'

'Why is that relevant?'

'Answer the question,' ordered the judge.

'I don't believe so … I, I …'

'So, how can you in fact know the baby in question was healthy when she left the asylum?' Charlotte stared hard at Negrone.

'Er … er … Dr Smith told me.'

'The same Dr Smith who is currently nowhere to be found?'

Sir Digby jumped to his feet. 'Your honour, the baby was taken from the O'Donohue residence almost dead, suffering from malnutrition—'

'Sit down, Sir Digby. Objection, if that is what you want, over-ruled.'

She sure is razor smart, thought Ambrose.

'Do you have any qualifications in paediatrics, Dr Negrone?'

'Er, er, no. Why does that matter?'

'Because Iris was a baby. Surely someone at the asylum had some training in dealing with the babies born there?'

'Er … er … there is no need for such a person.'

'Dr Negrone, you can provide no credible evidence that the baby was taken by deceit, and none that she was well when she left the asylum five days before you collected her from Mrs O'Donohue's house. As your witness testified in your initial questioning, the baby displayed no marks of violence or poisoning; furthermore, she was at the O'Donohue residence for five days, which is a comparatively short time, so it is extremely difficult to see how negligence, in that time period, could be responsible for her death. How indeed can Mrs O'Donohue be responsible if there is no certifiable evidence to prove the neglect of the baby in her care?'

'Miss Wong, do you wish to call any witnesses?' asked the judge.

'I have a character witness, your honour: Father O'Brien, a priest from Mrs O'Donohue's parish church.'

Father O'Brien outlined his view of Mrs O'Donohue's character, respectability, and a comprehensive list of the good works she had performed in the community.

Justice Cussen addressed the jury. 'Men and women of the jury, fortunately for us all this case has been short. I have read Sir Richard Butterby's piece in the *Argus* this morning about restricting the rights of the so-called 'lower classes' to breed. The law is against such theorising, as every citizen is equal before the law. Apart from the initial flourish on these matters, the prosecution has failed to give any credible evidence that could be used to find Mrs Kathleen O'Donohue guilty as charged. I instruct you to withdraw and find her not guilty.'

As a consequence of this very clear instruction, the jury's absence was short. When the foreman of the jury later stood and declared her innocent of the crime, a great deal of relief and joy filled the stuffy atmosphere of the court. The reporters, among them the *Argus* journalist, rushed out to write articles. Prominently, the phrases 'pathetic case' and 'the poor but good aunt' would make it into numerous prints.

Outside on the steps under the dome, Ambrose stood amongst the happy band. Dressed in his dark suit, he and Charlotte—in black, with her court robes on top and a horsehair wig—stood out from the working-class women around them.

Reggie wandered over. 'Congratulations and thank you. You were very impressive. The asylum people obviously did not expect you to be so good! Ambrose thought you would be ace!'

'I hoped you had no such negative thoughts?' Charlotte stared at Ambrose.

'Of course not!' he exclaimed rather too vehemently, blushing.

Charlotte stared at him quite purposely. 'I'm pleased for Kathleen, and I was delighted that the judge was fair and unbiased. I wish all the members of the legal profession were like Justice Cussen. I doubt I can practise regularly unless all the judges are as positive to female counsel. He really didn't mind a woman appearing in his court in the slightest, but regrettably, he is not the norm.'

Reggie interrupted: 'You're right, I've never seen the prejudice against female barristers in action, but I have heard about it.

It was nice not to see it in action today. Say, how about we all have a drink or something to celebrate?'

Ambrose watched Charlotte's reaction. It seemed obvious that she had been unprepared for the offer and was vacillating … or so he surmised.

'As long as it is not like the last time I attended a social occasion with Dr Pink,' she replied in haughty tones.

Ambrose closed his eyes, briefly in pain, and hoped that his wince was not visible.

'If you are referring to the college ball many years ago, I can only assure you again that it was an isolated incident. If you would be more comfortable meeting with me and a group of friends … you're invited too, Reggie. I am currently entertaining a foreign guest, a dear friend of mine and my parents. He only visits occasionally, and I am sure you will greatly enjoy his company. You could have dinner at my home in our company.'

A gust of wind caused the jabot attached to her collar to lift up. She smoothed the white bands down, paused, and then looked up.

'Very well. That would be most welcome.' She flashed a brief smile.

'Excellent, seven for seven-thirty, 44 Alfred Crescent, North Fitzroy. 7218 if you need to telephone,' he added.

She wrote the details into a notebook. 'I look forward to it.'

He watched her disappear into the crowd of barristers and their clients before he collected Rose and Kathleen into the Riley and headed off for what was sure to be a joyous celebration at their Faraday Street home.

'You know, Doctor,' Kathleen said in the car on her way home, 'I am very grateful for your help and so very happy to be free, but little Iris is still gone and I don't understand what took 'er from us. It makes 'er loss even harder to bear.'

'I understand,' replied Ambrose. 'We can't bring her back, but we haven't finished finding out what did happen to her. I promise to get you some answers so you can find some peace, for yourselves and for her.'

He again wondered what Cam had meant about Charlotte's unsavoury connections and if they might be any use to him now.

Chapter Nine
Young Charlotte Wong's Unfortunate Banquet

Bangkok, Khlong Sathon
Saturday, 1 November 1913
(eight years before the year of the adventure)

'Chen-Chen, get your hand out of the water. It's not clean.'
'But all the children are swimming in the canal, Auntie. Can I swim too?'

'Buddhists are required to bathe daily, but these children and their parents have not been taught about bacteria,' Chen Nom-chong answered, stroking the hair of her fifteen-year-old niece, Charlotte.

The odours of sewerage and rotting vegetation was mingled with the powerful scents of some nearby flowering golden rain trees and frangipani bushes. As if such an olfactory feast was inadequate, blended into the mix for the visitors' pleasure were smells of spicy charcoal cooking from the open verandas on houses supported by stilts built over the khlong, as many families had fired up the charcoal burners for the evening meal. Others were out on their boats paddling to the floating market and stopping at vendors' boats or the open structures over the water where food was sold to be eaten in situ or taken home. The khlong was teeming with all variety of boats and markets.

'Can I have some grilled chicken, Auntie?'
'No, Chen-Chen dear, it will spoil your appetite, and my sister

Apiradee has ordered a banquet tonight for our visit. They will have snacks when we arrive in a few minutes.'

The woman paddling the punt slowly turned it towards the bank. Their destination was a large pavilion jutting out from an expansive garden that ran from the bank of the khlong up on either side of a large traditional teak Siamese house. The women disembarked on the jetty attached to the wooden structure over the water and, climbing the few wooden stairs, found themselves in the outdoor kitchen typical of such houses. This comprised a teak floor and ceiling, held aloft by carved teak posts without walls. A number of single clay burners, along with some larger double burners, were smoking with burning charcoal. Many delicious scents escaped from the woks on the burners surrounding them, including those of various curries, frying meat, and grilling fish. Pots of rice sat on one of the larger double burners. Around a low wooden table, other women chopped vegetables and prepared salads and snacks. This entailed wrapping ingredients in rice paper or omelette nets that were being prepared on a nearby burner. A young girl, clearly not Siamese, with different features and darker skin, approached them with two ceramic cups. These contained jasmine-scented rainwater that had been ladled from large green clay pots in the open. As it was Saturday, she was dressed in shimmering purple silk fashioned into traditional Thai dress. A strict colour code informed the daily choice of colour. Chen and Charlotte bowed slightly, hands together, and the girl bowed deeply in return. She smiled at Charlotte and spoke to her in Siamese. Chen answered for Charlotte, and the girl darted off and came back with some of the snacks being prepared in the kitchen. Charlotte ate them at once as she hadn't eaten since breakfast and it was mid-afternoon.

'*Khob khun mak mak kah*,' she said to the young cook.

Much to the surprise of the two visitors, she added, 'I can

speak English as well. Please come through, Khun Chen and Charlotte.'

She smiled, turned, and led the two visitors deeper into the dark wooden house.

'*Lohk Gai, Lohk Gai*, how wonderful to see you. I could have collected you from the station. Why didn't you let me? I see you have met Hli, my beautiful Hmong daughter.'

The woman addressing Charlotte's aunt as '*Lohk Gai*' or 'Little Chick'—her Siamese nickname—was her sister, who was, to Charlotte's eyes, extremely similar in appearance to her aunt, although a little taller and older. She was also dressed in the traditional Siamese costume of a panang: cloth wound around the waist and then passed between the legs and attached at the back. Above it, a wrap-around piece of cloth under the armpits was pinned behind. Both pieces of cloth were in mauve silk, as it was Saturday. Her waist, arms, shoulders, legs, and feet were bare.

Chen replied, 'I wanted to come from the railway station in a boat down the khlongs, the way we used to travel, and meet you here at the family house so that Charlotte could experience it.'

'I'm so sad to have you here on this occasion, to mourn the death of your husband Yijun. We can talk about it at length later, but please introduce me to this beautiful young girl. This must be Charlotte, my niece and your ward.'

'You'll need to speak Mandarin or English, sister—she has no Siamese. She was born in Australia. Charlotte, this is your other aunt, Khun Apiradee.'

'Hello Auntie Apiradee, I'm pleased to meet you. Aunt has spoken of you often.'

Aunt Apiradee embraced Charlotte. 'I have taken the liberty of buying and preparing for you both some silk cloth so that you can wear traditional dress tonight to meet the family. A distant cousin in the family has just been elevated to the position of *Chao*

Praya Chodeuk Rajasrethi, which means that he has become the Head of the Department of Eastern Affairs and Commerce for his Royal Highness. This means he is in charge of trade and foreign affairs with China. The holder of this title also becomes the head of our Chinese community in Siam. His name is Narong Thamrongnawasawat. He is known in the family as *Kung*, meaning "little shrimp". His elevation is a great honour, especially as he is so young—just thirty. He wished to be invited to offer his condolences to you, Chen. Kung told me that he remembers your husband when he was just a little boy, and that he was more like a father to him and an inspiration. Kung is also bringing his chief wife, but it will be relatively informal as it is family, and we are here to honour you, and welcome Charlotte, of course.'

The two visitors were shown to their room.

'Aunt, are there many people in Bangkok who have both Siamese and Chinese ancestors like us?'

'The Chinese have been immigrating into Siam and intermarrying for centuries to the extent that it is difficult to find many wealthy families in Bangkok that don't have some of both in their history. The royal family is part Chinese. Your mother gave you an Anglo-Saxon name because you were born in Australia and she wanted you to fit in, but you were also named after me, which is why I call you Chen-Chen.'

'So, I am part Siamese?'

'Yes, Chen-Chen.'

'I like it here very much. I think I will come back many times. We aren't going to live here, are we, Auntie?'

'I haven't decided what to do yet, Chen-Chen. Nearby is a good girls' school run by the nuns, so we could stay here for some years—we'll see. Now wash, and I'll show you how to wrap and put on the traditional dress.'

Later that evening, the family sat around a large European

table. The sound of frogs in the khlong provided a cacophonous aural background to the dinner—perhaps they were complaining about the smell of the water. Children ran around the house, eating in the kitchen, but Charlotte, both as a special guest and as a developing young woman, was given a place at the table. The cooks, including Hli, presented the family with an increasingly exotic selection of various dishes. As it was hot, and the family were wealthy, Charlotte was surprised to find the rice was served on ice. Some flavours were spicy, sour, hot, sweet, and altogether quite unlike anything Charlotte had eaten at home, but some she recognised as similar to the Chinese dishes often served by her aunt Chen in Melbourne.

'I like the sweet and sour soup with prawns and the green beef curry best, Aunt.'

'The recipes are from the funeral books of your ancestors,' Apridee replied. 'That way, we remember them when we eat.'

'Khun Chen … may I call you "great aunt"?' asked Narong Thamrongnawasawat.

'Of course, Narong. May I call you *Kung*?'

They all laughed at using a nickname for one so important seemed incongruous.

'Please tell us about your trip, great aunt.'

'Yinjun died in August, as you know, and I couldn't stay in the house any longer as it was full of memories that I wished to banish. So I took Charlotte from school to accompany me and we sailed from Melbourne in September. It took some weeks to arrive in Singapore and we stayed for a week or two to meet some distant relatives. Then we caught the excellent train to Bangkok a few days ago and arrived today. We aren't too exhausted from travel. We both loved boating down the khlongs to here from the station, even if I had forgotten that the smells are sometimes challenging!'

'It was a bad cholera season this summer,' said Narong. 'His Royal Highness asked for some sanitary experts from England to come and give advice about the khlongs, and they threw up their collective hands in despair at the thought of how difficult it would be to sewer a city that is criss-crossed by canals and the great Chao Phraya river. One of them had been at Oxford with the king and me, and so he stayed in my house.'

Conversation and eating continued filling the evening with good cheer. The evening concluded with some traditional dancing by some of the young girls and then, out of respect to the newly arrived guests, everyone left rather early, with the promise from Kung that he would bring his motor car on Monday morning and take the visitors for a drive around the streets of Bangkok.

Sathorn Road
Monday, 3 November 1913, 9am

Charlotte and Chen climbed into the back of the large American car, while Kung and the driver sat in the front. Chen had reverted to European dress, but Charlotte was an adventurous young lady and she enjoyed wearing her new Siamese clothes, although because it was Monday, where yellow was the appropriate colour, her aunt had borrowed yellow silk for her to wear.

'Where has all the water from the khlongs gone?' asked Charlotte.

'They only fill twice a day at high tide, apart from the larger ones that have sluice gates to keep them permanently full,' replied Kong.

What Charlotte most noticed about Bangkok was its enormous variety. Singapore had been a shock, an amazing mix of the oriental and the occidental, but Bangkok was even more extraordinary. Buddhist temples covered in glistening gold sat next to filthy hovels or Italian Renaissance-style public buildings. Large shiny cars passed rickshaws being pulled by coolies, a motor tram car ran up and down the centre of Bangkok alongside elephants and horse-drawn gharries, and there was always that extraordinary smell of spices, charcoal braziers, fragrant plants, and fetid water.

They drove down New Road, a modernised thoroughfare leading from the king's palace to the far end of the city. Glued to the window, Charlotte spied the European department stores in front of which paraded Europeans, Siamese in traditional panung or even in European dress, and many others from different Asian places in their own native dress. Kung pointed out that European dress was quite often worn by wealthy Siamese, and they saw cars in which Siamese women sat with bobbed hair and dress that would have not seemed out of place parading at the Paris end of Collins Street in Melbourne. There were Chinese among the crowds, some of whom could be recognised by the traditionally compulsory cultural pigtail, and yet others who had discarded the tradition without the penalties that had not so long ago applied. Amongst all these wandered the saffron-robed monks who were so ubiquitous to the city.

From the main road branched out little lanes that were blocked by markets. Other large roads were lined and overhung with tamarind and other exotic trees. All around were people who were clothed in so many different forms of dress, with different physical features and hairstyles.

'Auntie, there are so many different races and people here, all living in peace. It's not like Melbourne at all.'

'Since 1901, much has changed in Australia, Chen-Chen. We can only hope it will improve.'

They stopped at stalls for food and snacks, and drove to the hill from which rose the beautiful golden temple Wat Sa Ket, in the royal district, with its grand mixture of Italian and Siamese architecture.

'Behind the royal palace is a school for the daughters of the royal family, princes, and aristocracy.' Kung pointed to the building. 'They remain at the school until they are married or become a concubine. Are you promised to any man, Charlotte?'

'It is not done that way in Australia, Narong,' interrupted Chen, suddenly looking oddly strained. 'I promised Charlotte's aunt that we would return by three. Would you mind if we were driven back to Sathon Road?'

'Of course not.'

When they returned, Chen took Charlotte up to her room and insisted that she change into her normal clothes. *What was happening?* thought Charlotte. *Why was Auntie so cross?*

Chen then left Charlotte alone. Intrigued with the change in mood, Charlotte opened the door. She could just hear her aunt having an animated conversation with her sister in another room in Siamese.

'Charlotte, come here please,' called Aunt Chen.

Charlotte walked down the corridor and into a library. It had a felt-top table, a desk, and comfortable chairs. The shelves on the side tables were adorned with fine blue china, if there was space for them among the countless books. Her aunts were sitting in two of the chairs; both simultaneously gestured for Charlotte to join them in the empty seat opposite.

'What we have to say to you is very difficult,' said Chen. 'I am sure that you are not ready for it, but Apiradee insists and is probably correct. Who shall start?' Auntie Chen looked quite flustered.

Aunt Apiradee began. 'When you were out today, I received a letter. Hand delivered to me, as head of the family in Bangkok.

Kung wrote requesting that I speak to Chen about his offer to make you, Charlotte, his concubine or second wife.'

Charlotte was dumbstruck. Her head swirled. He'd only met her at the dinner, and she was fifteen. 'No, NO, NO.' She almost screamed.

'I was a fool to bring you without thinking of such an outcome. I've been in Melbourne too long,' Chen whispered. 'It is not at all possible, for many reasons. However, I am now aware, the fool I've been, that the reasons I could give would not seem to be impediments in Siam.'

'It is not an unreasonable request from one so important, and you would be treated well and with great respect,' Apiradee interrupted. 'But I understand that you would not be prepared for this. If the answer is no, I suggest we think carefully about what we do. Kung is an honourable man, but it is not usual for a man as elevated as he has become to be refused. He won't see your problems, just the honour he feels he is bestowing on you and the insult if you refuse.'

The next day they fled Bangkok for Melbourne.

96 St Vincent's Place, South Melbourne
24 December 1913

'Auntie, there's a parcel that's just arrived from Siam.'

Charlotte ran excitedly into the front room where her Aunt Chen was reading the paper.

'It's addressed to you and me. Can I open it? It's probably from Aunt Apiradee.'

'Of course, Chen-Chen, open it.'

It took some effort to open, as it was heavy and packed in a great deal of paper and various cardboard boxes. With the last layer removed, both the women found themselves looking upon a magnificent white elephant, carved in ivory. A small card with Siamese characters accompanied it.

'How wonderful!' exclaimed Charlotte.

Her aunt, however, looked very unhappy. 'You don't understand, Charlotte. It's from Narong … Kung … the man who proposed to you. He says that he hopes the elephant does all that he expects it will do.' She paused and took a deep breath. 'That means he wishes bad luck on you unless you return. It is a threat!'

'What do you mean, Auntie?'

'White elephants are meant to bring great luck to the nation, and if one is born it is immediately brought to the king, who provides a most lavish lifestyle for it at great cost. When the king is displeased with a nobleman, he sends him a white elephant in the expectation that the upkeep of it will ruin him. If the prince or aristocrat returns the gift, he not only suffers a great loss of status, he also admits wrong and subjugates himself to the king. Narong did not send this to us with benign intent, Chen-Chen. I cannot see how you can avoid submitting to his wishes forever. Your refusal will create great problems for your family in Bangkok.'

Chapter Ten
The Dutchman's Warning

44 Alfred Crescent, North Fitzroy
Friday, 30 September 1921, 7pm

It was a late September night in Melbourne; therefore, it was dark, wet, and windy. As the taxi circled slowly around Alfred Crescent, Charlotte reviewed her expectations for the evening. She had tossed up whether to dress 'flapper' or 'traditional Chinese', and she had decided that, as she didn't know any of the company or her host socially, she would opt for traditional. *More intimidating*, she thought. She had borrowed Auntie Chen's black silk dress that she'd worn as a young woman—tight-fitting with a golden dragon wending its way from low hem to high neckline.

I have my doubts about Ambrose Pink, but he had gone to a good deal of trouble to help the O'Donohues and young Wally, so perhaps he is acceptable … perhaps even nice.

Charlotte disembarked from the taxi, opened the gate, mounted the short flight of steps, and knocked. Barking broke out and in a short time, Ambrose opened the door, holding a small dog by the collar, who immediately escaped and almost jumped up on Charlotte before Ambrose intervened.

Likes dogs … that's a good sign too.

Delicious odours of food wafted from the kitchen in the rear.

Ambrose seemed to be somewhat tongue-tied at first and stared, finally smiling. 'Um … Charl … um … Miss Wong … I mean … Molly will destroy your dress if she jumps on you. Please come in.' He held on firmly to the eager, straining dog.

Charlotte gave him a smile and entered, patting the over-excited Molly on the head. They entered the vaulted front sitting room with its painted ceiling and slightly old-fashioned but comfortable armchairs and sofas. Reggie and Hedley scrambled to their feet to greet her. Both seemed somewhat taken aback, and Reggie whispered to Hedley, which seemed to amuse him. Charlotte noticed Ambrose stiffen and whisper something curtly to his guests, who were obviously his friends. They were both introduced.

'May I introduce the great friend of my parents and, I hope, of mine—Pieter Valdemar Stein van Haandel … and Miss Charlotte Wong,' said Ambrose.

Charlotte's gaze was transfixed by van Haandel. *What an extraordinary looking man*, she thought.

He was dressed in what the inhabitants of the Dutch East Indies would call formal wear: a straight sarong, shirt, and loose straight-cut coat, all of wondrous colours and complexity, topped off with sandals on his feet. But what was truly astonishing was his size and presence. He was gigantic in every proportion: height, width, and girth, and he had an enormous salt-and-pepper beard.

'Absolutely delighted to meet you,' he boomed. 'Young Ambrose is certainly NOT a friend of mine. He is as good as FAMILY.'

'Please take a seat, Charlotte. What shall you drink?' Ambrose interrupted.

He looks nervous, thought Charlotte. She gestured to the bottle of Old Court already sitting on the small table next to van Haandel.

'It's Charlie to my friends. A whisky would be nice.'

The giant Dutchman had a giant crystal glass full himself.

He rose, poured a generous measure into an identical glass, and handed it to her.

'Please, you call me Pieter. This Australian whiskey is excellent.'

Ambrose offered the water jug, of which she partook frugally.

'Ambrose has told me all about your great victory, to which we must all drink.'

'Thanks, I was certainly pleased to win, and I hope to have more opportunities to represent such worthy causes. Unfortunately, everyone has little faith in the profession accepting women at the bar.'

'Never mind them,' replied Reggie. 'You have a supportive and captive crowd right here. I told everyone how well you argued the case.'

'Here, here!' said Ambrose, and they all nodded with great enthusiasm.

Soon the mood had become extremely amicable; everyone was on a first name basis, Molly was entrenched at the feet of her new idol, and any early awkwardness was banished. The conversation was punctuated regularly by the booming laugh of the Dutch visitor whose sociability and conviviality were infectious. Suddenly, Hedley put his hand up, demanding attention.

'I have been asked, don't you know, to play with the great diva herself!'

'Who and what?' Ambrose asked quizzically.

'Nellie Melba, of course. She's in town on a homecoming tour. Been invited to perform at some special dinner at the Exhibition Buildings, but she's also putting on a concert at Her Majesty's Theatre. They're getting together a scratch orchestra, and I've been chosen!'

'Congratulations!' they all chimed in and raised their glasses.

Drinks finished, they moved to the dining room next door for a delectable first course of oyster soup.

'How long are you staying here, Pieter?' asked Charlotte.

'I have an open ticket. Yesterday I was invited by my Australian political contact to attend the grand dinner that is to be held to celebrate the twentieth anniversary of the Federation in the Exhibition Buildings in Carlton. It is to be held in one month, and it seems of interest, especially in this such young country, so I will stay. I may have to find other accommodation, Ambrose. Won't do overstaying—'

'You can stay next door in 42 for as long as you wish, Pieter. I bought it recently. In fact, I insist,' Ambrose said.

'Tell us in great detail the sins of young Ambrose in his early life, won't you Pieter? We're all dying to know,' asked Reggie, smiling broadly.

'Definitely,' added Hedley. 'We all have strong stomachs here!'

Pieter continued with a smile.

'Ambrose's parents spent some years in Mojokerto in East Java where I was living, and we became great friends. Young Ambrose occasionally accompanied us on expeditions for artefacts and specimens until he returned to school here, of course.'

'I remember those occasions well,' Ambrose said. 'In fact, I have quite a few artefacts that my family collected in this house. Once I have them catalogued, I plan to donate them to a museum. I'll happily show you, Pieter, and Charlotte, if you are interested. These two chaps get bored as soon as I mention a word of my collection.'

'We wouldn't think it dull if you didn't go on and on.' Reggie's smile and dramatic groan belied his words.

Obviously old and close friends, thought Charlotte. She had decided that she liked them and was impressed by Pieter. His eccentricities appealed to her. Clearly a man of great intellect. Ambrose, she had thought before tonight, was an appealing but ultimately run of the mill young man. Altogether typical of his class and background, but this change of opinion made her wonder if her own prejudices were getting in the way of assessing him appropriately. It seemed that, along with his kindness to the downtrodden classes of society, he was intelligent and good fun. In any case, she was surprised at how relaxed she was in their company and was glad she had, after all, decided to take the chance to come.

'If you want to hear someone going "on and on" about collections, just let Reggie take you to Westvale. It's a treasure trove according to him, but a junkyard to everyone else,' said Ambrose.

'Enough joshing, you two. You have guests,' Charlotte said, smiling broadly.

'Joshing?' said Pieter, 'What is this "joshing"?'

'"Geinen" in Dutch, Pieter. "Joshing" is an American word,' replied Ambrose.

A smile of comprehension lit up Pieter's face. 'Such companionship reminds me of those times with your parents. Ambrose, I must tell you that they have so much inspired my interest in anthropology that I am returning for some years to study for my doctorate at the University of Leiden. I have a coffee plantation in Java, and I deeply love the region, its people, and culture, and so I will return also. I made a detour here when I heard of your father's death, but I will travel on to Holland soon. Enough of me—let us pay our respects to this wonderful roast beef Mrs Simpson has placed before us, and this excellent Australian claret. And then, tell me more about the sad case of the baby and the asylum.'

Ambrose explained the history of the case, leaving the matter of cholera and substitution to the end.

'Stop!' van Haandel exclaimed, placing his knife and fork on the plate. He stared long and hard at Ambrose. 'It seems we have, after all, even more overlapping interests. I had no plans to mention these matters to you, Ambrose, as I had no idea you might be connected. Can I tell you all what I know and be sure it will go no further?'

'All present here have been told the story and I assure you can be trusted,' said Ambrose.

Pieter raised his glass, emptied it in a gulp, and refilled it to the top. 'This may take some time, and I need fortifying!'

'Just last year we had a visitor in Mojokerto who claimed to be connected to the Melbourne medical school. It's quite a small European community and so one hears all the gossip. I met a man who was very interested in the human remains that had been found by my countryman Eugène DuBois—known now as Java Man, an early hominid with heavy brows and so on … Do I need to elaborate, Ambrose?'

They all nodded or murmured in the negative, but indicated for him to go on regardless.

'I took this man out and entertained him. I asked after my Brosie, of whom he could offer only a little. Clearly, he was a man only interested in "important people", and Brosie was too junior to concern him. I showed him various sights, but I soon tired of his company. I did not find him compatible in his views of my beloved Java. He expressed his viewpoint that the natives were, as he put it, "inferior"! I then heard strange stories about his activities: that he was in Surabaya, the nearest port, asking about which of the ship captains could be "bought"; where he could find cholera sufferers; that he was spending time with a French doctor of unknown past and dubious morals. I was surprised when I discovered that he had made arrangements for cargo to be shipped by the *SS Catalina* to Australia also. The captain was a well-known pirate called Salvatore Negrone.'

'I know that name—we all do!' Ambrose interrupted. 'A Doctor Negrone runs the Kew asylum. Could they be related?'

'It raised many questions for me also. Why was a surgeon

doing this? What was his interest in cholera, which was not his specialty? And what would he be shipping to Australia?'

Ambrose could hold himself back no longer. 'Who was the man, Pieter?'

'I don't remember his name!'

'Could it have been Butterby, I wonder?' said Ambrose.

'He was a youngish man, probably in his thirties, I would have thought,' replied Pieter. 'He probably used a false name.'

'Well, that cuts out Butterby,' said Reggie.

Ambrose continued: 'Butterby asked me to come to the lecture organised by the Australian Protective League, and it seems he has an unusual, almost obsessive, interest in my father's collection of skulls. I promised to keep it quiet, so I will need to trust you all, but my aunt thinks Butterby stole two skulls from my father's collection—Reggie and Hedley know. It must have something to do with his research on the racial superiority of the white race.'

'This is far more interesting and important than I could have known!' said Pieter. 'I have been asked to report on some sensitive information relating to the Dutch and their place in Southeast Asia, with a particular person of very high standing in the Federal government while I am here in Melbourne. Some of my countrymen would not be happy that I speak so freely with another government, but I trust my contact here, who is of the highest integrity. I can't tell you everything because I am sworn to secrecy.

'I had planned to mention to the authorities as well this little mystery of the cholera and the men making investigations. Since I have been here, I have already taken it upon myself to find out that the SS *Catalina* had, indeed, berthed in Port Melbourne also. I stayed long enough to see that skunk Negrone appear. Also with him was the young doctor I met in Java. I retreated as fast as possible, as I am aware that I am not entirely … shall we say … inconspicuous. I'm not sure whether they saw me or not.'

The group sat back as one to digest this new information.

'Miss Wong, are you all right? You seem uncomfortable. Surely you haven't encountered Butterby as well?' Ambrose asked.

Charlotte had sat immobile through Ambrose and Pieter's revelations, with her chin in her hand but mind racing.

Van Haandel clearly played some kind of quasi-governmental role for the Dutch in the region. Was he a spy? Whose interests did he serve? Surely a spy for any nation would be less conspicuous. Oh my God! What to make of Ambrose's story!

Decision made, she took a deep breath and began. 'I may be making a mistake in sharing this with you …'

The others all clamoured to assure her of their trustworthiness and discretion with an enthusiasm that brought a smile to her lips.

'I am a member of an unofficial Chinese organisation in Melbourne. We exist because, as a group within this society, we are under threat. Before the states united to form the nation of Australia in 1901, our circumstances were not perfect, but we were tolerated and growing. Since the White Australia Policy was introduced, more and more pressure has been put on my community in numerous ways. It is often small things, but each one is always threatening to us. Restrictions on working, a ban on families coming here, and, of course, the casual discrimination and violence that afflicts us almost daily. Many of us were born here, and are citizens by right, but life can be made difficult even for citizens.

'Ambrose, you were correct in thinking that Butterby is active in white nationalist circles. We have been watching him closely as we believe he is one of the prime movers, not only of the Australian Protective League but of a secret right-wing organisation for which the League acts as a more respectable front. As I'm sure you can imagine, both organisations have an anti-Chinese agenda. We follow these sorts of activities, and try to ensure that members of our community do not act in ways that could provide any excuse for further hatred towards us.'

She laughed suddenly and shot Ambrose a sideways glance.

'We also offer protection and intelligence for our community. So, for example, we not only keep an eye on but also clean up when we can the opium dens around Little Lonsdale Street.'

'My God!' exclaimed Ambrose. 'It was you in the alleyway beneath the brothel that night! No wonder you referred to my nocturnal habits! I can explain …'

Charlotte smiled and waved him silent.

'Please let me explain,' said Ambrose, who seemed to Charlotte to be clearly discombobulated.

The embarrassing moment was interrupted as Mrs Simpson appeared with a rhubarb steamed pudding and a jug of hot custard. The room went strangely silent, and Mrs Simpson took five small glasses from the sideboard and uncorked a bottle of sauternes.

'I think we may need bigger glasses, Mrs Simpson. I'll get them.' A still shocked Ambrose poured the wine generously.

'Most excellent meal,' van Haandel boomed at the retreating cook, who beamed.

'Dr van Haandel, you have been a most kind guest. If Dr Pink invites you to stay again, you are more than welcome as far as I am concerned.'

'After I went to the university, at the conclusion of the coroner's hearing, to see if I could find Hugo and the missing specimen, Hugo exited his office with Butterby and, following them the surgeon McBride left the same room. When he bumped into me, he invited me to dine at Café Denat,' Ambrose explained.

'Very posh,' Reggie interrupted somewhat jealously.

'He wanted me to go out drinking after we had finished our meal and I found myself agreeing. He was very drunk, and I thought he might spill the beans about the League. And I'd gone to the lab to find any answer about cholera, and since he came from the same room, I wondered if he might know something and let that slip too. Honestly, I truly didn't know that he was taking me to a brothel; I'd have never agreed for a drink if I knew where he was expecting to take me. And I would never have guessed a brothel. It's not my kind of place, honest.'

'Where was that brothel as you call it?' asked Reggie.

'On the first floor of a building in Jones' Lane,' Ambrose answered.

Reggie doubled over in gales of laughter. 'I always thought you were asleep in dissection classes—you didn't absorb a thing!' he said. 'I know that place, and let me tell you, 'Brose my friend, there aren't many women in that establishment. I can tell you that as sure as I can tell if it's raining on my umbrella. McBride must fancy you!'

'My God … they weren't …?' Ambrose exclaimed, a look of utter surprise across his face.

'Let's get back to the main issue, I think that would be the kind thing to do,' Charlotte said, smiling just as widely as Reggie. 'Why did McBride take you there?'

'Apart from the obvious?' asked a still chuckling Reggie, sub-siding only when the whole group turned as one to glare at him.

'I don't know really. He muttered something about headquar-ters,' replied Ambrose.

'Was he involved in the assault below? And why would he organise that if he invited you to join the League?' van Haandel observed. 'Are they frightened about the publicity for the chol-era? Why would that be, do you suppose?'

All at once, everyone started talking excitedly, creating a cacophony of questions and opinions.

Ambrose raised his arm. 'Stop everyone! There are so many loose ends but also so much implicit in what we have heard tonight. It affects us all to variable degrees. Are we going to let these people succeed in what looks like some sort of dangerous plot to advance their obnoxious racial and social views? I for one feel I ought to play a role against this. Who, then, shall be in this adventure with me? No blame, or disgrace, will be the outcome of withdrawing, but now is the time to commit if we are to proceed with this perilous and difficult endeavour at all. I think it is now time to firmly decide. Put up you hand if you're in.'

One by one everyone in the room raised a hand.

'Well, right then. All together now! To start,' said Ambrose, 'first of all, we clearly need to find out more about that ship and its cargo. My trainer at the football club, Paddy Murphy, knows many fellows who work at the wharves—he could possibly find out more.'

'Ah,' van Haandel said. 'There is a problem. That ship is unlikely to have any English-speaking sailors. It's an Italian ship that travels regularly through Java, so it could have Dutch, Italian, Chinese, or Javanese crew, or all of the above. He will need me as a translator, of course.'

Just looking at van Haandel—a giant—would have engendered fear in any he opposed. *How many men was he worth in a scrap?* thought Charlotte.

'We also need to get into the asylum and find out about the baby,' said Ambrose. 'I want to speak to Flora. It's very strange that, although she was at the centre of all of that business, she has never been seen or interviewed.'

'That shall be my task,' said Charlotte. 'After all, I did represent her aunt, and no one knows that I have any knowledge of cholera or Ambrose's theories—I certainly didn't put them forward in court. And of course, I will discreetly ask my Chinese compatriots to be even more vigilant in tracking Butterby's movements.'

'What am I to do?' asked Ambrose.

'You and I can join the Australian Protective League!' Reggie chimed in.

'What a ridiculous suggestion, Reggie!' snapped Charlotte. 'You will put yourself in great danger. You are not to do it, Brosie!'

'Why should you always be the one to be in danger, Charlie? Running around at night in black with armed fighters. I'm not afraid, and I think it is a good idea,' replied Ambrose.

He and Charlotte stared at each other, Charlotte registering that she had used his familiar name for the first time.

Ambrose blinked first. 'I just remembered, Pieter. You mentioned a French doctor of dubious reputation in Java. Do you remember who that might have been?'

'I believe so. He was thrown out of the Pasteur Institute in Paris because of some bad indiscretion … some French name I think. One of the famous ones, I think.'

'You don't mean Pascal Hugo?'

'Maybe, I can't quite remember. It may have been Pascal. Why do you ask?'

Chapter Eleven
The Wrong Note

44 Alfred Crescent, North Fitzroy
Thursday, 6 October 1921

The week following the dinner party pact, all the dinner party companions independently prepared for their various expeditions. Paddy Murphy agreed to help Pieter van Haandel over a pot of beer (or three) at the Great Northern Hotel. Paddy examined Pieter's linguistic *curriculum vitae* at the hotel and discovered that, while he was proficient in many of the languages of the sailors who frequented the port—including an impressive grasp of the most colourful words—he didn't speak Chinese. On reporting back to Ambrose and Charlotte, they both agreed that Wally Koochew was the one they trusted sufficiently to undertake the task. They spoke to Wally and explained what was going on, and he was delighted to go along with the scheme. Ambrose was quietly pleased that it would give young Wally the opportunity to spend more time with Paddy. He knew that any hope Wally had of cementing himself in the Melbourne football club would be greatly enhanced by Paddy's support. Paddy regularly regaled willing onlookers with the story of Wally's heroics in the game against Fitzroy.

Steeling himself, Ambrose contacted McBride. He gave off the impression that their shared evening of inebriation was merely a passing recollection.

'Bit of a blur the end of that night, Brosie. Must have imbibed too heavily at the trough. Hope you got home all right, old man?'

McBride informed him that he would get back to him soon with a time for the meeting, so Ambrose had nothing more to do but wait and watch from the sidelines as the others went about their plans. He felt that getting in with the enemy was a dangerous endeavour, and if he was suspected of deception, things would end extremely poorly. He hoped that his willingness to join the League would blind-side them sufficiently.

The week had also been taxing at the surgery. An early spring outbreak of influenza had made life very busy. On Thursday night, Ambrose arrived home later than usual and exhausted; the 1919 epidemic was constantly at the back of his mind, and he prayed that the present occurrence did not presage another epidemic as bad as that terrible experience. Mrs Simpson had gone down with the flu herself, so he had to scratch about in the kitchen to find some food. Too tired to bother going out for dinner, he sufficed a cold collation or omelette would have to do. Ambrose also had to admit to himself that he was becoming a little paranoid about being out on his own at night; too often he had the distinct feeling that he was being followed, which naturally put a damper on venturing into town. He was just sitting down with his humble attempt at a meal when Hedley burst into the room.

'Great news,' he said. 'I've something to entertain you!'

Despite, or perhaps because of, Hedley's cheerful demeanour, Ambrose knew enough to be immediately suspicious.

'Why would I need entertaining? And what have you done?'

'Well, besides waiting from news for McBride and possibly pining over beautiful lawyers you mean?' chortled Hedley. 'You know this flu that's going around? Well of course you do. Anyway, Maestro Heinze can't get together enough players to make up a proper orchestra, so it might mean that Dame Nellie's homecoming concert has to be cancelled. He said he could make do if only he could find more cellos. Apparently with the bad flu season, there are none available, so of course, I offered you as a replacement.'

'WHAT?'

Ambrose went pale, the blood seeping from his face to pool in his stomach even as he told himself this was an anatomical impossibility.

'ME! I couldn't possibly do it. I would make a public fool of myself.'

'It's not quite as bad as it sounds,' Hedley pleaded. 'You know only the core of the players in the orchestra are actually professionals. There are lots of amateurs like you. The maestro can just cover most of the main programme, but some of the patriotic songs at the conclusion need a larger sound and he needs backup. They're very easy. And she won't sing unless she gets exactly what she wants. I've looked at the scores—you can manage, with practice. Despite any objections you are about to make, we both know you can play.'

'I absolutely refuse. I will not be moved.'

'Well, I guess I understand. Some of her entourage are travelling with her and playing in the orchestra. I've already spoken to one of them about taking lessons if I can get to London. I need to impress them. Please, just for me. I'll help you with this case you're on. I got overexcited. I never dreamed you wouldn't want to do it when we both know you actually play so well.'

What could Ambrose do? As a friend, Hedley had been in to bat for him many times. He could already feel himself being sucked into the undertow of Hedley's enthusiasm and he did indeed know just how important this opportunity could be for him.

'Well, what's a little public humiliation between friends anyway? You'll owe me one. But I'll need to get the score to practise,' said Ambrose, giving into the inevitable.

Hedley removed some papers from his satchel with a flourish. 'I took the liberty of bringing it with me. You're a true friend. I'll play the piano accompaniment to give you the tempos and context. Quick, quick. Go get your cello.'

Her Majesty's Theatre, Exhibition St
Orchestra pit
Friday, 14 October 1921, 2pm

Ambrose found himself sitting behind the other cellos at the back of the orchestra pit for the rehearsal.

The concert was to be in Her Majesty's Theatre on the following day. It was to be the first of a short tour that would see the diva and her party travel to Adelaide and Sydney for the rest of the month and return to Melbourne for the celebration of twenty years of Federation on 29 October. Dame Melba would both perform and be guest of honour at the grand banquet and gala in the Exhibition Buildings in Carlton. An extra incentive for all the interstate visitors was the running of the Melbourne Cup on the following Tuesday.

As they had an odd number of cellos, and were in rows of two across, he was alone at the last music stand at the back, right against the stage—a dim light barely illuminating the now slightly crumpled score he had placed on the stand. As he contemplated the ornate and richly coloured ceiling high above him and the tiers of red velvet upholstered seats, his stomach churned and gurgled in a most unhappy manner. *Why did I agree to this humiliation?* he asked himself again. This, unsurprisingly, had become a frequent question since he had allowed Hedley to talk him into this. The concert's main rehearsal concluded and they moved on to rehearse the patriotic songs with the augmented orchestra, which included Ambrose. The world-famous diva stood on the stage directly behind him. He could feel her otherworldly aura shine upon him—or so he imagined. *Oh shit*, he thought.

'You know, I refused to sing here in 1909 unless they improved the acoustics?' She directed the question to the young conductor, Bernard Heinze.

'Of course, Dame Nellie. They are much improved, don't you think?'

'Yes, and considering the band was assembled at short notice, I must congratulate you. I am quite happy with the sound, even if it is not what I would tolerate *at home*.'

Ambrose resisted the urge to slump in his seat.

'Shall we begin?' The maestro tapped on his stand and raised his baton.

Ambrose was so nervous he suddenly, in a rush of blood, bowed out the first note on his cello on the down beat of the conductor's baton—a beat before the rest of the orchestra. A wobbly, single, slightly flat 'D' echoed through the auditorium.

Silence ensued, except for some stifled giggling in the pit. Dame Nellie, wearing her customary knee-high lace-up rehearsal boots, moved to the front of the stage in order to peer down at Ambrose.

'And what would your name be young man?'

Ambrose, feeling as if he was about to faint, stuttered out, 'Pink … Dr Pink.'

'Dr Pink … a medical doctor?'

'Er … er, yes, Dame Nellie.'

'Dr Pink.' She cut him off. 'I do not doubt that you have spent many years studying the instrument between your legs … but *not* the cello obviously!'

Laughter filled the theatre, and Ambrose unsuccessfully

struggled to contain a rising blush. The ice was broken, however, and Dame Nellie Melba returned to centre stage. Soon her signature 'Home sweet home' was concluded satisfactorily, as were all the other favourite ballads programmed for the following night.

'That was a bit hair-raising,' Hedley observed as the players packed up their instruments. 'You had better prescribe yourself something calming for tomorrow.'

'Shut up … and stop laughing when it's all your fault. I knew I should never have let you convince me into this insanity, and now, how can I forgive you?' replied Ambrose.

'Easily—a mistake in rehearsals practically guarantees you'll be all right on the night. Everyone knows that.'

Somehow, Ambrose didn't feel that Hedley took all this quite as seriously as he should.

A stagehand tapped Ambrose on the shoulder. 'Dame Nellie would like to see you. Please follow me.'

As he prepared himself for a private dressing down, Ambrose's one consolation was that Hedley had gone satisfactorily pale at the request!

Ambrose trod through the narrow back corridors pondering what she could possibly want, and knocked on the door indicated. It had a red star affixed and a sign that read 'SILENCE SILENCE'.

'Enter,' came a voice from within.

He entered to find Melba sitting in a chair in some measure of undress, a glass of champagne before her, while her dresser fussed with her wardrobe. An elegantly dressed man was also in attendance.

'Dr Pink … Ambrose. Please let me apologise for drawing attention to you so rudely before.'

She obviously found out my first name.

'I think I managed to draw attention to myself. I apologise again for the mistake, Dame Nellie,' he replied.

'Just Nellie, please. I would offer you a drink, but I must rush to a reception at Government House. I am told you are an amateur who has valiantly filled in due to multiple illnesses. I wondered if you would like to be my guest at the coming Federation anniversary banquet? Your playing skills will not be required on that evening, and I can enjoy the company of a handsome young man who has done so much for his country.'

'What do you think, Beverley?' she addressed her companion. He eyed Ambrose up and down briefly. 'Perfect, Dame Nellie.'

'Well, that's agreed,' she said briskly, and correctly apparently, taking Ambrose's acceptance as a given. 'You have evening dress, of course? This is my private secretary, Mr Beverley Nichols—he can organise anything. He will arrange the invitation and anything else you need.'

'A great honour and pleasure. I would be delighted!' Ambrose finally managed to reply.

'Now off you go.' The great diva waved him to the door. 'Until the banquet. Beverley will send you an invitation.'

Beverley accompanied him. 'And anything you require, sir, just let me know.'

As they reached the door, he leant towards him confidentially. 'Dame Nellie likes to have her way, Dr Pink, and you have obviously taken her fancy. She enjoys making unreasonable requests and will certainly get her way and have an invitation for you, even though the authorities will complain.'

Ambrose nodded.

'It is highly likely, however, that she will forget you or change her mind. So, I would not assume that you have an invitation until it actually arrives, and even then, she may well not sit with you, even if you go.' He stared at Ambrose's feet. 'But please, do ensure that if an invitation arrives that you do polish your shoes for the occasion!'

Her Majesty's Theatre, Exhibition St
Backstage
Saturday, 15 October 1921, 7pm

Ambrose, kitted up in his black dinner suit, nervously paced back and forth backstage as the main orchestra entered the orchestral pit in dribs and drabs. Maestro Heinze and Dame Nellie were nowhere to be seen. Ambrose would have quite a wait as his pieces were scheduled at the end of the concert. So he pulled himself together and found a hidden seat in the wings near the pullies and stuff that accumulates in such places and peered out into the theatre.

Spying on the audience was something he could enjoy. He could just make out Pieter, Reggie, and Charlotte enter to find seats at the back of the ground floor stalls. He hadn't managed to spend any time alone with Charlotte since their first dinner, but she seemed to enjoy the company of his friends. He admitted he was still somewhat concerned about McLeish's warnings, but he assumed that he had been referring to the secret Chinese vigilante group she confessed she was involved with. He'd known plenty of Chinese when he'd lived in Java with his parents, but it was different in Melbourne. *She's very attractive in so many ways, and I admire her independence.* Would she accept him? She was obviously single. Maybe it was difficult for her to find a companion. That was at least something they had in common, albeit for different reasons perhaps. Pieter raved about her charm and intelligence whenever he had the chance, and Ambrose had yet to decide if Pieter had intended these remarks as encouragement for such thoughts.

Scanning the theatre, he saw Giuseppe Favaloro and his wife Maria at the front of 'the gods' in the highest level. He would have waved, but they couldn't see him in his hiding place. In the audience were many medical people he knew, including the dean of the medical school, Professor Allen—a very proper but decent man—and his wife. With him was Professor Richard Berry and his wife. Ambrose knew Berry shared many of Butterby's views on heads and race. Professor Allen had earlier spoken gravely to Ambrose about the courtroom incident and his cholera comments, and indicated that he was safe, for now, from any further investigations or misconduct inquiries. He was discreet enough not to say anything too explicit, but Ambrose knew that his claims about cholera were being written off as the enthusiasm of an overzealous young practitioner, which needed to be diligently suppressed to avoid public panic.

Ambrose, although resentful that his concerns were being brushed aside so easily, felt considerable guilty relief that his career was not, after all, at risk. At least not at the present moment. The problem of the Australian Protective League and their thugs was an altogether different proposition—one that kept him awake and within reach of his pistol at night.

Then, suddenly, he spotted someone. *Wasn't that Dr Negrone, the Superintendent of the Kew Asylum, the man who had taken the baby from Faraday Street ... and Dr Hugo the bacteriologist with him?* And with them was another man who was obviously his twin brother—*another Negrone! That must be the captain of the ship Pieter talked about.* He certainly had a more weathered complexion than his brother and was wearing a uniform of sorts. An olive-skinned man was with them. Probably also Italian, Ambrose thought.

Out of the corner of his eye, he noticed some rapid movement. Giuseppe was animatedly tapping Maria's shoulder and pointing down at this group of four men who had just entered. He looked very upset. As the opening notes of the main programme began, Ambrose fell into speculation.

Heavens, what does it mean to have those three together? And is the fourth man involved as well? What does this mean about cholera?

The evening was a spectacular success, as much for Ambrose as for Dame Nellie Melba. He had not only made no mistakes, but even warranted a flirtatious smile and a flower thrown to him by the diva herself on the conclusion of the final encore. Her voice, although past its prime, did indeed seem like crystal, hovering in the air like a beam of light. Afterwards, at supper, his companions laughingly congratulated Ambrose for capturing the diva's affections.

Pieter informed Ambrose that he had seen a most extraordinary thing. 'You recall the French doctor I met in Java? The one with a dubious reputation, rumoured to have been thrown out of the Pasteur Institute in Paris because of some indiscretion? He was here tonight! With Negrone, the captain of the *SS Catalina*.'

'But I know him! He is the Dr Hugo I mentioned, who runs the university's new bacteriology lab. And he was here with Dr Negrone, the superintendent of the insane asylum.'

They all fell silent for a moment, considering the implications of the new connections they had discovered.

'So, can I summarise the situation?' said Reggie. He had been following the investigation with great interest while also bemoaning that there was no more active role for him to currently play.

'Dr Negrone from the asylum and Dr Hugo from the university, who we also now know as the disgraced French scientist from Java, were there with the ship's captain, Negrone's twin brother, along with another man, who we presume from his olive skin and clothing to also be Italian. Ambrose, you also mentioned that Giuseppe seemed to recognise the men and got agitated. You had better go and find out what he knows.'

'Excellently put,' said Charlotte. 'You are wasted on medicine when you could be summarising your arguments for a jury.' She twinkled at Reggie.

Ambrose noticed that she had warmed to Reggie immensely since their first slightly awkward meeting. Whether she knew that Reggie's interest in her was bound to be strictly platonic, or she had discovered, as many did, that his sometimes-puckish sense of humour overlaid an extremely thoughtful, loyal, and caring friend, he was glad. Although, of course, it would be nice if she was as demonstrative with him from time to time …

'There's mischief afoot. I don't like it one bit. Here's to finding the fourth man and discovering all he knows!' Charlotte finished her drink with a flourish, and they joined her in downing their glasses.

Ambrose slept particularly well that night. He hadn't had one of his dreams for ages. Despite the nagging worry that he and his friends were treading into deep waters, something was obviously doing him good. He was even cleaning his shoes.

Chapter Twelve
The Plot Thickens

Medical Surgery, Fitzroy
Monday, 17 October 1921, 10am

The door opened and Caitlin ushered in Giuseppe and Maria Favaloro.

Ambrose greeted them warmly. 'Sit, please. What can I do to help?'

'Dottore Pink …' Maria looked tired. 'I wonder if you could give Giuseppe a sedative. 'Ee is not sleeping and needs something to calm 'is nerves. My normal remedies, they do not work.'

'Why Giuseppe and Maria, what's wrong? I can give you something, of course, but it would be better to address whatever is causing these vapours.'

Giuseppe and Maria exchanged glances.

'We can't tell you that, Dottore. Sorry, no offence meant, but it's better I just take the pills,' replied Giuseppe.

Suddenly Ambrose couldn't help himself, as he suspected it might be related to the night at the theatre. 'I wanted to speak to you about those four men at Melba's concert on Saturday night. When I was behind the curtain on the stage, I saw your reaction when you saw them. Do you know them?'

Giuseppe blanched. 'What do you know, Dottore?'

'I know three of them, and suspect they are covering up some secret. The fourth I did not know. If you will forgive me saying so, you seemed distressed to see them that night.'

Maria and Giuseppe looked at each other again in silence. Maria nodded and, laying her hand on Giuseppe's, said, 'Tell 'im, *amore.*'

'I trust you, Dottore. I will tell you if you swear by God Almighty that you will tell no one. There is big trouble coming in Melbourne.'

'As a doctor, I keep many secrets, and I promise I will keep yours,' said Ambrose. 'Giuseppe and Maria, you have my word.'

'Dr Negrone 'oo runs the asylum, 'ees well known in the Italian community, but he is not much liked. 'Ees past is murky, but the local officials they do not know it. 'Ees brother is Salvatore Negrone, the captain of the *SS Catalina*, we know already that 'ee is a rascal. And the other Italian man in the suit? 'Ees much worse, 'ees name is Mario Bertolini. Nobody likes to speak of it, but we know 'ee has come to bring Fascism to Australia. The others, they must be helping him. And the ship, it has berthed in many other cities, probably to drop off other Fascisti.'

'The Fascisti … fascism?' Ambrose asked. 'What do you mean?'

'A journalist, Benito Mussolini, 'ee has started a political movement to fight socialism in Italia. They are called the Fascisti, and they are violent thugs. They beat members of my family back home. Many of my countrymen 'ere will resist them, but there are also many who are dazzled by the promise of a new Italia based on our noble history. Ee is promising a new Roman Empire,' said Giuseppe.

Ambrose was stunned.

'The fascists!' continued Maria. 'So many of us hoped that they would not come 'ere,' she explained. 'But suddenly they are 'ere, and we 'ear the rumours that they want to take over the fruit and vegetable market from the Chinese. They already 'ave taken over all the Italian ice-cream carts and a dairy! If they don't persuade, they threaten our famiglia back home!'

Ambrose was stunned; he had stumbled on a much larger

conspiracy and could not imagine how these pieces fitted together. 'Which dairy?'

'The one down on the Yarra River in Kew,' replied Maria.

For now, he could only despatch them with further assurances of his discretion, reassuring words and a prescription for a mild opium tincture.

Ambrose stopped to telephone Charlie and Reggie, requesting them to visit him at home presently. After the arrival of the pair, Ambrose summoned Hedley from upstairs and Pieter from next door for a conference (with dinner included, of course). Ambrose was sharing his shocking new information with the group when there was a knock at the door. He was surprised to find Maria Favaloro, who lived nearby, on his doorstep. Ambrose's look of concern was met by a worried glace from Maria.

'Come in, come in.' He quickly ushered her through the door and into the parlour where the others were discussing their news over drinks.

Maria looked apprehensively at the visitors.

'Would you like to speak with me privately?' asked Ambrose. 'Although I can absolutely vouch for my friends' trustworthiness.'

Maria fretted a moment, but on being reassured by all present with warm welcome, she agreed to speak.

'Dottore, Giuseppe didn't tell you everything—'ee 'as become ... how do you say eet ... paranoid? The four men we spoke about ... they were at the Café Denat on Friday night for dinner. They 'ad a private booth in the corner. 'Ee knew who they were, although they did not know 'im. Giuseppe didn't wait on their table. But, as you might remember, the booth 'as a high wooden panel to obscure the door to the kitchen. Eet is possible to stand behind it and 'ear what diners are saying ...'

Ambrose handed her a glass of water, as she had refused any wine. She took a sip and a deep breath before continuing.

'Giuseppe knew them, and 'ee was worried, so 'ee tried to hear everything. Eet was mostly in Italian so they weren't too careful, not knowing Giuseppe could overhear what they were saying. 'Ee's worried now that they will recognise 'im from the restaurant and work out that 'ee's Italian and maybe heard more than he should have. It is not only the fascists, though.' She crossed herself. 'The good Lord knows, that is bad enough. Dr Negrone and Dr Hugo, they work with the fascists, but they have another purpose. Giuseppe couldn't quite work out the name, but eet is another organisation, it is secret, to protect Australia.'

She paused to take another sip of water.

'But I don't think they mean "protect" in a good way, at least not for people like me and Giuseppe. The two doctors organised some cargo in Java, and Negrone, the captain, brought eet out secretly. Eet's on an island somewhere south of Melbourne and is guarded. Giuseppe said the island's name is "Isola Acqua Casa". They talked about a grand banquet and exhibition or something like that. Dottore, I don't know why you are interested in them, but I hope you can do something. The police, they will never listen to someone like me, so what can I do?'

Maria looked exhausted and drained, but relieved. *What a terrible burden she has been carrying*, thought Ambrose. After more reassurances that they would find a way to act without revealing Giuseppe's identity, or letting him know that Maria had spoken to them, Ambrose showed her to the door. When he returned, it was to find his friends sitting in uncharacteristic silence. Charlotte was the first to speak.

'My Chinese companions had warned me about the fascists' arrival. The Chinese underworld is not taking kindly to it, as you can imagine. But I hadn't dreamed that they would be connected to the Australian Protective League, which is surely the other group Maria is talking about. In retrospect, though, it seems obvious, as they both have the same aims and enemies.'

'It seems as if they intend to target the twentieth anniversary bash,' said Reggie. 'We'll need to figure out their plans and make sure we are all there to stop them. Pieter has an invitation. Hedley is playing in the orchestra. Brosie will be with Dame Nellie, causing dismay in the hearts of Methodist debutantes. I, of course, have an invitation.'

This went without saying. Reggie's friends had long since ceased to question how it was that he managed to get invited to all the significant events on the social calendar, many of which he attended with relish despite his complaints as to their tedious nature.

'So, we'll have to work out how to get you in as well, Charlie.'

'Actually, that's easy,' she replied. 'The organisers want a grand spectacle provided by every community in Melbourne, and my uncle is president of the Chinese association that has been asked to provide entertainment. We are going to have our traditional dragon parade around the hall so I, along with some of my fellow practitioners of the Shaolin martial arts, will be under the dragon. But if there is any possibility of violence, I think it would be good to have as many reinforcements there as possible. Can we find a way to get Wally and Paddy inside?'

'I'll have to give that some thought,' answered Ambrose.

Agreeing to convene again soon, the group slowly dispersed. Reggie was the first to leave with a distance to travel home, and Pieter returned next door shortly after. Hedley retired to bed upstairs. This, as Ambrose suddenly realised with a flutter of nerves, left him alone with Charlotte. Pausing only to give the adoring Molly a last pat, Charlotte rose to leave.

'You won't stay for another drink?'

'Ambrose, I really shouldn't stay here, in your home, alone with you now that the others have left. My conservative Chinese aunt wouldn't approve, and besides, it isn't dignified in private settings, as well you know. I should go now. I'm already taking enough risks as it is.'

Well, that's me sunk. Still, it was worth a try. I must redeem myself; can't have her thinking I'm undignified…

'Charlie, I enjoy your company a great deal. I'd very much enjoy spending more time with you, in whatever a setting you deem most appropriate, of course.'

'Yes, of course, Ambrose. As much as I enjoy your company, and that of your friends, my career means a lot to me, so this does not change the fact that I really must get home.'

She paused, and then, seeing the look on Ambrose's face, continued in a softened tone.

'In other circumstances, I would perhaps be tempted to stay. But I can't spend my days forging my way in a hostile profession, my nights attempting to help preserve my community, and then instigate or even accept a close relationship with anyone. You must see the impossibility here.'

Even when she is being gentle, Charlotte doesn't pull her punches. Ambrose took a breath.

'I can only respect your wishes. I understand your commitment to your work. But please know, my admiration for you grows as I spend more time with you. I, myself, have found a cause within all this nastiness and poor baby Iris, and I am aware it may be difficult for you, as an intelligent Chinese woman, to form a close relationship with someone like me. Your life must be very constrained. And your illegal activities surely wouldn't help to encourage possible suitors, so I understand … but I do wish you to know that I would be pleased of your company, should you find the loneliness that I can only imagine you must feel become burdensome.'

If looks could kill.

'I don't believe your arrogance, Dr Pink. I thought you were better than the run-of-the-mill wealthy white men populating this city. And yet, you have proved yourself otherwise in a matter of breaths. How condescending! Honestly, I am surprised that you have managed to keep such charming and intelligent friends if you carry attitudes as low-level and bigoted as that.'

He blushed, hanging his head and reluctant to meet her gaze. She turned her back swiftly and left in a huff.

What a hot-headed person she can be. I had no intention of being insulting. The arrogance of it! Well, that's that. He shrugged and ushered Molly to follow him up the stairs to bed.

Chapter Thirteen
Action

44 Alfred Crescent, North Fitzroy
Tuesday, 18 October 1921, 10am

The group met again the next morning. The dinner was to be held in less than two weeks, so they had to make sense of the information given by the Favaloros and move fast. Ambrose felt relieved that Charlotte maintained her usual ease among the group. He hoped he appeared the same after the emotional—for him at least—conversation of the evening before. Although he felt conflicted and confused in her presence, he didn't want her to back out, although he wasn't quite sure why he felt that way.

'I apologise for making us meet here so often. It's not because it is my place, but rather it suits Pieter, Hedley, and Wally. Charlotte, you don't have permanent chambers, do you?'

'No, I don't.' She glared at him.

Maybe not so at ease. She's still got daggers out for me.

'And there isn't much work around,' she continued. 'Thanks for pointing it out, Ambrose! I may have to give up the bar before I have really started. I live reasonably close by with my aunt—this is fine. As long as my aunt doesn't know of my excursions, I'm in the clear. I'm determined to be involved if you want me, as this cholera plot will be disastrous for the Chinese living here. It is important that we succeed.'

'Et moi?' exclaimed Reggie.

'If you want to invite us all to stay at Westvale, we'll be up there in a shot. Your flat in town is too small, and not salubrious enough for a lady, retorted Hedley.

A cushion was thrown at him, and Reggie composed himself, having flung his frustrations in padded form, and went on to provide the summary of their information at hand.

'We need to know more about the nature of what "disaster" is being planned. The leads point towards the Kew Asylum, the Italian fascists, and the Australian Protective League. We need to investigate the illegal doings at the docks and the mysterious threat contained on Bass Strait Island—we don't yet know how these things link up. Where should we start?'

'Well, since it's our fresh lead, let's start with the island,' Ambrose replied at the same time as he opened his most detailed atlas, placed it on his reading desk, and invited the others to have a look. Unfortunately, Bass Strait was littered with hundreds of islands, and none of them were called 'Isola Acqua Casa'. After a frustrating and fruitless period of review, and a small argument between Reggie and Hedley over whether 'Isola Acqua Casa' could possibly have been misheard for 'Isabella', they turned their collective attention to the other items on Reggie's list.

It was decided that Pieter would take Wally to the port to meet Paddy and see what they could discover about the *SS Catalina* and its cargo.

'I have plenty of pound notes—they may help,' Pieter said, laughing.

Charlotte chimed in. 'I'm going to take Kathleen to see her niece Flora at the asylum today. We've already sent in a request for her to visit, and as I represented Kathleen, they shouldn't be able to stop me visiting with her. We also need to know what, if anything, the fascists' interest in the dairy next door means. Is it relevant that it is right next to the asylum on the river? We need someone to explore the dairy.'

'Perhaps young Will can accompany you to the asylum. He's not going to school because too many of the teachers are sick. and there is no one to keep an eye on him. He will have to go with someone as Mrs Simpson is not at home during the day. I insist, however, that he isn't to enter the dairy. It is too dangerous,' said Ambrose. 'I'll speak to him as soon as possible.' He ploughed on. 'As for me, I'm not giving up on that lost faecal specimen either. I'm going to snoop around Hugo's office and the bacteriology lab to see if I can find anything useful. Hugo's giving lectures between 1 and 3pm, so I know when he'll be preoccupied. How about we all meet here tomorrow evening to report back? I'll feed you, of course—or rather, Mrs Simpson will.'

This was an idea that cheered up everyone, including Molly, who barked enthusiastically.

'What can Hedley and I contribute?' asked Reggie.

'Well, you laughed about infiltrating the fascists, but maybe there's a way you can explore what they are doing. Maria mentioned that they'd taken over the city's ice-cream businesses as well as the dairy, so maybe it's time the ice-cream vendors were inspected, perhaps by a public health officer and his observant assistant?'

'Righto,' they both chorused, happy to have a task.

All of a sudden Ambrose struck his brow with the palm of his hand. 'Stupid!' he cried. 'I've just realised!' He ran to the map of Bass Strait on his desk. 'Isola is not the first name of the island. "Isola" is the Italian word for "island". "Acqua Casa" means "water house". He jammed his finger down on the map. 'Look here, Waterhouse Island and little Waterhouse Island—just off the north-east coast of Tasmania!'

'Genius!' Hedley cried. Reggie suggested that finding out more about the island, and the best way to get there, be added to the list of tasks, after which everyone dispersed.

Kew Insane Asylum
Outside the main entrance
Noon

Charlotte, young Will, and Kathleen O'Donohue walked up the steps and entered the grand foyer of the asylum. Will was a transformed figure, with some decent clothes, regular washing, and the knowledge that people cared for him.

Built in the mid nineteenth century in open countryside on a high and commanding position, the asylum looked down to the Yarra River. Over the years, Melbourne's affluent had encroached on the surrounding land around its expansive grounds, building large houses surrounded by extensive gardens, thus giving the poor inmates something to aspire to.

'We've come to see Flora O'Donohue,' Charlotte announced to the surly looking character behind the desk.

'Dr Negrone received your request and would like to know your reasons for visiting her.'

'Mrs O'Donohue here is her aunt, and I represent her as her lawyer. This young man is my assistant. May I see her record first?'

'Well, family can visit her, and I guess her lawyer can join, but only for thirty minutes. One of the junior doctors will take you to see her. Here is the register with her record.'

Charlotte looked carefully at it, took some notes, and handed it back. They waited for ten minutes until a young man, who was obviously distracted and indicated that he was too busy to worry with visitors, arrived and asked them to follow him out the front door. They walked around to the left along a path until they stopped at a small cottage amongst many others in the grounds.

'Only the bad cases are kept in the wards in the main building,' the young guide explained, seeming to anticipate her question. 'Flora had an attack of hysteria when we took her baby off her, and she sank into a state of stupor. Seen it many times myself—deep depression. She's a permanent resident, but can't keep a baby. Dr Negrone said it was going to the orphanage when he took it from her originally. She has been heavily sedated, but is coming to now,' he said, then departed abruptly.

'Can I go off and explore, miss?' asked young Will.

'Only if you stay nearby and don't go off the grounds,' Charlotte said as they entered the room.

Will ran off across the grounds.

Before them was Flora, a very beautiful young woman in ragged but clean asylum clothing. She seemed surprised to see Charlotte, but nodded quietly when Kathleen explained who she was. Initially she seemed to express no interest in why they were there, but as Kathleen and Charlotte described the events that had led up to her aunt's trial, she became visibly distressed.

'Shall I fetch a doctor?' asked Charlotte.

'Oh no, miss,' Flora said in a rush. 'They'll only sedate me again. I want to be able to feel things again, even if it means I'm sad.' She took a deep breath and said, 'Please continue. I'm so sorry they blamed you, Aunt. Miss, are you here now to tell me I might also be held responsible for my baby's death?'

'No, not at all,' Charlotte rushed to assure her. 'I don't want to give you any false hope, but what your aunt told me about your story made me wonder if we could get your case reviewed. I can't say more, but if you could fill in these pages please, it would be very helpful.'

Flora looked slightly uncertain, but she took the pages and pencil Charlotte offered her and sat at the small table in the room to fill them out.

Due to the competency of the staff—or rather, lack of—it was nearly 2pm before a very irritated attendant arrived at Flora's cottage and escorted them from the asylum.

Standing outside the gates, Charlotte looked very pleased with herself. 'I think we've done very well, Kathleen. Very well indeed.'

Kathleen looked less than convinced. 'I hope we have, miss. I hope we have.'

She and Flora had bid each other a painful farewell. It was clear neither believed there was any likelihood she would be leaving the asylum soon.

Will was waiting for them at the car.

'Where have you been, Will?' asked Charlotte.

'My apologies, but I went next door to look at the dairy.'

'That was very naughty of you. What did you find?'

'Miss, the dairy is next to the asylum, and a big house and garden is next to both places. There are some nasty looking men, like military types, wandering around the grounds of both the dairy and the big house. I'm sure that at least one of 'em 'as a gun.'

'Did you find out who the house belongs to?'

'I spoke to a boy who works in the garden and 'e told me it's owned by a doctor named McBride, and 'e comes to the asylum and visits the dairy with people as well. Do you know 'im, miss?'

'McBride? No, but I believe Ambrose does. We'll have to ask him. Let's get back to North Fitzroy.'

At that moment, a car pulled up, and two men stepped out and headed into the main foyer. One was a powerfully built man in his fifties with a large head crowned with distinguished grey hair. The other was a younger man with short blond hair.

'That's the man who kindly brought us the fresh milk to feed Iris!' Kathleen exclaimed.

'Which one?'

'The younger one,' Kathleen replied.

In light of young Will's information and Ambrose's earlier descriptions, Charlotte wondered whether the man they had just seen was McBride.

Perhaps his companion is Butterby. Why are all these disparate people connected? They are all medical, of course, and most medical men in Melbourne know or know of each other. Apart from that, the only obvious connecting thread is the Australian Protective League. She just hoped the pieces made more sense to Ambrose.

Port Melbourne Wharves
Noon

Pieter found Paddy having a smoke behind one of the landing cranes used to move cargo, and they set off together to find Negrone's boat. It didn't take them long to spot a couple of larrikins, cigarettes hanging off their lips, guarding a gangplank. As they got closer, the writing on the hull was visable, *SS Catalina*. Giving each other a nod, Pieter and Paddy approached.

'You can't go aboard. Clear orf!' said the larger of the two larrikins as the visitors began to climb the gangway. The only flaw in his argument was that, large as he was, Pieter and Paddy were considerably larger.

'Do you want a fiver or a fist?' Paddy made his point by assuming a boxing position, while at the same time Pieter took out his wallet and started counting out five-pound notes.

'They 'en't payin' us much,' said the other one to his companion, who nodded. 'We'll take what you've got in yer hand, mista.'

The two guards, satisfied with the day's takings, presumably headed off to choose one of the many pubs that served the wharfies' thirst and drink to good fortune.

After some searching onboard, Pieter and Paddy finally came across a crew member taking a nap.

'Halo, Asmanipun panjenengan sinten?' asked Pieter, having shaken the man awake.

Once the crew hand had recovered from the shock of coming to under the shadow of a giant who somehow inexplicably spoke his language, the sailor had a lot to say. It turned out that he held plenty of grudges. Some animated conversation revealed that not only was he from east Java, but he had been effectively shanghaied, plucked off the street as he went about his business and forced onboard. This was a naval tradition with a long history, whenever ships were short of crew or navies lacking sailors. He had no love for Captain Negrone, knew little about the other crew members, and just wanted to go home.

'Paddy, he tells me he was forced into service in Java, and this is their first port of call, but they dropped some others who had also been shanghaied in Java onto an island not far from here. He thinks some provisions were unloaded with them.'

Pieter thanked the sailor and they headed back to Fitzroy with their intriguing news.

Swanston St Bridge, over the Yarra River
Midday

Reggie and Hedley met 'under the clocks'—as the rendezvous point was referred to by the locals—at the domed Flinders Street railway station on the busy corner of Swanston and Flinders streets.

'Leave it to me,' said Reggie. 'I speak the lingo. I was in Italy last year. Also, I'm wearing a cravat I purchased in Milan—bound to make them take me more seriously.'

Hedley shook his head and decided to keep his reflections on the possible efficacy of the cravat to himself. He would go along for the ride; he was just the assistant after all. Just opposite were a group of ice-cream carts and their vendors. The two men sauntered up to a little group of men talking animatedly in some form of Italian Reggie couldn't understand.

'Bon giorno a tutti,' he said with all the false bravado of one functionally illiterate in the language. He waved his hands in an exaggerated manner, as that is how they talked in Italy, he had explained to Hedley.

The group eyed the two intruders rather suspiciously.

'No ice-cream, good sirs ... niente ... finito ... fatto ... finished,' answered a rather bow-legged older man.

'Oh, that's all right, we don't want ice-cream,' Reggie replied cheerfully, 'just information about the Fascisti.'

The little group seemed stunned for a moment, and then, in what looked like the caucus race in *Alice in Wonderland*, they dashed in circles trying to disengage from each other's carts while avoiding the two interrogators until, finally becoming disentangled, they headed off at speed in different directions.

'Well done,' said Hedley. 'Very subtle, bloody brilliant result! If ever I write a comedic opera, I would choreograph a chorus just like this scene.'

'On the contrary, I think we have learnt a great deal. We have certainly confirmed that they are all upset by the mention of the fascists,' Reggie responded with dignity, and a flick of his forelock.

Outside Hugo's office
Medical school, 1pm

Being a graduate and part-time surgical student, Ambrose was not accosted as an intruder as he embarked on his own personal mission at the medical school. He knew the place intimately and its rhythms were familiar to him. After 1pm, if the students had no lectures after lunch, they would be in the library or have gone home. Those in the clinical years would be in the various hospitals scattered conveniently around the medical school. Any who did have lectures would most likely be quietly nodding off in their lecture theatres. He hoped the same pattern of behaviour was true for the staff, leaving the vast majority of the public parts of the building empty.

Ambrose waited for some time, seemingly perusing the specimens, as it wasn't unusual for the ghoulish to ponder at length the little one-legged recorder player from Paris. So he feigned interest, even though it was a familiar sight, while making sure Hugo was not in his room. When all seemed clear and he could hear no sound, he utilised a well-known technique in the ancient art of breaking and entering Paddy had taught him, which involved a thin piece of sturdy balsa wood. He quickly closed the door after entering and secured it, as he hoped he had a couple of hours to search.

Where to begin? He rummaged through the drawers and cupboards, looking in and behind every vessel, test-tubes included. He even knocked on the cupboards and walls in an attempt to find any secret hiding places. He got quite a shock when someone knocked back. A faint 'Shut up!' emanated from the neighbouring office, and Ambrose decided to cease knocking around for hidden compartments. It looked like he had come to a dead end; he had found nothing so sat down to reconsider his plans. All that was left was a small shelf of books. Searching here involved taking each volume off the shelves one by one, holding the spines, and shaking vigorously. Now, one of Ambrose's weaknesses was books and he couldn't help looking at the titles and dipping into them to try to understand the mind of the man who owned them. He was not surprised to see that, mixed with texts of the new field of bacteriology, were numerous books on theories of race.

On this particular shelf, quite a number were about how

superior the white race was compared to the other races, including J.H. Curle's *Today and Tomorrow*. He finally came upon two Jack London books that had numerous place-markings sticking out. One was titled *The Unparalleled Invasion*. He'd heard something about that—it was a science-fiction tale in which China was wiped out by the West using biological weapons. *Well, biological warfare was older than the Middle Ages, when besieging armies catapulted diseased corpses into the defending cities to create chaos and disease.* The other, *South Sea Tales*, had only one piece of paper sticking out. The marker was placed on a story called 'Yah! Yah! Yah!' It was about deliberately exposing a Polynesian population to measles and killing many of them. Ambrose was transfixed. His eye wandered to the piece of marking paper in his hand. It was his own handwriting! The very note he had left with the specimen jar. One word written on it: cholera. This was incontrovertible proof that Hugo had indeed received the sample!

All of a sudden, he heard steps approaching. Then a knock on the door. He froze.

'Pascal … are you there? We need to talk. I've just been at the asylum. They've been talking to the girl. You were right about Pink, I think.'

It was McBride, sounding angry. Ambrose's heart was beating so loudly he wondered if it could be heard outside. McBride tried the door—it was locked. He heard McBride swear under his breath and stride away. *Thank Heavens*, he thought. *Thank God I locked the door.*

As soon as the footsteps receded, Ambrose carefully stuck his head out the door, checking to see if all was clear. At no sign of anyone, he bolted with the piece of paper clutched in his hand. *It would have Hugo's fingerprints on it at least. Maybe I can prove that he was lying about his ignorance of the specimen jar I left.*

CHAPTER FOURTEEN
A PLAN EMERGES

North Fitzroy
Wednesday, 19 October 1921, Late afternoon

When Ambrose, Charlotte, Pieter, Hedley, and Reggie met at number 44 Alfred Crescent, they all had news they were eager to share. Charlotte went first with what she had discovered.

'Flora was committed to the Kew Asylum by McBride. He acts as an honorary there. I looked at the register and it was just his signature against her name. As a child, she had spent many years inside with her own mother, the record claiming she was mentally defective as well, but I have little faith in that diagnosis. It also recorded the heavy sedatives she was receiving. But between the register and my discussion with the junior doctor, it seems clear that she was primarily traumatised by the birth and loss of her child, as well as the rape that had almost certainly caused her pregnancy. Also, Ambrose had the idea of trying out some new tests to ascertain her intelligence, and so I took them along and had her fill them out. As we were leaving, Kathleen recognised the man who had brought Iris milk that night and, based on Ambrose's description, I think it must have been McBride. Butterby may have been with him, but I couldn't be sure. Will discovered that McBride is the owner of the house and grounds next to the dairy. Surprisingly the dairy had armed guards, and we've been told it is connected to the fascists!'

'Sorry Ambrose,' she said, noticing him glaring at her. 'Will's curiosity got the better of him and he escaped and went searching the adjacent properties.'

"Well, he is safe and uncovered valuable information. So I am grateful for that,' said Ambrose.

'Who raped her?' asked Ambrose. 'McBride, Butterby, and Hugo had easy access to the asylum grounds; McBride as he owned the property that abutted it. Negrone must have taken Iris back to the asylum from Kathleen O'Donohue's house in Carlton. As superintendent of the asylum, Negrone seems to be in cohorts with McBride and possibly Butterby.'

'Did she know who raped her?' asked Hedley.

'She thinks it must have happened when she was drugged. She has no idea.'

'Well,' said Pieter, 'we discovered at the ports that the ship dropped off some other captive sailors on an island before coming to Melbourne, with provisions also.'

They all stared at him in shock.

Pieter placed his hands solemnly on the table. 'I shall speak to my contact in the Federal government.'

'Thank you, Pieter,' said Ambrose. 'There's someone in the police force who plays with me in the Melbourne seconds, Cam McLeish. He's a good man, but does it by the book. I can go to him, but we need to have more concrete evidence.'

'Well,' said Hedley, 'I've asked for some maps at the university library. Never knew there was so much there outside the music collection. I'll need someone who understands topography to have a closer look with me, but maybe it should be possible to land on Waterhouse Island. We definitely need to have closer look at what is going on there.'

'Don't you feel we're getting out of our depth here?' said Reggie. 'Just asking, in case anyone wants to withdraw.'

Silence descended on the room as they each considered the situation.

'I can't see any way out of it,' replied Ambrose. 'We'll ask the police discreetly through my contact, and Pieter can through his, but there seems to be powerful figures involved and we don't know who else is involved. I would be happy if you all withdrew as I don't want any harm to come to you and prick my conscience!'

'Well said,' Charlotte interrupted. 'It seems that we could all withdraw, but Ambrose will be a target, and if we don't stick beside him, he could be in trouble. I'm in.' She avoided Ambrose's gaze but seemed a bit flush on the cheeks.

A chorus of agreement followed. Glasses were raised to cement the pledge. Ambrose tentatively looked at Charlotte out of the corner of his eye, but she resolutely ignored his gaze.

'Paddy and I have been planning a trip to Waterhouse Island already,' said Pieter, 'and we reckon it would take the best part of twelve hours on a boat. We need to think some things through. What is the best time to land, and where, and what precautions should we take if any trouble eventuates?'

'We will need to make a trip as soon as possible,' said Charlotte. 'So, which of us should go?'

Ambrose sighed. 'I'd hoped to make the trip myself, but so many of my colleagues at Oddfellows are ill, and the influenza season is in full swing. Everyone is still spooked by the 1919 epidemic. I'd be negligent to leave my patients at this time.'

'There's plenty to do here,' said Charlotte.

Pieter spoke up. 'In any case, I am not sure how many people can make the journey. I'm finding it very difficult to get any boat big enough at short notice. I could look and see if I could hire a seaplane, but it would limit our numbers even further. We also don't know how many prisoners were dropped off by the *SS Catalina*.'

'My father bought a seaplane,' Reggie said nonchalantly. He

had been rather subdued after being forced to describe, with frequent interjections from Hedley, his lack of success with the ice-cream vendors of Melbourne. 'I could twist his arm to let us have it.'

'That's brilliant,' said Charlotte. 'I think it's a better plan than a boat in any case. We can't invade Waterhouse Island by boat anyway and rescue the prisoners, if indeed there are any on the island. We don't have the manpower, and we don't know how many guards or prisoners are on the island. We need to leave that to the authorities, but we need to give them evidence to get them to act. I know a few people with a pilot's licence. Reggie, do you think you would be able to convince your father to lend it to us? We can then find a pilot.'

'Oh,' Reggie said triumphantly, 'that's not an issue. I can fly it …' In a whisper, he added, 'I think.'

'Excellent, you truly contain many mysteries, Reggie,' said Charlotte. 'We can land near the island and pretend to be out of fuel. We can then establish who is there and what is going on, and if the opportunity to free the prisoners arises, we can take action with an escape route back to Melbourne already in place. Where is this seaplane, Reggie?'

'It's moored in Corio Bay near Geelong and nobody uses it. My father imported it after the war, hoping to set up a passenger service for the wealthy. Foolish idea. He got the wrong plane for his purposes.'

'Can I come too?' Hedley interrupted. 'And why do you say it was the wrong plane?'

Reggie continued, ignoring the interruption. 'It's only a three-seater, and it's one of the French biplanes, *Georges Levy G.L. 40 HB2*. It's got a range of 177 miles, which would normally just get us there. But its armaments have been removed and it has been fitted with a second equivalent fuel tank, so we'll be able to fly and return. Just. Otherwise, you will need to swim.'

'You didn't answer the question,' said Hedley. 'Why is it the wrong plane?'

'You don't know the nickname of the G.L. 40? It's called "the flying coffin". No one would hire it.'

'I'll certainly come,' said Charlotte. 'If the captives are Chinese, you will need me.'

Ambrose watched as his friends excitedly discussed flight paths, fuel usage rates, and emergency procedures. Finally, he couldn't help himself.

'You're can't possibly be thinking of going, Charlotte. It sounds far too dangerous!'

'Yes, Ambrose, I am going. Since when has it been up to you to decide what I should or should not do?'

'As your friend, I have the right to express my concern for your safety.'

'Your concern is noted,' Charlotte said icily. 'Of course, it should also be noted that I'm not the one who has needed to be rescued on the streets of Melbourne. How many times is it now?'

'Very droll,' Ambrose replied through clenched teeth. 'The situations are not at all the same and you know it.'

The two combatants stared at each other with flaming eyes.

As Charlotte drew breath to respond, Pieter interjected quickly. 'You'd better both calm down. We all need clear heads ... and if you want to enjoy arguing as much as you obviously do, you should marry also.'

As a tactic, it was magnificent. Both collapsed immediately into an embarrassed silence that filled the room, only slightly broken by what sounded suspiciously like muffled giggles from Reggie and Hedley. Luckily, this caused Ambrose and Charlotte to unite in turning their glares towards them. Pieter remained majestically calm, as if all these doings were beneath his notice and had not in fact been precipitated by him. A slight curl embellished the corner of his lips. Mrs Simpson's appearance, with the suggestion that they should stay for dinner, was welcomed by all.

'I'm delighted that you're so worried about my safety and Hedley's, Brosie, not just Charlie's,' Reggie remarked as they moved into the dining room, causing both of them to fall into gales of laughter again.

It started as a rather tense meal interspersed with discussion on what needed to be done next. Mrs Simpson served *navarin d'agneau avec legumes de printemps*, although she didn't know it was called that when Pieter pointed it out.

'Mother's spring lamb stew is what I call it,' she remarked rather proudly.

Molly sat quietly on the side with her sweetest, most expectant face, because that was the best way to get some secret handouts from the softer guests. She soon discovered that the best touches were Reggie and Charlie, so she upped and moved her camp between them. As he opened first the Seppelt's sparkling wine, followed by Shiraz from the excellent 1919 vintage, Ambrose realised with some surprise that, despite his earlier conflict with Charlotte, and the gravity of the plot they had unearthed, he was happier than he could remember being.

'More port anyone?' said Reggie.

'Certainly,' they all replied.

Ambrose suddenly hit his forehead. 'I've been so focused on all the strands of the cholera saga, I completely forgot to mention that McBride rang before you came asking me to a meeting of the Australian Protective League at his house next Tuesday night,' he interjected into the noisy clamour of voices.

'Are you going after all this?' exclaimed Pieter. 'Let me come with you. I'd like to meet this man also!'

'I think I'll go to McBride's on my own. I would like to go to

Waterhouse, and we don't really have much evidence to fly over and barge in. Reggie's plane will be ready if we need it. I insist we put the Waterhouse flight on hold until we have more evidence that going over would accomplish something.'

'All right, if you say so,' said Reggie, and the others murmured agreement, except Charlotte, who just stared at the floor.

CHAPTER FIFTEEN
THE FACTS ARE IN

Melbourne Teachers College, Parkville
Monday, 24 October 1921, 10am

Charlotte and Ambrose arrived at the 1888 Building on Elgin Street in Carlton and climbed the grand double staircase. Charlotte was holding the papers she had asked Flora to fill in on her visit to the asylum. They knocked on the door of the office of Professor John Smyth, expert in the new science of intelligence testing.

'Come in.'

They entered to find the professor, a dour looking Scot in his late fifties, as well as a younger, rather good-looking man—dark-haired, open-faced.

'Hello Ken,' said Ambrose, shaking his hand.

'Welcome. This is Prof Smyth. Ambrose and Charlotte, sit down,' Ken Cunningham replied. 'How did your research go?'

'Most interesting. We'll show you,' Charlotte removed a wad of papers from her bag and placed them on the desk.

'Perhaps you could bring me up to date, Ken?' asked Smyth.

'I knew Ambrose a little at the university. He was interested in my research on intelligence testing. He and Miss Wong visited me a short time ago and asked if they could have copies of the latest testing methods in order to test someone and get our professional opinion of their intelligence. I gave them one of the Binet-Simon tests and some of Porteus Maze tests from Fitzroy.'

Cunningham picked up the wad of papers Charlotte had placed on the desk and took them to the professor. The two men became lost in reading for some minutes. Cunningham took note on a sheet of paper, and they conferred quietly.

'What's your conclusion, gentlemen?' Ambrose asked after waiting a polite amount of time for the professors to finish their discussion.

'Well,' said Cunningham, 'based on these results, Professor Smyth and are in agreement that the subject is rather above average intelligence.'

Charlotte and Ambrose looked at each other and smiled.

'Would you be willing to swear to that in court?' asked Charlotte.

Smyth replied, 'Intelligence testing is a very new science, but we think it is highly accurate and has the potential to shape the future of education. There have been exciting developments in recent years in France, the United States, and England, as well as here in Melbourne. So yes, I would certainly be prepared to give expert advice to that effect and to the particular case in front of us. The real question is: would the judge accept it as relevant or significant?'

'That will be *our* problem, Professor. We would be grateful for your support. Thank you, gentlemen, for your time and expertise,' said Ambrose.

Cunningham intervened as they were on the point of leaving. 'I don't suppose you would tell us something about your subject?'

'She is currently residing at the Kew Asylum, Ken. She has been diagnosed by an eminent medical professor as a mental deficient. Her mother was in and out of the asylum with various episodes of hysteria over a long period, and in fact Flora was born there. There are apparently other instances of mental deficiency in her family, so it was easy to mount a case to commit her. But we think that she has been kept there to keep her out of the way.

She seems to have inadvertently become involved in an evil plot. With her family background, we'd never imagined she would score quite so highly on your tests, but this only reconfirms our suspicions.'

Smyth replied, 'Extraordinary. Well, it would be good to bring a test case to court, especially one that examines our less fortunate members of society. This would indeed help to establish the credibility of our work. We will most certainly do all that we can to help.'

The offices of the Federal Department of Health
Spring St, Melbourne
Tuesday, 25 October 1921, 9.30am

'Come in, Pieter, sit down. I'm delighted you were able to visit Melbourne and report to me about those important matters we have been working on together. This episode with the *SS Catalina* was a side issue, of course, but it is most certainly worrying. I've invited you to the Department of Health for the Commonwealth government so you can inform this gentleman here of the situation. Pieter, this is Dr John Cumpston, head of all federal health matters, including quarantine. Would you please tell him your story?'

Pieter van Haandel outlined to the two men all the details he and his companions understood to be linked with Ambrose's curious case of cholera. He also advised of the conclusions they had surmised based on their suspicions.

'An extraordinary story—stranger than fiction really,' replied Cumpston, who had remained silent and stony-faced through Pieter's story. 'In fact, I should say that I do know something of your special task that has been undertaken for us in Java, and I would like to thank you for all that you have achieved on our behalf.' He paused and frowned. 'It is only because of this knowledge that I feel I must take your otherwise fantastical tale seriously. If true, the matter concerning the *SS Catalina* will be very difficult to resolve satisfactorily.

'I trust,' he said, gesturing towards Pieter, 'that you have spent long enough here to realise the importance of the individuals and institutions you have named? Accusations of illegality could easily lead to questions about the very integrity of some of our most important and respected medical institutions. We must be sure that the risk of panic and instability is not greater than the need to bring any miscreants to justice. I have very few people under me, and I rely on state enforcement bodies to implement any action I wish to take. Without a clear-cut case or enough evidence to act, it will be difficult to get the police to investigate. I am willing to introduce you to some of the few in the police force whom I trust. But I suspect you will be told the same thing, and you will need to gather some more evidence yourselves before he is able to act.'

Cumpston smiled grimly. 'Please be aware that if you did not have the strong support of the man sitting here beside you, even this much would not be possible. The Australian Protective League includes members of the highest standing in society. No one will wish to see them drawn into a scandal. But if it can be proved that there is an extremist group in their midst—unbeknown to many of their members—I am sure we will be able to help. If I can be assured of the accuracy of your information, of course. I know the dean of the medical school, Professor Allen, is of the highest moral character, and I believe he would support you also, if evidence was forthcoming. But it must be inconvertible evidence if you are to have any chance of success.'

Pieter and his anonymous contact departed.

Chapter Sixteen
Man's Best Friend

27 Redmond St, Kew
Tuesday, 25 October 1921, 7.30pm

A car pulled up next to a parkland in the eastern suburbs of Melbourne. The door opened and two large figures dressed in black, complete with blackened faces, quietly got out. One of them was carrying a small wriggling bundle, which he placed on the grass as they slinked into the parkland in the dark. The small bundle became four legged and followed.

Meanwhile, nearby, a taxicab pulled up outside 27 Redmond Street, Kew. After a brief moment, the door opened and Ambrose disembarked. He was dressed in loose-fitting but fashionable slacks and a jacket. Strangely enough, no dress code had been specified on the invitation to the dinner. He would have expected formal wear. He knocked on the door, which was opened by a waiter who beckoned him in. It was a large Federation-style mansion, surrounded by an expansive verandah with gargoyles representing native animals at each corner of the sweeping, red-tiled roof—a residence befitting a successful young surgeon. McBride welcomed him in with a wave from the back of the crowded room, and a waiter with a military bearing offered him a glass of champagne from a silver tray. The room was wood panelled and relatively dark, and it seemed to be full of men in various modes of dress representing a broad spectrum of the middle and upper ranks of society. Scottish paraphernalia, including crossed swords, a stag's head, and pictures of the highland glens decorated the walls. It was a very masculine room suitable for a wealthy bachelor. Ambrose surveyed the room and recognised a few familiar faces. But none of them he warmed to.

'Let's begin. Move into the ballroom,' McBride announced loudly.

They all shuffled into a large room with two extremely long tables with food set down the middle of both, and a card with a person's name in front of each chair. Ambrose found himself placed towards the back of the room. Cornelius Hamon was sitting further down the front. *What are Butterby's dresser and assistant in the dissection room doing here? He must be a member of the League.* A few of the military-style waiters moved around pouring wine and beer.

'Help yourselves!' cried out McBride, loud enough to be heard at the end of the room. 'We're not having waiting on table tonight. All the food is before you. Our wine waiters will take away your plates later.'

The spread included oysters, savoury mousses, terrines, cold chicken, sliced meat, and salads, as well as hot bain-maries with various potato dishes and hot stews, and many baskets of bread. *Clearly, the aim is to keep staff to a minimum. What is all the secrecy and security for?*

Across the end of the room was a smaller high table at a right angle to the others. At this table seated next to McBride was Richard Butterby, Herbert Brookes, and to Ambrose's immense surprise, Prime Minister William 'Billy' Hughes. Beside them were a number of well-known businessmen and politicians. As a lectern had been placed next to the high table, it seemed obvious that there would be speeches. After about thirty minutes, McBride rose and stood before the lectern and knocked with a gavel.

'Attention … your attention please!' The racket of conversation and clatter of knives and forks on plates stopped. 'As you know we are gathered here to raise money for the Australian Protective League.'

'Hear, hear,' shouted a few diners.

'I would like to welcome all of you, but especially Mr Hughes, the Prime Minister of Australia, whose support for our cause is much appreciated.'

Applause rippled around the room.

'Later, we will gather in smaller groups to discuss the various strategies we have begun to keep Australia free from the Bolshevik threat. But first, tonight, we have the great pleasure to welcome Sir Richard Butterby—surgeon, anatomist, and one of the giants of Australian medicine. He is going to talk on his research and explain why the lower classes, especially the union bosses attempting to destroy capitalism ('hiss, boo' from the room), are inferior members of our great Australian White Race.'

Butterby stood and walked to the lectern. 'Dr Joseph DeJaienette, a great American patriot, has written a poem about the dangers of letting inferior men and women and inferior races breed. It is titled "Mendel's Law: A Plea for a Better Race of Men". I shall start with a recitation of some of it.'

Oh, why are you so foolish—
You breeders who breed our men
Let the fools, the weaklings and crazy
Keep breeding and breeding again?
The criminal, deformed, and the misfit,
Dependent, diseased, and the rest—
As we breed the human family
The worst is as good as the best.

The poem continued in a similar manner for many stanzas, during which Ambrose concentrated on trying to commit other faces in the room to memory. After the thunderous applause that followed the end of the poem, Butterby then outlined at length, and with illustrations, how his measurements in the anatomy laboratory had proved that most members of the lower classes—Aboriginal Australians, criminals, prostitutes, homosexuals, in fact anyone who deviated from the norm he set—were degenerate because of their small head size. Ambrose shifted uncomfortably as he wondered how many of his patients, neighbours, and indeed friends would fall under Butterby's opprobrium. He suspected the list was long. The crowd listened with rapt attention and applauded regularly. As Butterby went on to explain the current state of affairs in anthropology, Ambrose motioned for more wine from the waiter. He was going to need it to get through the evening.

'You will all be aware of the huge gulf between the educated white man and the savage aboriginal (hear! hear!). I want to assure you that, despite some misguided fools who argue that they share our recent past and that their current form reflects useful adaptations to the Australian environment, this is not true. I have evidence, and am in the process of gathering more, to conclusively prove there has been no recent evolution of the primitive races since they separated, at an extremely early date, from the ape-like creatures from which we are all descended. The White Race, as we know it, is ancient beyond belief in its current form and has always been the superior race. Thank you!'

The crowd clapped enthusiastically, and many stamped their feet.

He's talking about Dad's collection and skulls. What's he up to? I must remain calm.

After Butterby, other speakers gave talks on the dangers of Russia and Bolshevism and about the threats posed by the leftist revolutions occurring in Europe. With the drink and all the spleen and hatred, the night was becoming quite animated. Ambrose sat quietly until, in a break before the small groups were meant to form, McBride approached him.

'Good to see you, Brosie. Great night, heah!'

'Absolutely,' Ambrose said in the sincerest voice he could muster in the circumstances, thinking, *He seems a bit inebriated.*

'Let's step outside in the garden. I'd like a smoke and to chat about something that's on my mind.'

'Given up smoking, Gus, and I'd hate to miss the small groups,' replied Ambrose.

'Later then … later, hold you to it,' McBride said as he ambled off.

A few minutes later, one of the waiters came to Ambrose and discretely whispered that a visitor wished to speak to him privately in the corridor. Ambrose raised his eyebrows; it seemed McBride really was determined to speak to him tonight. He pushed back his seat and went through the back door into the corridor.

'No one's here. I'm not waiting, they can find me inside,' Ambrose said to the waiter who'd followed him out, and he turned to re-enter the ballroom.

'They're waiting outside. I'd prefer it if you came.'

To his utter surprise, Ambrose felt something poking into his back. 'Don't be ridiculous,' he said, turning back to find Cornelius Hamon, who was holding a pistol.

Ambrose's mind was running full steam on escape options as they walked the short distance down the corridor and finally out into the extensive garden that ran down to the Yarra River, sheep huddled together halfway down.

They eventually stopped at a gazebo near a thicket of trees. The clear night sky was dominated by a half moon and brilliant stars. It was completely silent, other than a dog barking in a garden nearby. Dr Hugo appeared from the gloom.

'What the hell do you think you are doing?' Ambrose hissed, keeping his voice down in consideration of the pistol still held at his back.

'Pink, you've been meddling. You should 'ave just forgotten the baby and cholera and you wouldn't be in this fix.' Hamon produced some rope and began to tie Ambrose's arms behind his back.

'Are you insane?' said Ambrose. 'You can't be serious.'

'On the contrary,' said Hugo. 'About these matters, I am very serious indeed. First you come to me with your crazy ideas about cholera, and then you won't stop talking about them … in the newspaper … everywhere. Also, McBride is too impulsive. First, he experimented on the baby without telling me, and then, when 'e discovered the child was missing, he took some of the cholera milk to finish it off at the house in Carlton. Then 'e thinks 'e can keep you quiet by getting you to join us. He was so excited; he tells me he has convinced you to join us in our great work and 'e does not stop to think. He then brings you to our headquarters in the back of the brothel. Idiot! Me, I watch more carefully. You are not here tonight because you agree with our mission. I have been told you were once considered a young man of promise. But you choose to live in the slums and consort with deviants and Asiatics.' He paused to spit. 'You are a traitor to the white race.'

'And the other baby—the one in the morgue?' Ambrose was sweating with fear now.

'That was disposable too. Those babies were of no value, so we swapped them. Those young mental deficient women are like coloured races. Inferior. I and some of my friends have enjoyed them for a moment's pleasure, but not for breeding. There are plenty of babies that shouldn't be born. No loss,' he scowled, 'there can be no question for the coroner that there is cholera in Australia.'

'Cornelis,' Ambrose gasped, 'what about the section of the pregnant girl in the anatomy museum? The one we were supposed to believe had died of tuberculosis?'

Hamon merely shrugged his shoulder and smiled. Hugo recollected himself and gestured to the waiter behind Ambrose to take over the task of tying his arms.

'What do you think you are doing, Hugo … Cornelius? You can't possibly think to shoot me here and get away with it. The Prime Minister's inside, for God's sake.'

Ambrose was terrified; fear gripped him as it had at the battlefront. He was aware that his mind was racing for openings. How could he get out of this?

'Who said anything about shooting you? Terrible accident … drank too much … wandering around on a dark night, slipped, 'it his head on a rock.' Hugo waved a piece of granite in his hand. 'And rolled into ze river. That Asiatic woman you 'ave been seeing will be so unhappy … thought she'd got a real white man.'

The dog next door barked again furiously.

Ambrose just had time to think, *I know that bark*, when suddenly it was Molly heading at full speed towards the waiter who was binding his arms. All turned towards the sudden arrival of the little dog. Ambrose took a few steps and head-butted Cornelius Hamon, who dropped the gun at the very moment Molly stuck her teeth into the leg of the waiter tying Ambrose's hands. Ambrose turned and ran towards the sheep and the river, zig-zagging and calling Molly over his shoulder as he ran. He had natural speed, but it was reasonably dark, and his hands were still tangled in a half-finished knot behind his back. The sheep scattered in all directions as he hit top speed. Then, just as he was about to reach the river, he was suddenly grabbed, thrown up into the air, and somersaulted down to earth on his back. Had he been shot? Molly meanwhile had abandoned her juicy leg and quickly caught up with him, now sitting beside him wagging her tail as if the danger was past. He was winded and, looking up, could see the waiter perhaps forty yards away, holding the gun in a very professional way in both hands and pointing it at him. Hugo and Hamon stood by him. Despair overtook him. *At least I'll die with my dog. If only I'd told Charlotte what I really feel*, thought Ambrose, though why and how Molly was there was a complete mystery.

Unexpectedly, the gunman suddenly screamed and threw the gun up in the air. A bullet whistled past Ambrose's ear. He could see that Hugo was running as fast as he could back up to the house, followed by Hamon. They both looked back briefly and then continued, clearly of the opinion that luck was against them that night. Two darkly clad figures came from the trees and stood briefly over the remaining waiter writhing in pain on the ground. They then came quickly down to Ambrose.

'Sorry to keep you waiting, Brosie,' said Pieter, 'but I needed to get that gun and retrieve my dart from his hand also.' He held up a dart about six inches long and slipped it back into a blow pipe. 'Given to me by a descendent of the last Sultan of Mataram—very useful.' He threw the gun into the river.

'What happened? Why are you here?' replied the completely stunned Ambrose.

'We decided to visit the dairy, and Charlie suggested we do it tonight. She was most insistent that we keep an eye on you. And that we bring Molly.'

Paddy grinned as they hauled Ambrose up, and between them helped him to the dairy fence.

'We'll cut through the grounds of the dairy to the car. There are no guards in the dairy now—well, not any that can cause harm at least.' Paddy smiled. 'We watched you with your three captors. Pieter had his dart aimed at the gunman all along. When you decided to make a dash, you obviously hadn't seen the barbed-wire fence that ran along the river—too dark. It's there to keep the sheep in, and in return they keep the grass down. You ran full on into it and catapulted over it—very impressive three-quarter somersault. You'll have a few scratches, but no bullet holes.'

They both chuckled. They reached the car without incident and drove back to North Fitzroy.

'What happened at the dairy, gentlemen? I'm very concerned that the assault on the guards last night will mean they'll close up shop and we'll lose our lead on the cholera,' Ambrose said as he bandaged his few scratches and then poured everyone drinks.

'Don't worry about the guards, Brosie. There were two,' said Pieter. 'We jumped them and trussed them up also. Paddy put on a most excellent accent and boasted about being in the Fitzroy Roses gang—Squizzy Taylor's henchman no less. Paddy talked about looking for cash, and made it clear when we left that we had been disappointed and that it was not worth our while to come back. I stayed in the shadows, so I don't think they would have doubted my credentials, also.'

'What did you find?'

'They have a laboratory and everything you would need to culture and store disease organisms. We went through their rosters and schedules. They have weekly boat trips to and from somewhere that is written as "maison de l'eau". You know what that means, of course, Brosie.'

'Yes, it's definitely "Waterhouse", and Hugo is obviously deeply involved. Pieter, I'm meeting Detective Inspector McLeish tomorrow. Perhaps you and Paddy might dine at Café Denat and see if you can discover more about the menu for next Saturday. We need to be certain what food will be adulterated with cholera.'

'There was something else, but we didn't take it,' said Pieter. 'In one of the drawers I managed to open, we found a medical prescription that looked as though it had been signed by you. And with it were a number of sheets of plain paper with your signature written out many times. I think they are practising forging it. I made sure they wouldn't know it had been disturbed.'

'Hell. This is getting very dirty indeed. What are their plans?'

'I think Paddy should move in next door with me temporarily so we can take turns watching over you. This situation is escalating, and you are definitely a target.'

'I'll get my things today and drop by this afternoon. I'll get guns for us both,' replied Paddy.

Chapter Seventeen
Ambrose Takes a Risk

Police Headquarters, Russell St
Wednesday, 26 October 1921, Noon

'What can I do for you, Brose? I'd say it's nice to see you off the football field, but I have had some seriously worrying phone calls this morning and I think trepidation might be a better reaction. What on earth have you and that giant Dutchman been stirring up?'

Cameron McLeish was of Scots descent and had many of the better characteristics of his type. Understated in his dress and manner, with long angular features, he was deceptively powerful and could hold his own in a brawl. His intense eyes had unsettled many a criminal, but he also had an excellent sense of humour, which was used sparingly. Ambrose believed he was highly intelligent and utterly trustworthy.

Ambrose went through the whole business from the arrival of the sick child until the attempt on his life the previous evening, ending with a shrug.

'Look, I do know this all sounds incredibly outlandish, but there's no other conclusion we could come to.'

McLeish let him speak without interruption. 'Now,' he said, 'these are serious matters indeed.' He paused, a worried look on his face. 'I have a problem, however. I'm not sure I should tell you this, but I have recently been given some other information regarding you. Complaints have been made to some of my superiors about your claims that there is cholera in Australia. These complaints have been connected to your work and domicile in Fitzroy, and unpleasant connections have been made. The inference is that you are a front man for Bolshevik underground revolutionaries and that you have been stirring up trouble. There has even been a suggestion that you have somehow introduced this deadly disease secretly. Apparently, these high sources claim to have evidence. What do you intend to do? Are you going to press charges against Hugo? It would end up being your word against his, and if he is part of the Protective League, they'll have sympathisers right through the judiciary and the police force. Lots of prominent people in the League, you know.'

Ambrose went pale. 'I had no idea that they're trying to blame me for their plot. We'll have to get to Waterhouse now. The proof of their plot must be there.'

McLeish nodded briskly. 'You will need to bring me some good evidence before I will be willing to get too involved. As of yet, you have nothing strong enough on Butterby concerning the babies, in any case.'

'We have better evidence against Hugo being involved in a plot related to cholera,' replied Ambrose. 'But we will need to get another sample and organise another laboratory with authority to independently prove the existence of the disease, as well as prove they had the expertise to manufacture it. We then have to show they have brought it here and are intending to use it.'

McLeish interrupted. 'Not to mention, we'd need to pass over your, ahem, unofficial knowledge of the activities at the dairy and go in again knowing that we'd definitely find what we are looking for. I'd look a fool raiding a dairy for a microorganism that the best medical minds say doesn't exist in Australia, only to come out emptyhanded. You need the evidence of Flora, and perhaps others. You have considered that these young women will have to stand up in court and be believed. As you well know, Brose, poor women often choose prostitution out of desperation. You know the argument the legal teams will put up, and they'll probably be members of the same clubs as the judge.'

Ambrose's spirits had fallen somewhat during his response.

'Look, don't worry, Brose. I'll throw my support behind you as soon as I think we have a good chance at success. You seem to have convinced some key people in high places already, and Cumpston's backing will be crucial. I can organise raids and arrests, but it must be at the right time and with incontrovertible evidence. As they have sympathisers in the force, I'm keeping this to myself, and you would be wise to be careful as well—you've experienced what they are willing to do. Don't forget, take care, some very powerful people seem to be out for your skin. Unofficially, get yourself a weapon.'

Café Denat
215 Exhibition St, Melbourne
Thursday, 27 October 1921, 3pm

'Good tucker,' said Paddy, rubbing his ample midriff.

'Exshellent repasht … delightful cwuisine,' echoed Pieter, cleaning out his mouth with a toothpick and then proceeding with the considerable task of removing crumbs from his beard. On the table before them lay the ruins of *Canard a l'Orange*, along with almost empty vegetable platters and a number of empty bottles of wine. They had each devoured a whole duck, and Paddy had requested extra servings of the scrumptious orange gravy.

'See now why the toffs get excited about this 'ere French food,' he said.

'I'll bring you your crème caramel now, sir?' Giuseppe Favaloro inquired.

'Yes please,' replied Pieter. 'But please don't forget we ordered four, Giuseppe, and bring the cognac bottle also. And would it be possible for me to present my compliments to the chef in person? I wish to ask him a question.'

'I'll ask Signor Handeel, but the chef … ees very excitable. I wouldn't criticise anything … not even a little thing … if I were you.'

Pieter assured him that they wished to pass on nothing but compliments and settled down with a sigh of contentment to wait for the next course. Giuseppe returned laden with desserts and a bottle and glasses.

'Signor, the chef wishes to thank you but to excuse himself as 'e 'as an 'eadache.'

'Giuseppe,' said Pieter, 'you may be able to help me. I believe that your chef has been chosen to run the banquet next Saturday at the Exhibition Building to celebrate the twentieth birthday of the Federation of Australia. Do you happen to know what is on the menu?'

'That ees a big secret and has caused 'is 'eadache, signor. 'e organised it in honour of the great diva, who the chef cooked for 'imself when 'e worked under Escoffier at the Ritz in London,' said Giuseppe. 'I can only tell you what will not be served: the *Pêche Melba*, which would have so perfectly honoured the dame.'

'What went wrong?'

'They will serve the *Pêche Melba* to the highest table, but not made by 'im. 'e is very upset … 'e feels it ees a terrible insult. 'e 'as just been asked to serve fruit and sweetmeats to the "*hoi polloi*", as 'e calls them. 'e feels that it ees beneath 'is dignity. Also, ice-cream from the Italian ice-cream vendors will be served to all of the guests.'

'Who is to make the *Pêche Melba* and ice-cream, waiter?' asked Pieter.

'I don't know. That worries me.'

'Me too,' replied Pieter. 'Eat and drink up, Billy. When we finish this, it's back to Fitzroy to report what we have found.'

Chapter Eighteen
A Flying Coffin

Corio Bay
Thursday, 27 October 1921, 1am

It is a little too windy, Charlotte thought. *This biplane—'the flying coffin' as it is affectionately known—seems very flimsy. This* was despite Reggie assuring her that all would be well. *I hope it will be able to make the trip.*

She had read that a similar aircraft had gone down in Bass Strait in the previous year attempting a search for a missing ship. She had lied to Ambrose. She figured that if only she and Reggie went, it would lighten the load, giving them a slightly greater range. She had persuaded Hedley to stay in Melbourne and decided that if she told Ambrose they were going, he would have bullied Reggie into excluding her. Also, if they had a spare seat, they had the capacity to bring one more back. She had also managed, through her secret contacts, to get three hand grenades and two pistols—the hand grenades to create the diversion she planned. After poring over the map of Waterhouse Island in the university library with Hedley, Charlotte formulated what she thought was a simple but effective plan.

Charlotte went over it with Reggie once more in the darkness before they began the flight.

'Waterhouse Island is about three quarters of a mile wide and a bit under three miles long on an angle of about two o'clock from north. There is a lighthouse at the north-eastern point, and

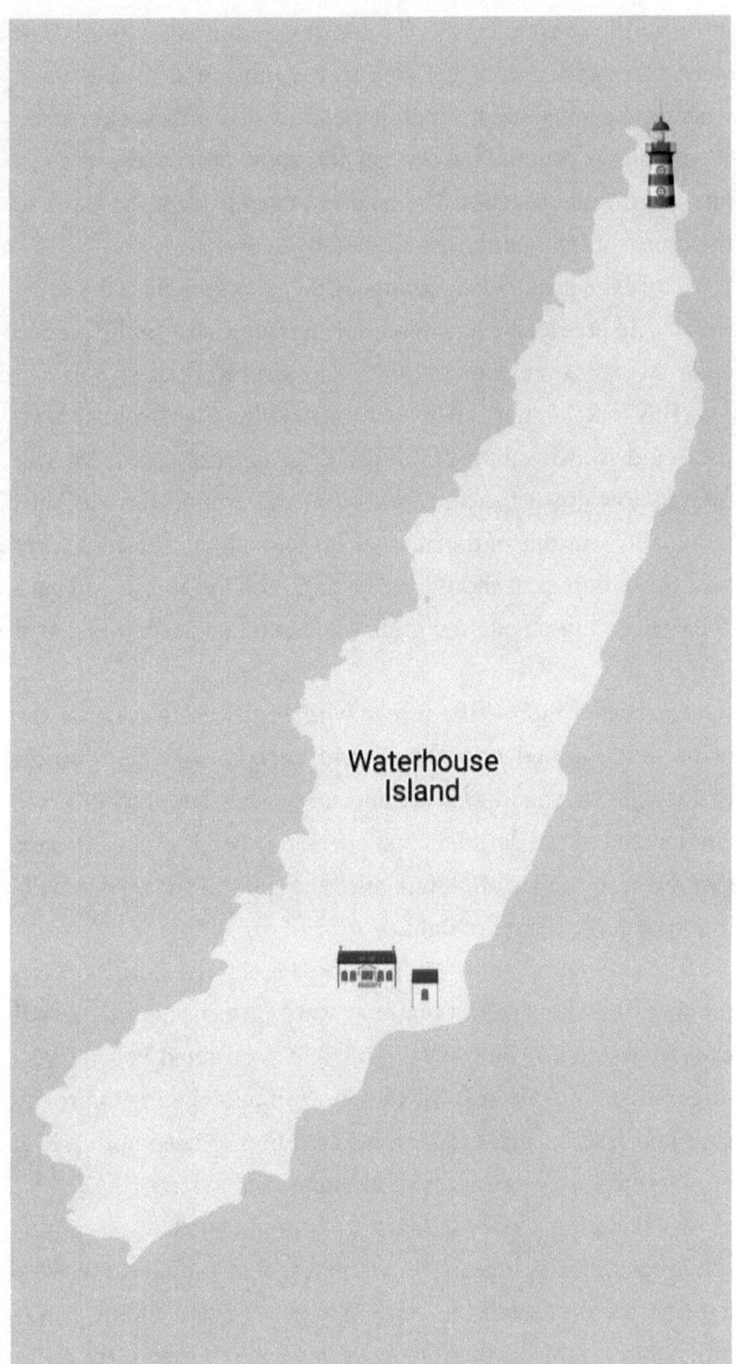
Waterhouse
Island

most of the coast is rocky. The only exception is the south-east coast three quarters of the way to the other end of the island where there are some fine sandy beaches. The only buildings on the island—a colonial homestead and some outhouses—are just inland from the beaches. The land rises gently from the shore to the centre of the island, with limited tree cover.'

'I love the plan to drop grenades,' Reggie chimed in, shivering in the cold breeze. He had agreed with enthusiasm to the plan to cause an explosion near the lighthouse just before dawn.

'This was the most effective means of drawing any guards on the island away from the buildings,' Charlotte explained. 'We will then fly low down the northern coast and around the southern tip to land near one of the beaches on the southern-eastern coast near the buildings. It should still be dark, and the guards will have departed to investigate the grenades exploding at the other end of the island.'

Charlotte grabbed the flimsy wire and cloth fuselage of the plane and climbed into the second cockpit. The nervousness that surged through her body and turned her knees to jelly was emphasised by the darkness that enveloped her. It was a darkness that didn't forbid vision—stars filled the sky and the waxing half-moon cast a dim haze of light.

The engine roared to life, blowing diesel fumes into her face, the shock of which meant that they were airborne before she had time to register the bumpy take-off. She interpreted Reggie's gestures in the cockpit in front of her as an apology for the rocky start and resisted the temptation to tell him to keep both hands on the wheel, or whatever it was that he used to steer.

For Charlotte, once airborne, the flight took on an atmosphere of timeless infinity once the few lights of Geelong were left behind. Even with the eerie light of stars and moon, it was difficult to see the distinction between sea and horizon. The noise of the engine and slipstream further added to the unworldliness of the trip.

She found her mind wandering towards Ambrose—something that had happened quite a bit lately.

He can be pompous and was almost insulting when he propositioned me, and yet he shows plenty of kindness to Will and Wally, who are not the sort of people that a pompous snob would help or associate with. And the Favaloros. Maybe he's just compensating for being an orphan. He is certainly confronting and confusing—I don't know what to think. Perhaps I am being a little proud. I do think he has some appealing features and someone that I find attractive ... extremely ... in some ways. But what good can any permanent attachment mean for my work and independence? After Bangkok, I swore to never be attached.

Such musings occupied much of the flight over Bass Strait.

Waterhouse Island
40.7997° S, 147.6323° E
4.40am

Reggie's frantic hand gestures jolted Charlotte out from her reverie. They were approaching the lighthouse, just on schedule. Charlotte threw a grenade and, signalling Reggie to turn back, she threw another one. Multiple explosions shattered the silence. They were so low to the land it looked as though they would crash as the nautical twilight only just illuminated features on the land. Up until now, the trip had been relatively uneventful as the prevailing westerlies had died down. After the diversion caused by the explosions, they then swooped down just above the sea and headed north-west away from the island. The three-mile route down the northern coast took only a few minutes and was hidden from the buildings on the beaches. They looped out to the north to give the islanders time to wake up and head to the lighthouse. She signalled to Reggie to turn and fly back towards the south-western tip.

* * * * *

'What was that?' The guard struggled out of the bunk and shook the shoulder of a sleeping figure in the bunk above.

'Fuck off! What do you want? It's still dark.'

'There was an explosion. Didn't you hear it?'

On the other side of the bedroom, another figure lit a lantern, and by this time the four men in the room were in various degrees of wakefulness. *BANG!* A distant explosion. Wide awake now, the men rushed into the corridor and out the front door into the burgeoning dawn light.

'Nothing happening here, so it must be on the other side of the island,' the first man said. 'It's still too dark to see properly, so we had better get to the top of the island to get a decent line of sight in all directions. It may be at the lighthouse.'

'I hope it's not the supply ship in trouble—it was due today,' said another of the party. 'I'll go and get some guns from the house just in case it's trouble. You three go and I'll stay here if you like?'

'No need,' said one of the others. 'If they're friends or enemies, it makes no difference. It'll take a while for a boat to get around the northern end and we will have a better look at them from the hill in the middle of the island or from the lighthouse. The natives are locked up safe and sound. We'll all go.'

Quickly armed and each with a lantern, the four men headed north-east diagonally across the island to the lighthouse. Fifteen minutes from the first explosion, the four guards were already about a mile away from their camp. The path they took across the middle of the island meant they had just crossed its highest ridge and descended into a dip about one hundred metres long. So they didn't see the plane or hear its engine above the wind and the waves as it skimmed low above the ocean around the southern tip.

*****

Dawn was starting to illuminate the sky, and Charlotte and Reggie could just make out the beach and the buildings scattered beyond it. A small boat was moored to a jetty, but there was enough space to land as long as no underwater rocks or snags were hidden from view. The plane touched down and stopped just off the beach. Charlotte jumped out, waded in towards the shore, and looked hard. She could see perhaps three or four lanterns along the ridge about halfway up the island and, as she ran up the beach, it seemed that no one was nearby.

Quickly moving from the homestead to the nearest and largest outhouse, she discovered the padlock on the door and risked discovery by shooting it off. The door swung open, and inside she could just make out about five or six figures, some in bunks, the others backing into the corner. Charlotte spoke to them first in English and then in Mandarin. The latter provoked immediate responses, and one of the men replied to Charlotte's urgent request to know where they had come from and explained that they had been working on a plantation in Java.

'Were any of you ill?' asked Charlotte.

'Our village was struck down with the cholera, but all of us here didn't get sick like the others,' he replied. 'We don't know why we were kidnapped. We have been kept under guard and have no idea where we are.'

Charlotte assured them that they would be freed in time and handed a pistol to the self-appointed leader, who led other men to the main house at a run.

'Who are you? Have you come to rescue us?' called out a dishevelled figure lying on a bunk in the corner, looking equally hopeful and afraid. The English speaker identified himself as the lighthouse keeper. As he approached the light, Charlotte noticed he had a bandaged head.

'How did you get that?' Charlotte asked, pointing.

'I got too nosey a few days ago when I came out from the mainland to check the light. These buildings have been empty for years. What's going on?'

'There's no time to explain, but I can get you out of here. Are you all right to move?' asked Charlotte.

At that moment, a shot rang out from the house. Charlotte and the lighthouse keeper ran down to discover that the prisoners had found the rifle and ammunition cabinet and had shot the lock off. They were now all armed and apparently under the command of the leader, who obviously had had some sort of military training. He had two climbing on the roof and others covering the way back from the lighthouse. He and Charlotte spoke rapidly in Mandarin.

Charlotte turned to the keeper. 'He says we should go and get help, and that he can easily hold off the guards. There are only four of them, and all the food is in the house. There are spotlights in the house, and they will never be able to rush the house now that the prisoners can put up a good defence and are well armed. He said I should take you as you are injured, and you won't understand any instructions he gives you. You may compromise their defence. Can you make it to the aircraft?'

It was quite light now, and the lighthouse man nodded resolutely, if unenthusiastically. As they both waded into the sea,

Charlotte was delighted to see that Reggie, as promised, had remained in the cockpit, ready to take off at a moment's notice. It had taken all of the persuasion she had learnt at law school to convince him that he needed to stay behind while she investigated, as having the plane ready was critical to their success. He scrambled down to help get the lightkeeper onboard and returned to the cockpit to prepare to take off. Just then, an explosion behind them destroyed the boat tied to the wharf.

'What was that?' Reggie yelled from the front.

'Oh, I gave a grenade to them,' she replied. 'They must have decided to cut off any escape route.'

'Well, next time can I get one too?' he grumbled. 'I'm the only one who's missed out.'

Charlotte didn't bother to suppress her grin. Amazingly, it seemed that not only had they guessed correctly as to the whereabouts of the Chinese carriers, but they had pulled off a rescue plan to the letter.

Soon the aircraft was in the sky, gaining height as it flew over the island. Suddenly, shots whistled past the plane. Looking around frantically, Charlotte found the guards in the centre of the island returning from the lighthouse. She was relieved as Reggie banked below the shooters' horizon and sped northwards. There seemed to be no damage to either the passengers or the plane.

Suddenly Reggie gesticulated wildly to her left. She leant out as far as she could, the slipstream tearing at her face. Finally, with dread, she saw fuel sputtering out into the air. They had hit the spare fuel tank—and now getting back to Geelong would be impossible.

What to do? Go back to Waterhouse? Go to Tasmania … but where? It was her job to navigate. If they went to Waterhouse, they would all be stuck on the island. Eventually the boat that resupplied the island and took whatever it was they needed to produce the cholera in Kew would arrive and they would be finished—they could only last for so long and the only boat was destroyed. It would have to be Tasmania.

She signalled to Reggie to turn back, but not to Waterhouse—they needed to go west along the coast until they came to a reasonably sized settlement. She opened the map she had brought with her and struggled to stop the draught tearing it from her hands. Bridport was only twenty-five miles away, but it was in the middle of nowhere and they would not be able to get a message to Ambrose and the others. George Town was over fifty miles away, and she remembered that the telegraph station between Tasmania and Victoria was there. They'd have to fly to George Town. She tapped Reggie on the shoulder and pointed west.

The westerly is building up. Will we have enough fuel? The range is about 170 miles, so we can't lose more than two thirds of the tank.

The next thirty minutes seemed like the longest of Reggie and Charlotte's lives. She couldn't stop leaning out and staring out at the stream of fuel leaving the tank. Finally, to her left was the mouth of the Tamar River, and she signalled to Reggie to head for the estuary. As they flew over the giant trees on the point and followed the river upstream, the town appeared about three miles ahead. As they came closer, the engine started to misfire, but they just managed to land and taxi to the pier in Stone Quarry Bay when the engine cut out completely.

The inhabitants of the town had gathered to see the rare sight of a seaplane landing in the river and were even more surprised when Charlotte and Reggie jumped out. Charlotte saw to it that the lighthouse man was taken to the town doctor, and then asked the way to the telegraph station. When she returned to the plane, Reggie was showing off its beauties to a group of enthralled children.

'If we patch up that hole quickly and get some more fuel, we can be back in Melbourne sometime in the late afternoon,' said Reggie.

He had maintained his insouciant attitude throughout their journey, which impressed her all the more, knowing they had really been in danger.

41 Alfred Crescent, Fitzroy North
3.30pm

Pieter had just arrived home after his excellent lunch when he was disturbed by Mrs Simpson banging on the connecting doors between the houses.

'Dr van Haandel, Dr van Haandel, come quickly!'

He opened the door and Mrs Simpson thrust a telegram into his hand.

'Dr Pink is at the surgery and I know he would want you to read this.'

Pieter opened it. 'Stuck in George Town STOP Waterhouse in trouble STOP captives free STOP need police STOP home tonight.'

All thoughts of an afternoon nap vanished as Pieter sped out the door to find Ambrose.

Chapter Nineteen

Standoff

Police Headquarters, Russell St
Thursday, 27 October 1921, 4.45pm

'This could finish my career, Brosie. I suppose you are ignorant of the Wong girl's unsavoury connections?'

'What do you mean, Cam?'

'I know she has had dealings with a secret Chinese organisation. She runs a fine line in her operations within the Chinese community. She won't do you much good.'

So that's all Cam has on her.

'Whether what you say is true, I believe her in this instance and can give no reason why giving us false evidence would gain her any benefit at all. If she knew they were there for some nefarious purpose, why would she try to expose them? Besides, Reggie is with her,' replied Ambrose.

'Do you realise the logistics? I'll have to pull rank over someone in the water police and go all the way in one of their boats with about half a dozen police to a remote island, which happens to be in a different state and out of my jurisdiction … Very well, I'll do it—and I'll probably miss the Cup on Tuesday if we find anything. You have no idea what you owe me!'

'I'll put a tenner on your pick for the winner of the Cup for you as thanks.'

'You can do that, and you can come with me.'

The Heads, Port Phillip Bay
Thursday, 27 October 1921, 11.59pm

McLeish was as good as his word; Ambrose was feeling rather sick leaning against the side of the cabin of the water police's largest vessel. Normally the boat of choice to board any large ship near the coastline that aroused suspicion, tonight it was to serve a different purpose and take to the high seas to Tasmania. The phrase 'it was a dark and stormy night' came to mind, but he couldn't remember where he had read it. In fact, the weather wasn't too bad, but the passage from the enclosed Port Phillip Bay out into Bass Strait was notoriously rough and difficult for any landlubber like Ambrose. Five policemen made up the crew aboard, along with the two friends, and they all seemed to manage the rough seas better than Ambrose. The pilot of the boat had told them it would take about nine hours to reach Waterhouse Island. Ambrose had telegraphed Charlotte and Reggie at Boyd Town explaining what he was doing, but had no expectation that they would receive it. He wasn't going anywhere in the next nine hours and so he climbed into one of the bunks underneath the cabin and attempted to sleep.

Waterhouse Island
40.7997° S, 147.6323° E
Friday, 28 October 1921, 9am

Ambrose was wide awake, but not because he'd had a good night's sleep.

What will we find?

The boat was coming into the beach, and they could see the Chinese captives waving to them from the house. A shot landed in the water to their left and made some on the boat duck for cover.

'We'll lower the rowboat and head in I think,' said McLeish. 'Those must be the guards shooting at us. They must be up behind the ridge, which is about four hundred yards from the house. They're not likely to hit anyone at the house unless they get lucky. They won't stop us landing. You stay here.'

'With pleasure,' replied Ambrose.

McLeish and three of the police climbed into the rowboat, and two manned the oars. Ambrose watched as they landed and ran doubled up towards the house. Suddenly they turned, and McLeish began gesturing at him wildly. He couldn't make out what was going on until a shot landed in the sea just near to him. He turned to see another vessel some distance off had just come around the north-east tip—it must be the supply ship. He grabbed some binoculars and tried to steady himself on the rocking boat. At the stern of the boat was Captain Salvatore Negrone. One of the men still on the police boat fired some warning shots across the bow of the intruder. It was a standoff.

What could he do? He remembered McLeish had brought the latest camera equipment to record any evidence, and so he ducked into the cabin. He emerged with a Kodak, luckily just like the one he owned, and began taking photos. At least they would have some evidence if they could get out of this mess.

One of the policemen tapped Ambrose on the shoulder while he was photographing the island and pointed to the other ship. 'Look, something is happening.'

The sea had become quite choppy, but they could see the men on the supply ship were winching a smallish boat over the side. As the larger ship was clearly too big to dock at Waterhouse, this smaller vessel must be what they used to ferry people and goods to and from the island. Ambrose and the others on the police boat watched the proceedings through their binoculars.

'It looks like Negrone is abandoning ship,' Ambrose said.

'Or heading to the mainland for reinforcements?' replied one of the officers.

'According to the maps, there is a tiny settlement called Ducane about five miles south-east around the point. Looks like he might be heading there.'

With a roar, the outboard motor sprung to life and the boat, with Negrone, followed an arc that kept it out of firing range but on course to Ducane. In a few minutes, it had disappeared from view.

Ambrose returned to documenting the scene at the house when shots started again from the boat. Ambrose and the police ducked as it seemed to be moving towards them and attacking. He then heard what sounded like the distant sound of an engine. Suddenly, a seaplane appeared flying perilously low, heading towards the attacking supply ship—after which an explosion rocked the deck of Negrone's boat. Ambrose saw a figure fall into the water ... then some more explosions and random bullets firing—an ammunition store must have been hit. The plane passed on into the distance so quickly that the shocked crew on the damaged boat had no time to fire at it with their guns. The boat seemed to list and all onboard scrambled to get into the one remaining rowboat. The boat seemed to be overloaded with passengers and it tipped into the sea.

'Let's get over and get any survivors,' said Ambrose.

In a few minutes, they had arrived at the spot where the boat had been. Ambrose and one of the officers dragged three men aboard while the other kept them covered with a gun. They were quickly handcuffed and stowed below. Two bodies of those who had seemed to have drowned when the lifeboat tipped were dragged onboard, but Negrone was well gone. Turning back to look at the shore, Ambrose could see the four guards walking down to the house with their arms held high; they'd seen enough to realise it was all up for them. McLeish was herding the guards together as they arrived at the house. He joined the officers in a small boat that took them to the shore to meet McLeish.

The seaplane returned overhead, and two figures waved from the cockpits—Charlotte and Reggie, as expected.

The plane landed near the beach, and Charlotte clambered down into the shallow waves and walked to the beach. Ambrose knew he couldn't resist anymore. Like Aphrodite, Charlie had enchanted him. He was speechless and yet faltered. What if she didn't reciprocate again? What if he wasn't good enough? They met on the beach.

'Charlie, why didn't you bring me? You could have been …'

'I say, Brosie, this has been fun.' Reggie had waded in as well. 'Did you see those explosions? My turn at last.'

'What caused them?' asked Ambrose.

'My last hand grenade,' replied Charlotte, 'thrown by Reggie right into the ammunition stores. Amazing aim, I've never seen anything like it.'

'Cricket,' Reggie said modestly with a shrug.

'A hand grenade can cause damage like that?' Ambrose asked incredulously.

'Certainly can, if it either hits the right spot or, in this case, some ammunition stores,' said one of the officers who had now joined the group on the beach.

Ambrose turned to an amused looking McLeish and made introductions.

'Thank you all for your help. Now I don't want to sound like I'm hurrying you, but I've got a serious crime scene here to contain as well as more bodies to search for. I radioed Launceston, and they will have some men here in a few hours. I'm grateful for your part in proceedings, but it might be better if I gloss over your role when describing recent events to the local police. How much petrol have you got in that plane, Dr Robinson … Miss Wong?'

'You're lucky we couldn't repair the fuel tank in time to fly home to Melbourne yesterday,' said Reggie. 'I got your telegram in George Town and thought I might come and have a look before I flew back to Geelong. I have enough fuel for a double crossing, and so I have plenty to fly past here on the way back.'

'I think our unwilling guests on Waterhouse Island in Bass Strait may have cholera. Are they the secret weapon that will be used to create the disaster at the Exhibition Buildings?' added Ambrose.

'They do. I asked them and they were chosen because they have no symptoms,' said Charlotte.

'Explain,' McLeish demanded.

'Cholera kills, but not everyone who contracts it. A few in every population will even carry the bacteria without symptoms and others will get better. They must have only carriers of the disease on Waterhouse,' replied Ambrose.

'But why not just bring cholera bacteria in some medium from Java, like petri jars? Why do they need the humans?'

'The cholera bacterium can survive in food and drink, or even better in a petri jar, for a maximum of about ten days at room temperature. If they used ice, they could keep it alive for longer, but they couldn't rely on a good supply using this method. They'd have to keep shipping it and if it failed in the Melbourne lab, they'd have to start all over again.'

'They must have been testing cholera patients and their families in Java and picked out the asymptomatic members who continued to have signs of the cholera organism in their stools but no symptoms of the disease. Cholera carriers can persist with chronic infection and the production and shedding of organisms in their stool for many years without showing any signs of sickness. By shanghaiing a few of these human carriers and bringing them to Waterhouse, they would be guaranteed a fresh and constant supply of infected stools for a long time.'

'But it is still unclear to me why they would introduce cholera to Australia? What would they gain? And how many of the infected victims would die in this country?' asked Cam.

'Many would be infected, and as cholera doesn't currently exist in Australia, it would be some time before the medical community realised what they had on their hands and got themselves organised to deliver the proper treatment. Once it spread, it would become endemic, never to be truly eliminated. Those who die in a cholera epidemic are usually the weak, young, and elderly, and of course the poor, living in unsanitary conditions. In other words, all the kinds of people Butterby and his ilk like to refer to as "degenerates" or "the unfit", said Ambrose. 'So, perhaps their plan is to "cleanse" the nation and reinforce the idea of white superiority.'

'And, if the arrival of cholera can be linked to some Chinese sailors, that will serve their argument too,' remarked Charlotte.

'So', said Cam, 'if I've got this right, they have a plan to create an epidemic to rid the country of the people they don't like, which somehow involves cholera and the grand banquet on 29 October. But it's hardly as if any of the people you describe will be invited. The whole thing sounds insane.'

Ambrose had to agree. 'You are right, it does sound insane. But we know they are targeting the event, so we have to focus on preventing their plans, then figure out what the thinking is behind their plan.'

'It's the ice-cream,' Charlotte cried suddenly, waving a piece of paper. 'Pieter telegraphed us yesterday and said that the dessert had been changed to ice-cream and that it would come from the dairy in Kew. We've been wondering where the fascists and the ice-cream vans fit in, not to mention the shared interest they and the asylum officials seem to have in the dairy. They are going to introduce cholera via milk. Giving infected milk to a baby would infect her, isn't that right? Iris might have been accidently infected, or they might have been deliberately experimenting on the best way to introduce the disease. And it worked. So now, they have the supply of cholera, the supply of milk, and an ally who controls the ice-cream trade. They are going to serve ice-cream at the banquet!'

'Clearly McBride and Negrone at the asylum had been working with both Negrone's brother and the fascists. But was Butterby involved? Who was the mastermind?' asked Ambrose.

Cam interjected. 'But my original question is still not fully answered. To introduce cholera, yes, it will cause much distress and misery for the working class, many of whom are not the middle-class white men that these madmen so much love. But why not simply infect the milk from the dairy and introduce it to the poor this way? Why also bring it to the banquet, where they themselves will be eating?'

'I think I understand,' Ambrose said slowly. 'An epidemic would certainly cause chaos, and, as you say, primarily affect those that Butterby and his ilk would like to see purged from the country. Cholera is known to be common in Asia, and if it it's been introduced to the country by Chinese sailors, as outrageous as it sounds, I think they see it as an opportunity for some kind of *coup d'état*. A claim that the disease has been introduced as part of a plot to destabilise the nation, by those unhappy with its new policies, such as the international movement, gives them their chance to claim that the government is not capable of running the country or protecting its borders.

'If they just wanted to wipe out some of the poorer parts of the population, there are lots of ways to introduce cholera. But instead, they are choosing to use an occasion crammed full of the country's great and good to introduce the disease. Which would make more sense if it *was* a leftist plot, and if a few conservative politicians die, well, that only makes it easier to pin on the Bolsheviks … and me.'

'Also, apart from their inner circle, they clearly don't care if it even kills some of their own. It literally kills two birds with one stone if some conservative politicians die, as it then becomes easier to explain it as a leftist plot and, at the same time, they get rid of moderates in the movement,' Reggie observed.

They all stared at each other in silence at the enormity of such evil. It was hard to credit, but it certainly brought together all the disparate threads they had been pursuing.

'Look, everything you've all said makes a certain kind of sense,' said Cam, 'but, and it's a big but, I could hardly credit your story if I hadn't heard all the evidence as you brought it together. How on earth can we take this story to someone in authority and not get sent to the asylum ourselves?'

McLeish continued, 'In that case, may I suggest that you head off—immediately! After the events of today, I'm willing to believe even your most outlandish theories, Ambrose. I'll contact my trustworthy superiors and get them to make arrangements for the banquet. I can see you have a spare seat. You three get back to Melbourne and deal with the problem we are facing at the dinner at the Exhibition Buildings. I might not make it in time. No hand grenades mind, and Miss Wong, I've already forgotten that I saw any today, but if any more do make an appearance, we might need to discuss where you acquired them …'

Chapter Twenty
Another Poisoned Chalice

Exhibition Gardens, Rathdowne Street, Carlton
Saturday, 29 October 1921, 9am

It was a grand fête day. The gardens surrounding the Exhibition Buildings were already full of booths selling all manner of trinkets, tents with women in bright scarves reading palms, a boxing tent with a line of hopeful and foolish young men outside, and many food carts, of which not a single one was selling ice-cream. In nine hours or so, it would be the venue for the great celebration.

Ambrose and Charlotte approached the entrance of the enormous Exhibition Building, built for the Great Exhibition in 1880 and set in Victorian public gardens with palms and flower beds of annuals separated by wide lawns. The huge building, modelled to some degree on the original Great Exhibition building at Crystal Palace, had become the home of the Victorian Parliament since Federation in 1901—the Federal Parliaments having camped in the Victorian Parliament House until the new capital was built in Canberra. Tonight, it would relive its days of grand political glory as it acted as the venue for the celebration of twenty years of Federation and of Federal Parliament.

For a while, Ambrose and Charlotte merely strolled around the fair like many other young couples. Together and yet separated by uncertainty.

'So, do you think it's definitely in the ice-cream?' asked Charlotte.

'No. But I can't see what else it could be in—and Giuseppe's information about dessert changing despite the chef's wishes suggests something is up. Anyway, let's get in and see what we can see.'

It didn't prove to be too hard to get in—the security was very lax. They lied to the policeman on the door by claiming they were preparing one of the entertainments. They entered the main hall, which was in the final process of being prepared for the dinner. Multiple long trestle tables with hundreds of seats were being put into position. The room—if that was an adequate word to bear the weight of such volume—was a huge cruciform shape. The tables were aligned down the longer east-west axis, while in front of both the east and the west doors, two stages faced each other approximately eighty yards apart, at right angles to the long rows of tables. The painted wooden ceiling towered above them, with a multi-coloured painted Florentine style cupola dome above the intersection of the four wings. The whole interior was ringed by an elevated wide balcony running the whole circumference of the cross-shaped interior. One of the stages—the western one—was obviously for the VIPs, as a number of workmen were labouring to lift some large, heavy wooden tables onto it and about fifty ornate wooden chairs stood by the side. Behind this western stage was a duplicate stage for the orchestra, which blocked the entrance doors. The other stage, near the eastern door, faced the main stage and was obviously for the entertainment.

There was a pile of menus on one of the tables.

'So, what's for dinner, Brosie?' said Charlotte.

Ambrose picked one up.

'They'll have trouble getting through all that,' said Charlotte, looking over his shoulder.

'Obviously the chef favours the old style of service. The *Argus* today said that it's a copy of a menu served at one of the

Oysters on shell

– o –

Potage: Tortue Claire

– o –

Poissons: Saumon Sauce Ravigotte,
Blanchailles

– o –

Entrées: Vol au Vent à la Toulouse,
Cotelettes d'Agneau aux Champignons

– o –

Relêves: Dinde Farcie à la Perigourd,
Jambon d' York, Asperges Glacés

– o –

Rôti: Perdreaux, Grives

– o –

Entremets (Desserts):
fruit, nuts and small sweets.

– o –

Café

celebratory dinners in 1901. They obviously haven't had time to change the dessert to *Pêche Melba* and ice-cream,' said Ambrose.

They followed their noses and headed towards the kitchen, downstairs in the shorter southern arm of the building. They paused just inside the entrance as it was almost impossible to enter. The cavernous kitchens were full of smoke and steam, provisions piled high, chefs in uniform running everywhere with red faces and screaming orders in French. What sounded to be the head chef—the chef from Café Denat—was doing most of the shouting.

'Can you hear all that shouting? Listen!' Ambrose remarked. 'MERDE … IMBÉCILE … MERDE …'

Giuseppe appeared out of a fog of steam like a lost soul escaping Hades. He seemed very agitated. 'Dottore, what are you doing here? I am most concerned … about the *Pêche Melba*,' he shouted above the din. 'I don't know who to tell.'

'Let's get out of here and talk.'

They backed out into the corridor that ran by the kitchen, where the din was slightly less.

'The chef … 'es crazy mad … there ees no time to prepare all the desserts or entremets as 'e calls them. Do you know that they are serving the ice-cream to everyone? I just discovered that Bertolini the Fascisiti has said he will get it. 'e has told all the ice-cream vendors to come tonight and we will serve it from the carts outside the door of the kitchen!'

'That's what we have heard too. But what about the *Pêche Melba*, Giuseppe? What's happened to that?

'The 'igh table will be served with a plate weeth some peaches—canned—and some boats of raspberry sauce. The waiter for the 'igh table—which ees me, Dottore—will serve the ice-cream and pour the sauce, but the ice-cream and Bertolini, Dottore …'

'I know … I know,' said Ambrose. 'We need to think about this.'

It was a beautiful spring day. There was not much more they could do to prepare for whatever it was they would face this evening. By common accord, they turned back to the fête, each of them unknowingly thinking of the other but fearful to make a move that could be rejected.

'Do you think Cam has returned?' asked Charlotte.

'He said he would call me when he'd arrived,' replied Ambrose. 'I am so overwhelmed at the moment, Charlie. I am so fearful of what might happen tonight, but I am even further confused, because at this moment of great danger, I feel as though I can't tell you how much I have fallen in love with you. I know I was foolish before. Can you forgive my prejudice?'

'And you forgive my pride?' she replied as they embraced and kissed long and passionately.

At that moment, a young couple walking down Rathdowne Street, hand in hand, stopped. 'Oi Jessie. Look over there. A posh boy is kissing a Chinese lady. You don't see that often.'

'Shut up, Norman. They're probably in love.'

Chapter Twenty-One
Carrying a Dragon

44 Alfred Crescent, North Fitzroy
Saturday, 29 October 1921, 4pm

All were in attendance for the last briefing before the big event.

'I've received my invitation, so Melba obviously didn't get cold feet, but I'm not sure who will be there from the Australian Protective League,' Ambrose announced, 'and I'm not sure how to be prepared. As we discussed earlier, it seems to me that the only aim of the mad men running this plot is to cause a major disease outbreak amongst the leading politicians and dignitaries, after which they will blame it on Asians and communists. This will create chaos and allow them to stage a *coup d'état* as they have so many people of influence under the same roof. What do you think?'

A babble of voices broke out and Ambrose was forced to raise his arms. 'One at a time. You first, Charlie.'

'There will be over forty Shaolin warriors under the dragon with me. After our performance, we'll spread out and keep an eye on what's happening. I've warned them that there may be trouble, but on no account to create any.'

'You will also have the eyes and arms of everyone in this room. We all will be there; in one way or another, we are all going,' said Pieter.

'Is all the ice-cream laced with cholera, or just that for the high table?' asked Wally, who, after the fight at the football match, had been forbidden by his father to get involved in any of Ambrose's escapades.

'We don't know, so I suggest we stage some distraction before dessert—or entremets as they are called. We can't stop them earlier, because they could have different ways and avenues of delivering the disease. Pieter, can you get a message through to your high-ranking friend in the Federal parliament? He will be there, I assume?'

'Yes, Brosie, both he and I will be there.'

'What if I get to the kettle drums and beat a drum roll at your signal, Brosie?' asked Hedley. 'I'll be in the orchestra. You could warn everyone, and if the ice-cream isn't eaten, it could be tested later.'

'What if some start eating the ice-cream before Hedley's distraction?' asked Paddy.

'Because there are so many entertainments, the toast to the king has been put back to just before the ice-cream course, which means everyone is expected to wait until the toast before they start eating dessert,' replied Ambrose.

'You can count on me too. I'll be with the *plebeians* in the main section, keeping an eye out for possibilities for action,' said Reggie. Plebeian being very loosely defined in the case of this evening. Only the highest of Melbourne society would be attending.

'Very well everyone, I can't think of a better plan, so let's go and keep our eyes open. I'll be on the high table with Melba, so I should be visible to everyone.'

With all in agreement that they were as prepared as they could possibly be for whatever the evening might hold, the friends dispersed, preparing for their respective parts to play in their final plan.

The Exhibition Building, Carlton
29 October 1921, 6.30pm

The best cars money could buy, including a Studebaker Big Six, entered the driveway on Rathdowne Street and slowly navigated the large roundabout in front of the western entrance to the mighty Exhibition Building—temple of progress or a palace to industry, whichever you preferred. In the middle of the roundabout was a giant circular ornate marble fountain surrounded by flowerbeds. It was topped by young marble statues of cupids. Water gushed between serried rows of bright flowers, planted in honour of this special occasion. Unable to ceremonially mount the staircase to the western entrance, as the orchestra stage blocked the way immediately inside, the very important people had to disembark from their grand vehicles and turn left, then right and walk around to the northern entrance. A fair bit of waddling ensued.

Upon entering the hall, the very important people encountered hundreds of less important guests milling about, sipping on champagne and trying to catch elusive waiters for a nibble or two. The orchestra on the western dais behind the elevated high table were belting out some arrangements of well-known folk tunes by Percy Grainger, luckily loud enough to drown the foul language still emanating from the direction of the kitchen in the basement of the southern wing. Grainger was living in the United States and had received a special invitation to the celebration, but refused point-blank to attend when he learned they were playing only his folk-song arrangements. Also, he did not get on well with Nellie Melba. His reply had been quite rude.

Many in the crowd had been annoyed at the heightened security. Numerous uniformed and undercover police patrolled the entrances and searched any sizeable bags before they entered.

'What are we looking out for exactly?' said Reggie to Pieter, both sipping champagne in the crowded foyer.

'Anything suspicious. I'm not sure what they will do when Ambrose pulls his stunt, so we have to be on our toes, also.'

'Should I start a big food fight or something? I don't have any weapons,' Reggie complained. Ever since his first grenade, Reggie had become addicted to things that went *bang*.

'We have enough supporters spread around the venue; we will be fine if they don't have guns. The police are searching for weapons also. Cam's boss is in charge.'

At the same time as the guests were being treated to food, wine, and music, a dazzling diversity of performers were being corralled by exasperated organisers outside the eastern entrance on Nicholson Street, ready to make their entry through the door and onto the stage. A group of Scottish dancers resplendent in kilts with the obligatory gaggle of bagpipes tuned up—if that is what you could call it. Fur-clad Cossack dancers frightened passing children waving sabres, but not as much as a large Chinese dragon with about forty men (and one woman) in black underneath carrying it along. American Indians, or those purporting to be, with tomahawks completed the exotic spectacle. A group of Victorian footballers in club uniforms supported by a few men dressed as umpires and trainers (with McNamara, Paddy, and Wally among them) kicked footballs to each other. With his football contacts, Ambrose had been instrumental in getting Paddy and Wally included in the entertainment. There were music hall entertainers, including jugglers and sword swallowers, and at the rear was a group of skeletons—actually medical students in costumes and masks who had prepared a gruesome song. All the acts regularly proved popular at fetes held in this huge building. It was going to be a grand procession.

The security team had been extra vigilant with the

entertainers, checking that the swords were not real and demanding that weapons of any sort be handed in. The comments that went around the crowd indicated that many surmised the police were expecting some sort of trouble. Many wondered why this would be so.

'Don't forget to keep an eye out for anyone unknown approaching Ambrose. He's been told to stay on the high table so that we can keep an eye on him. The cops are making sure no weapons get into the building, but you never know whether any of them are bent,' Paddy said to Wally. 'It's our job to protect him. Charlotte thinks they might try to kill him.'

7pm

At the beating of the giant gong, all the guests filed into their places. Melba had decided that while her young guest had turned himself out nicely, quite nicely indeed, she really should be sitting next to the Prime Minister. So, she had her name card removed from the place next to Ambrose, who would never have been invited on to the high table without her insistence. This was made abundantly clear to Ambrose by many sitting around him as they studiously ignored him, especially Sir Richard and Lady Butterby—Butterby occasionally stared coldly through him. Hugo was the opposite. He sat at a table just near the stage on which the high table was placed, and he stared at Ambrose constantly—or so Ambrose thought. Taking Melba's lead, Pieter had slipped up to the dais and changed the cards around so that he was sitting next to Ambrose. He also managed to slip a largish bag under the table where they were sitting. Giuseppe had avoided the police with the very obvious ruse of smuggling it into the hall through the kitchen.

Ambrose looked around after sitting down. How could he

possibly pick anyone out if they were towards the back of the crowd? Perspiration dribbled down his starched white dress shirt as he listened to the Premier give a rambling speech introducing the evening; so nervous was he that he took in not a word. His reverie was broken by Giuseppe placing the first course in front of him. He just stared at the food—his normal healthy appetite had deserted him. He toyed with his food until the half-full dish was whipped from under his nose to be replaced immediately with the next course. All seemed a bit of a blur, but he noticed that, under the wide internal veranda that ringed the interior, tables and chairs had been set up for the performers, who were also enjoying refreshments. He could just make out Wally and Paddy, but Charlotte eluded his gaze. Food, drink, and performances followed one another, minus Ambrose's attention as he frantically kept searching the crowd for McBride and his co-conspirators. Finally, the time was approaching for the toast to the king, and then the dessert.

Surely something will happen soon, he thought.

The penultimate exhibition involved the footballers playing out one of their training drills, weaving in and around amongst each other on stage, while passing the ball either by hand or foot, all accompanied by the 'Blue Danube Waltz' by Johannes Strauss.

When asked after the event to describe the entertainment, Ambrose couldn't remember a single act, so nervous was he, eyes darting everywhere trying to pick out any enemies in the crowd.

After the footballers vacated the stage and settled in the alcoves with considerable appetites, the orchestra struck up an arrangement of Mozart's 'Rondo alla Turca', and the Chinese dragon entered with drummers and firecrackers to the great delight of the audience. The director of music didn't have any Chinese music, but he thought Turkey was oriental enough to give the right mood. It was a great success.

The entertainment ended and it was the moment for Dame Nellie Melba to stand and sing her favourite patriotic tune, 'Home Sweet Home'. This would be followed by the royal toast to His Majesty the King.

During the previous two performances, a line of Italian ice-cream vendors with their handcarts had been growing fast along the length of the building, finishing at the entrance to the kitchen. Upon reaching the entrance to the kitchen, the vendors, one by one, scooped the vanilla ice-cream on to trays of dessert plates, which were then being whisked away by waiters to be placed before the guests. As each ice-cream man emptied his cart, he moved off, and the remaining vendors moved forward one place. Ambrose and Pieter became tense as they watched the diners' places being slowly filled up with plates of ice-cream.

'They are beginning to melt,' said Pieter.

'I noticed that. Someone might break protocol and start eating,' Ambrose replied anxiously.

'They must act soon. We must be on full alert,' whispered Pieter. 'They know we are here and must suspect we are on to them or they wouldn't have attacked you at the dinner in Kew. What will they attempt? Where is McBride? I can't see him.'

Their table was to be served last, as obviously someone had sensibly calculated that those served first would most likely end up with a puddle on their plate, and that would not be appropriate for the high table, especially as the dessert was being served in honour of Melba's attendance. On the high table, the plates in front of each diner had canned peaches artfully placed in boats carved from melting ice, with a small jug of raspberry sauce on the side. The ice-cream would be served by Giuseppe when the diva had finished her performance.

Melba stood and the orchestra began playing the long introduction.

Almost as if her performance was a signal, Ambrose noticed shadowy figures appearing at intervals of about twenty yards right around the top floor on the internal veranda. This development seemed ominous.

He poked Pieter and pointed. 'They must be planning a *coup d'état* tonight under the pretence of stopping a revolution.'

Melba's crystal voice soared into the high recesses of the hall:

'Mid pleasures and palaces though we may roam

Be it ever so humble, there's no place like …'

Crash!

All of a sudden there was a disturbance in the orchestra behind Melba, followed by a shout as Hedley pushed the percussionist off the podium, grabbed the sticks, and commenced an extremely loud drumroll.

Melba was transfixed mid-tune.

Ambrose had seen the figures on the balcony come forward at the start of the song, but it was when he observed McBride stepping forward as well that he knew he couldn't wait. McBride was waving a gun! He must have smuggled it in. He had the only weapon in the hall.

Ambrose signalled Hedley to action. As soon as Hedley's drumroll started, Ambrose immediately reached underneath the table and dragged a megaphone from the bag Pieter had hidden.

'Don't eat the ice-cream—it's poison! I repeat, don't eat the ice-cream in front of you.'

Bang!

A shot rang out, and Ambrose dived under the table. McBride stepped up onto the balcony rail, holding one of its slender wrought-iron columns for support, a rowing cox's megaphone strapped to his head. A man with a gun stood beside him.

'Stand up, Pink, or I'll be forced to shoot one of your friends!'

McBride and his henchman pointed their guns at Pieter

sitting next to Ambrose. Pieter couldn't hide under the table, as he was being restrained by four men who had jumped up from behind the stage.

Ambrose stood up, and all around him moved away, leaving him entirely exposed.

'Nobody move, and nobody touch their desserts! This man, Ambrose Pink, is a Bolshevik who has poisoned the ice-cream!'

A gasp rose from the diners.

'I am Dr McBride from the Australian Protective League. We are patriots dedicated to the health of this great young nation. We have discovered a plot by communists led by this man. Make no mistake, their goal is revolution! For too long, the government has allowed Bolsheviks and their fellow travellers the freedom to poison our society with their words. Now, they intend to literally poison the best among us, who are gathered here tonight! We have proof that they have introduced cholera into the ice-cream in their attempt to destroy the foundations of our great civilisation. They are targeting its most prominent members. Ambrose Pink made it at the dairy at the Kew Asylum. And our government, those who should have protected us from this menace, have been too weak to act! Most of you have nothing to fear from us—just remain seated.'

Out of the corner of his eye, Ambrose noticed movement under the balconies in the dark as figures moved silently up the stairs. He was really going to die this time. He felt sick.

*****

At this moment, two young men were about to intervene in history. Unknown to Ambrose, young Will was hiding in an alcove on the veranda, about twenty paces behind McBride, trusty slingshot in hand with a good supply of stones. He had overheard their plans and, with all the wiles of his previous education on the street, had planted himself there with a good stash of food.

The second coincidence involved young Wally Koochew. He was below at the entertainers' tables, as he had been in the football exhibition, and he was sizing up his options. He wasn't about to see Ambrose shot. He was a superb kick of the football, and he had one in his hands. He was under the balcony on which McBride was standing, and he could just see where McBride was positioned, about eight yards vertically and twenty-five yards along.

It is worth a try, even if it just distracts him, he thought.

He took aim, took a few steps, and the sound of boot on leather filled the stunned silence. Seemingly in slow motion, the ball went up and out into the hall, turning over and over on its end, and then, as if by magic, it began to boomerang back in an arch towards McBride.

Ambrose, mouth open in astonishment and admiration, could only say, 'It's a boomerang punt … a banana!'

The crowd gasped and, at the last moment, McBride realised the ball was heading towards him. He turned and was almost hit in the face. He wobbled to avoid it, but slipped on the handrail and tried to regain his balance, dropping his pistol to the floor below. Wally rushed over and grabbed it. McBride's offsider turned to aim his gun at Wally and young Will, invisible in the shadows behind him, took his chance and unleashed a stone, which struck the gunman on the back of the head. He fell forward and dropped his gun as he fell.

As if released from a daze, the crowd now went wild. Melba and the other dignitaries were ushered hurriedly from the platform. Guests scrambled for the doors as best they could while fights broke out all along the upper balcony as Shaolin warriors, footballers, Indians, Scottish dancers, skeletons, and Cossacks jumped the militia men and battled for control of the balcony. A few of McBride's followers planted amongst the diners also jumped up, but van Haandel, after dealing with his assailants with the help of Ambrose, was soon amongst them creating chaos. Reggie did his best as well, only occasionally muttering the word 'grenades' when he paused for breath.

Chaos engulfed the hall as guests turned against each other until Detective Inspector McLeish entered from the northern entrance of a hall with a large band of police who immediately fanned out across the hall. He stood on the performers' stage and fired a shot in the air.

'Police! Everyone, stay still!'

The situation was under control within a surprisingly short amount of time.

Ambrose hurried to meet Charlotte as she emerged down the stairs from the balcony. Pale and obviously shaken, Ambrose took Charlotte into his arms, and she kissed him for what seemed a very long time.

'I say, you two, give up,' said Reggie, who had appeared at their side with a grin from ear to ear. 'You're leaving us to hunt for the others. We can't find McBride, Hugo, or Negrone, and Hedley said he saw Butterby and his missus hurrying out the side door.'

McLeish came up to the group. 'Leave this to me, you lot. Go off and get over your ordeal and we will speak very soon about what happens next.'

Satisfied that McLeish had things in hand, Ambrose drew Charlotte under his arm and guided her from the hall, both of them ignoring the melted ice-cream that dripped and pooled around them.

Chapter Twenty-Two
Laid to Rest

96 St Vincent's Place, South Melbourne
Sunday, 30 October 1921, Noon

Ambrose drove the Riley through town to South Melbourne and the grand residential enclave of St Vincent's Place. He parked, walked through the gate of number 96, and knocked on the door of the large, double-storied terrace house. It was answered by a diminutive Chinese woman of late middle age, neatly dressed in a Chinese silk dress, with her greying hair tied tightly back.

'Come in, Dr Pink, please come in. I am so pleased to meet you at last. Charlotte has told me a great deal about you. Come in.'

She led Ambrose into the front room that was decorated in the Chinese style, with calligraphy and ink paintings framed on the wall and black and red lacquered furniture. Some fine porcelain graced the shelves and tables.

'I am delighted to meet you, Mrs Nomchong. You must be very proud of your niece.'

'I am, Dr Pink, but it is very difficult for her. Not only has she chosen a career normally not open to women, but also being Chinese is a considerable burden. She is strong-willed—I only hope her future prospects are not damaged by her willingness to test the boundaries of propriety. I know standards of behaviour for young women are changing, but it is still possible to make mistakes. We are all concerned about the risks she takes. I sometimes think that I am too liberal.'

'And I think you are too strict, Auntie.' Charlotte entered the room laughing. She gave her aunt a hug as she left the room. She approached Ambrose, and they kissed once they were alone.

'What's the outcome of last night's discussion, Brosie? I'm sorry but I was just too exhausted to stay late.'

'Everyone split up early. We are to meet in an hour, and I have come to collect you for the meeting in Fitzroy. Hop in the car.'

North Fitzroy
Sunday, 30 October 1921, 1pm

Reggie stood before the gathered clan in the sitting room. All were seated post lunch with coffee or tea.

'Well, I think I worked it all out after you left last night. I think they were planning to poison the food at the dinner, or perhaps just release the disease and think of a way of using it to their political advantage, but when Ambrose announced that Iris had cholera, they had to improvise or abandon their plans altogether. One of their problems was that they weren't at all disciplined or in agreement about strategy, and so McBride went off on his own little adventure, which infuriated Hugo. So probably some of what happened has to be ascribed to incompetence. McBride initially wanted to get Ambrose on their side while, at the same time, Hugo wanted to get rid of him.'

'Hence the shouting I heard in Hugo's office and the invitation to the meeting followed by the attempt on my life,' Ambrose interjected.

'Exactly,' exclaimed Pieter.

Reggie raised his hand and continued. 'Butterby, on the other hand, wanted to encourage his co-conspirators to produce some sort of outrage, while being exceptionally careful that he left no evidence of his involvement, while the Negrones' and the fascists' representative, Bertolini, just wanted to sow discord and gain a foothold. His brother was the backroom person running the asylum—involved and supportive but not central. Basically, McBride and Hugo went out on a limb but couldn't work together until right at the end. They knew that when their cholera plot had been discovered, the best plan was to try to pin it on Ambrose.'

Hedley interjected, 'Brosie lived and worked in a working-class suburb, and they managed to get a copy of his signature and forge a document that seemed to be a rental agreement for the dairy. McLeish went to the dairy this morning and found it locked away. If Ambrose was dead, then they could frame him as he couldn't defend himself. McLeish also found a typed manifesto that they would have claimed was written by Ambrose.'

'But why would you announce you had found cholera in a child if you were introducing it to the country?' remarked Charlotte.

Ambrose replied, 'According to their plan, that would be understood as me attempting to look like I was innocent. I would pretend I was exposing the plot knowing no one would believe me as it seemed so outrageous. All they had to do was say I had no evidence and was just a junior general practitioner, and then I would be innocent when cholera killed many of the worthies at the dinner and Bolshevik leaders hopefully would have started a revolution.'

'So if McBride shot you at the dinner, he would look like he had foiled your plot after producing the forged documents. If they killed you earlier, they would have let the crowd eat the ice-cream and produce the evidence against you later,' Charlotte continued.

'Exactly. I got some other good news so hop in the car and I'll tell you.'

Ambrose and Charlotte left the others and drove to Faraday

Street where they picked up Kathleen and Ruby, and then proceeded to the Kew Asylum.

'I've been busy this morning and got the necessary signatures to have Flora released. Then we are going to have a little ceremony by the Yarra to remember poor Iris and the little girl who replaced her in the morgue.'

'I'm so excited about having Flora again,' said Kathleen in the back seat.

They all piled into the car at Kew, having arranged Flora's release and collecting her few positions. They took her down to celebrate her freedom at a boathouse serving lunch, after which they stood together and said a few prayers for the two babies. Tears were shed.

Ambrose and Charlotte left the family clan happily chatting on the grass and walked down through the gardens on the riverbank.

'You know, I feel less and less Australian, Brosie. We are made to feel like foreigners even when we are citizens. My uncle has a photograph on his wall of the march organised by the Chinese down Swanston Street in 1901 to celebrate Federation. We were more part of this country then.'

'Charlie, you see that group of Magnolias down near the riverbank? They were introduced here and are one of the most loved plants in European gardens all over the British Empire. Do you know where they come from?'

'Yes, Asia.'

'Times are difficult, but you and I mustn't give up. Action can always make situations better, especially if it is sustained and intelligent.'

They spent the afternoon walking along the river and then drove the O'Donohues home to Carlton.

Finally, Charlotte spoke. 'I'm always worried about what will happen to my family and friends in the Chinese community. I know I have done things that I now regret, but I sometimes can see no way forward.'

'Let's go and get dinner. We have an important meeting tomorrow, and I have some unfinished business in the Anatomy Department at the medical school as well. We can discuss your troubles over some good tucker.'

Outside the offices of the Prime Minister
Spring Street, Melbourne
Monday, 31 October 1921, 10am

'The Prime Minister will see you now,' a man announced as he opened the door and ushered Charlotte, Ambrose, and Pieter into a large office with an enormous desk. Behind the desk sat William 'Billy' Hughes, and above was the coat of arms of the Commonwealth of Australia.

'Welcome, welcome.' The Prime Minister enthusiastically greeted them, nodding his head while circling around the desk to shake each by the hand. 'Let's sit down ... terrible business ... the nation owes you a debt of gratitude ... which of course will never be publicly acknowledged ... you understand, of course?'

'Of course,' replied Ambrose. 'What will be the consequences of all this, Prime Minister?'

'Waterhouse Island is off limits for the moment, but the poor captive Chinese are being taken home to Java. Apparently, they were collecting their ... (he looked a little embarrassed) ... doings, so to speak, and using them to manufacture a good supply of bacteria. The dairy has been closed down, but Bertolini says he rented it out and, as we have no evidence against him, we can't do much. Unfortunately, McLeish broke so many rules that he has been put on leave with pay, and an investigation will take place ... not public, of course. As a favour to you, I have arranged that the members of the inquiry committee know the details. It won't be pleasant for him, and you may have lost a friend, but he will come out all right in the end.'

'I was attacked in Fitzroy and then again in Little Lonsdale Street by members of the League. What is to be done?' asked Ambrose.

'The problem is that the Australian Protective League,' replied the Prime Minister, 'which is a fine organisation, I must say ... lots of good people in it ... had in its midst some bad eggs, but the bad eggs are gone now ... locked up a few of those men bearing arms at the Exhibition building ... could only charge them with public nuisance offences in a public place it seems. McBride is a bit more of a tricky case. He's out on bail and has hired the best legal advice around. I've been told that he's going to plead that it was all due to the drink and a bit of an over-reaction ... and that he knew nothing of the island, the Chinese, and the cholera. He has a good chance of getting off, what with his powerful friends and his position in society and the Australian Protective League. As for the "brothel" as you call it, it seems the office at the back was known only to a few of McBride's close associates. It's been closed down. The membership of the League knew nothing about it ... or McBride's degeneracy. I am appalled!'

It certainly sounded like people had been working hard behind the scenes in the last few days. He obviously didn't know Ambrose attended the meeting in Kew at which he was present. The look given between the three guests indicated that it was a theory they all shared.

'Nothing will appear in any of the newspapers about the fuss on Saturday night. I've made that clear to the editors of the press, and even the Leftist newspapers will be quiet as they are scared of being connected with any suggestion of a *coup d'état*.'

'What about Butterby, Hugo, Hamon and Bertolini, and the Negrone brothers?' asked Pieter.

The Prime Minister looked uncertain and didn't look them in the eye. 'Butterby has made a magnificent contribution to this country … he assures me he knew nothing about all this illegal behaviour. I do believe, however, that he may be going on extended leave and taking a trip back home. There is nothing to be done about Dr Silvio Negrone as there is no evidence that he did any wrong. The fate of the babies cannot be ascribed to him, and we have no evidence of any cholera in the O'Donohue baby as it has disappeared. Hugo, Bertolini, and Salvatore Negrone have gone missing … we think they may be being hidden by extremists and will attempt to leave the country. We're looking for Cornelius Hamon too.'

Charlotte interjected. 'Young Flora O'Donohue was kept in that institution because her mother was in there, not because she deserved to be. Then evil men gain access to the asylum and abuse the innocent girls. This makes them even more traumatised and so gives their abusers proof that the women need to be kept in the institution. It's a vicious circle of abuse that is almost impossible to break unless you take some action. Flora and the others can't testify against powerful men in a courtroom—you know that well, Prime Minister. She has been tested by the most up-to-date tests at the university and is above average intelligence. What are you going to do about that?'

'I am truly disturbed by what you say, but it is a State matter, not a Commonwealth matter as laid out in the Constitution. I will speak to the Premier.'

The Prime Minister stood up, making it clear that the interview was finished.

'As a gesture, in consideration for the wonderful work you have done for this country—not to be declared publicly, of course, your names have been recorded and will be looked on favourably in the future. I believe there were two other gentlemen who should be thanked who are not present today. Their names have also been noted.'

He escorted them to the door, and they departed.

'Wow!' Charlotte said as they drove back to Fitzroy. 'No one is ever going to know about this at all. It's all been hushed up. If there is a cholera outbreak, however ...'

The dissection theatre
Medical school, Swanston St
2pm

Ambrose was looking for something. After a little research, he had ascertained that the dissection theatre would be empty that afternoon. It wasn't unusual for him, as a post-graduate surgery student, to be in the gruesome place amongst the partially dissected cadavers spread out on the twenty or so tables. The room smelled primarily of formaldehyde, although the scent of rotting flesh did seem to come through. He was looking through the assorted boxes of bones and skulls placed on the shelves along the walls. No luck, as he had half expected. He quickly moved to the locked back door and opened it, à la Paddy Murphy, and entered the room beyond. In it were filing cabinets and more archive boxes, which he knew held the Butterby collection—assorted remains of individuals of interest to anthropologists. Aboriginal remains predominated, but Ambrose knew and could see on the labels on the ends of the boxes that they had arrived from all over the world. He moved to the box labelled 'Cohuna' and opened it—it contained no skulls, just assorted limb bones. He moved across to the wooden filing cabinets, opened the drawer with the 'C's, and found the corresponding file marked 'Cohuna'. In it he found a handful of sheets in his father's hand. He placed them in a briefcase he had brought for the purpose.

'What do you think you are doing, Pink?'

He turned to face Butterby. 'Just collecting my father's belongings. I have the notes—now where are the skulls?'

For the first time Ambrose could see uncertainty in Butterby's eyes.

'I don't know what you're talking about. You have no right to be here or to take those notes.'

'You are in no position to threaten me *Sir* Richard. You are on shaky ground, and I have more information about your relationship with the asylum that could make things even worse for you. You were behind the cholera business. McBride was merely your willing puppet. I want the skulls!'

Butterby became momentarily flustered when faced with Ambrose's aggression. He wasn't used to juniors standing up to him. He quickly regained his composure, however.

'You have no evidence of anything. You are as foolish as Hugo and McBride. What you don't understand, Pink, is that it isn't violent revolutions or a cholera outbreak that change or mould societies—rather it is ideas. I preach my message about the superiority of the White Race in all ways possible. In the press, in public lectures, in my teaching at the university—even in films and public slide shows. I don't want mere objects spoiling my message, and so I destroyed the skulls.'

'Why did you destroy them?' Ambrose asked angrily. 'They weren't yours to destroy!'

'Because certain anatomists have recently been arguing that the native population are what they are because they represent a perfect expression of their environment. The young anatomy professor in Adelaide is recruiting young minds to *undermine* the truth that white man has, and always will be, superior. And I know that we are superior—not because of a benevolent European environment in which we evolved, but because we were superior from the earliest times when we separated from the inferior races.

'The German anthropologists I have met and whose work I read are better—they understand what I mean: the English are becoming weak minded. I will admit that some of the coloured races are clever enough. That is why we must exclude them from this continent and breed a true super white race—better than even the English. Then the future will be ours!'

Ambrose stared at Butterby. 'I'm keeping these papers! Your extremist views are unpalatable to me.'

This time Ambrose pushed past Butterby and headed out of the building and into the car with the others waiting.

'Did you find what you wanted?' Charlotte asked as they drove off.

'Only half. He stole at least two skulls from my father's collection, and I hoped I could find them. I did find the notes that went with them.'

'How could you recognise the skulls as your father's if you found them?'

'That would not be a problem,' interjected Pieter. 'You know, don't you, Brosie?'

Ambrose nodded.

'He always used indelible ink to mark his bones with a very small catalogue number somewhere that is hard to see. It's easy to recognise if you know you are looking for it and you have his notes also—is that not true, Brosie?'

'Yes, the Java skull I have has the mark recorded in his notes. I now have the numbers in his notes for the Cohuna skulls but no skulls. How infuriating!'

'Why did he destroy them?' asked Charlotte.

'He claimed that he doesn't want any evidence of evolution within the so-called 'inferior' races. It suggests change and the moulding effects of environment, and he wants the whites on top forever, as a matter of principle unrelated to outside influences. For him, whites are virtually a separate species. It's all part of the right-wing agenda.'

'You have made powerful enemies in Butterby, McBride, Hugo, and the Negrones, Brosie,' remarked Pieter.

Charlotte slapped Pieter on the shoulder. 'Forget them. Let's go and buy those tickets to the show at Her Majesty's next Thursday night. I want Pieter to see Mo Rene before he leaves for Holland next Saturday. He may not understand all of the humour in the show, but it's a Melbourne institution that needs to be paid homage to at least once.'

CHAPTER TWENTY-THREE
EXIT, PURSUED BY A BEAR

Her Majesty's Theatre, Exhibition Street
Thursday, 3 November 1921, 7pm

'I attended the farewell lecture given by Butterby today … told the assembled crowd that he'll be back in Melbourne one day but is going for a long stint in Britain,' said Ambrose.

'I wonder if he's on the ship you are on this Saturday, Pieter,' said Charlotte. 'If he was, it would be rather Shakespearean.'

'Why?' asked Ambrose.

'Exit, pursued by a bear.'

They all laughed uproariously as they sat in the front row of the first tier of seats in the theatre waiting for the curtain to rise.

'Now that you have all three sets of notes but only one skull, what will happen?' asked Charlotte.

'I'm not sure, but Butterby alluded to them in his lecture today and said that his main purpose in going to London was to pursue "important research on such matters", while looking at me the whole time. Only time will tell, but they are obviously part of his larger plan.'

The show was full of light-hearted entertainment, mainly comic acts interspersed with songs from operetta sung by that versatile tenor from Bendigo, Cyril Warne.

The main act, 'Stiffy and Mo', appeared after interval and was as 'blue' as Ambrose had ever heard, and had the audience in stiches, especially Pieter. As their final act, they put on some sketches that were spoofs of Shakespearean plays, the final play being *Hamlet*. Mo was dressed as Hamlet and Stiffy as the listening Ophelia.

Mo pulled a skull out of the bag next to him and declared: 'To be, or not to be—zat is za question!'

'Make up yer mind, luvy,' cried Ophelia. 'Strewth … is that yer mum?' She pointed at the skull. The crowd roared.

Ambrose grabbed Pieter and Charlotte both and pulled them up. 'Follow me,' he said, moving as fast as he could, pushing past the complaining audience.

'Follow me,' he repeated as he ran up the aisle, down the stairs, and out the front, waiting for the other two to catch up. Silencing their anticipated questions, he waved them to follow as he ran around the side and to the stage entrance. A fiver got him in until eventually he was standing with his puffing friends outside the star's door.

'Whadda yer want?' Mo asked as he arrived, carrying his props, the applause slowly dying down in the background.

'A word,' said Ambrose, and he whispered in the star's ear.

'Just you then,' Mo said as he opened the door, and they entered, leaving Charlotte and Pieter outside.

They waited some time before Ambrose came out.

'Well?' said Charlotte, 'what was all that about?'

'I was mistaken, but he has given me a lead to go on. I'll tell you all about it when I have followed up his suggestion.'

Flinders Lane, Melbourne
Friday, 4 November 1921, 10am

Ambrose paced up and down the footpath outside the large red brick building under the cantilevered sign swinging and creaking in the wind, which read 'Berry's Collectables and Second-hand Goods: Est. 1860'.

'When will they open?' Ambrose interrogated Reggie, as it was a place he frequently visited.

Reggie either ignored his remark, or more likely didn't hear him, as he was gazing intently in the large front window, which was stuffed higgledy-piggledy with treasures.

'Why are you looking at all that junk?' Ambrose asked rather pointedly.

'Eye of the beholder, my friend, eye of the beholder. Never know what might turn up,' replied Reggie.

They were disturbed by the sound of a bolt being drawn and slowly the door was opened by a tall cadaverous man. Ambrose entered behind Reggie.

'Good day, Dr Robinson, delighted to see you,' remarked the man, who no doubt could see a good sale coming early.

'I brought my friend, Mr Berry. He's interested in your memento mori,' said Reggie.

'What sort, young man?' said a white-haired elderly lady who appeared from behind one of the many piles of furniture. 'We have paintings, statues, trinkets ...'

'Good morning, Mrs Berry,' said Reggie.

She smiled and nodded.

'It's skulls I'm looking for,' Ambrose interrupted.

'What sort? We have plain skulls, native skulls, decorated specimens from the Pacific and French medical teaching skulls with wax additions. Follow me to our special room, please.'

They walked through the treasure trove to a room at the back of the building. Ambrose often had to grab hold of Reggie, who was easily distracted. The old lady unlocked the door.

The memento mori room was quite some place.

'I don't think this is going to cure anyone's depression,

dear boy,' Reggie remarked, staring wide-eyed at the grotesque collection of items grouped together, and all because of one theme: death. There were shrunken heads, death masks, bones of all sorts, small shrines dedicated to all manner of deities and departed relatives, and even mummified cats and ibises, but by far the most grotesque were the shelves and shelves filled with skulls of an infinite variety of species (mainly human) of all sorts and sizes, many of them decorated.

'We have more in the cupboards out back if you wish to look, young gentlemen,' remarked Mrs Berry. 'I'll leave you alone, as Dr Robinson is one of our best customers.' She exited the room at the sound of the front doorbell.

'I draw the line at buying this stuff, Brosie. Remind me, why are we here?'

'We're looking for my father's Cohuna skulls. Unadorned, old, and with some catalogue number inside is what we need to find. One of them should have large brows and a proportionally smaller skull size than a modern skull. The other perhaps will look more modern.'

'Physical anthropology 101, I get it,' replied Reggie.

Sometime later they could be seen walking down Flinders Lane looking in the windows of cafes, obviously craving refreshments, a brown paper parcel under Ambrose's arm.

44 Alfred Crescent, North Fitzroy

7pm

It was a grand night for a grand farewell dinner, and Mrs Simpson had been cooking up a storm for days.

The meal had begun with numerous delicious hors d'oeuvres and then, by special request, Mrs Simpson's delicious oyster soup, followed by devilled kidneys with unctuous port wine gravy ordered by Paddy. This was then followed by *Sole Normande*. Pieter had specially instructed Mrs Simpson in the making of this dish, most particularly in the making of the velouté sauce, to which were added mushrooms, butter, egg yolks, and cream. Reggie said it was 'very nice'. Then, also by special request, was *canard a l'orange*—many ducks had been purchased, such was the appetite of some of the guests. It was some business roasting them all, as well as the vegetables to go with them, but the Favaloros lived nearby and some ducks were chauffeured in the Riley, roasted, from their oven to be finished off at the appropriate moment by Giuseppe and Maria.

Finally, Mrs Simpson had decided to make Peach Melba (not *Pêche Melba*), which had everyone very amused, although she didn't use vanilla ice-cream, but rather vanilla custard and home-made raspberry preserve, as raspberries weren't in season either. Ambrose had brought out yet more of his best wines and, over dessert, they drank his best Seppeltsfield 1910 tawny port.

'Ambrose, the waiting is over—what happened last night at the theatre?' said Hedley. 'Charlotte and Pieter have left us on tenterhooks with their incomplete tale.'

'Very well, everyone. I was sitting there when all of a sudden I looked hard at the skull Mo had in his hand—it didn't look modern. It looked a lot like the Java skull my father had left me, which is ancient and has much larger brows above the eye-sockets than a modern skull. It didn't have my father's mark inside, but Mo told me that he had purchased it from Berry's in Flinders Lane and that they had quite a few.'

'Quite a few … that's a bit of an understatement,' remarked Reggie.

'Shut it, Reggie,' said Hedley.

Ignoring the bickering, Ambrose continued. 'Reggie and I then went to Berry's this morning to see what we could find.'

Reggie stuck his tongue out at Hedley. 'Some reminded me of you.'

'After combing through all the skulls,' said Ambrose, 'we found one with the catalogue entry of one of my father's Cohuna skulls written inside in a hard-to-find spot. It was one of the missing skulls, but it wasn't quite what I expected in a number of ways.'

'Why?' asked Charlotte.

'First, Reggie asked where the skull had come from. Mrs Berry told us confidentially with a little badgering, and a cash gift, that she bought this skull, along with lots of material regularly, from Cornelius Hamon, Butterby's assistant. Apparently, he usually sent a young messenger to conduct the transactions—a girl called Issy. Mrs Berry said she hadn't seen her for a while. I don't imagine Butterby knows about this. I can't imagine he would want this skull to turn up.'

'Why would that be?' asked Pieter.

'The skull doesn't fit in with Butterby's racist theories at all because it isn't "robust"—it doesn't have the heavy brows and disproportionately small brain case. It's what the anthropologists call "gracile". Although it was stained with the minerals of the Cohuna soil as well as it being heavier than a recent skull—both indications of great age—it looks a bit like a modern skull. According to the notes my father made, it was found in layers that can be dated to the Pleistocene, which is also the period of the "robust" skull from Java … any time from about twelve thousand to two and a half million years ago. When I read his notes more carefully, I realised that the two skulls from Cohuna for which I had his notes were, in fact, different—different species of human, if you like. What does it all mean?'

'It means that modern human anatomical humans existed in Australia in the Pleistocene, also. That would mess up Butterby's theories about Aboriginal Australians being primitive types from the earliest times, wouldn't it?' said Pieter.

'It certainly complicates things,' said Charlotte. 'Clearly, Mr Hamon has been moonlighting to earn a bit of extra cash. Butterby won't know about its existence. But what about the other skull he claimed to have destroyed?'

'I have no proof,' answered Ambrose, 'but I would bet a tenner that he is taking the robust Cohuna skull to England as part of his plan to denigrate the Aboriginals and elevate the so-called "white race".'

'I don't think we have heard the last of it yet, also,' said Pieter.

'Two other matters came up at Berry's,' Ambrose remarked. 'Mrs Berry wondered if we were interested in other things Hamon brought in. There were two items of interest. She opened a box with various trinkets and other personal belongings that he had sold to her. Amongst them was a cheap necklace with a lock of hair encased in glass and inscribed: "Isobel" on the back. I haven't plucked up the courage to show it to young Will yet.'

'Do you think that is young Will's sister?' remarked Reggie. 'And could that be our specimen of the pregnant girl in the anatomy museum?'

Ambrose nodded. Everyone looked gloomy.

'There's no way that I am going to let this pass,' exclaimed Ambrose. 'I won't rest until I find her killer!'

'The other object she showed us was a large tusk, which she said was a Diprotodon tooth from the Pleistocene age. She said Hamon collected such teeth for Butterby and sold her any others he could find.'

'They're useful for dating other anthropological finds—extinct, of course.'

The evening drew to a close far too soon for Ambrose, and he managed to draw Charlotte aside from the others as they left.

'We've had a great adventure, Charlie. Can I see you again lots, even though I have no excitement to offer in the immediate future? We could go for a walk, and I could trip up, and you could catch me—that's one way to save me again.'

Charlotte laughed and kissed him gently on the lips. 'There is no way you can keep me from your arms … but my aunt will need to be happy with any arrangements. I wish I could have stopped myself falling in love with you, as I can see all the impediments my family will raise against our liaison. Some you know nothing about. I do not want to have you caught up in all the trouble, Brose … my love.'

'I am prepared for anything that means I can keep you close to me, Charlie.'

They kissed passionately, then she hopped into her car and drove off.

Molly whined a little.

'You miss her already too, Mol.'

Chapter Twenty-four
Sweet Sorrow

96 St Vincent's Place, South Melbourne
Friday, 25 November 1921, 6pm

Ambrose was seated in one of the lacquered chairs with a cocktail in hand.

'When are you going to tell me the news?' Charlotte was sitting opposite, and the sounds and smells of a meal being prepared could be discerned coming from the back of the house—exotic smells, it must be said.

'All right, I shouldn't keep you on tenterhooks anymore. That conservative State Attorney-General Arthur Robinson—or Sir Arthur, I believe—rang me yesterday with a proposal. I don't think he was too keen, but it seemed like his arm was being bent in every conceivable way. I have been asked if I would consider the Coroner's job when Cole retires next year.'

'Congratulations, Brosie!' She jumped up and leant down and gave him a big kiss on the cheek. Ambrose beamed. Charlotte continued, 'It seems like Pieter and the others and I have missed out so far.'

'I'm not so sure. You see, I was also asked about how I saw the position, and I remarked that I thought it was time a full-time legally qualified deputy was appointed, and I suggested you. I hope you don't mind?'

'I'm very surprised. And I'm torn, Brosie—torn between the excitement of the possibility, but I also don't really want to be your deputy. I want to strike out on my own, be my own boss.'

'I understand, but you would really be your own boss as you would be the senior legal officer in the Coroner's office.'

At that moment, Mrs Nomchong entered the room. 'Dr Pink, Charlotte … the other guests have just arrived and the cook is ready to start serving. Charlotte assures me that you are a gourmet and would enjoy eating a traditional Chinese banquet. So we thought it would be a good way to introduce you to other members of the family. Please come through. I believe the men have brought an ample number of bottles of cognac to accompany the meal, Dr Pink. I hope you enjoy cognac.'

'I'm greatly looking forward to the meal, the cognac, and most of all, meeting Charlie's family,' said Ambrose—and he meant it. As he stood, he remarked, 'I can't help noticing the impressive number of white elephants you have displayed in this room, Mrs Nomchong.'

'They are nothing,' said Charlotte, looking anxious, 'just something that my cousin in Bangkok likes to send.'

Charlotte's aunt looked quite cross.

As they went to leave the room, Charlotte said to Ambrose, 'There is also the possibility that some of my illegal activities could surface. I shouldn't be associated with you in any way—it could ruin you. Oh, I forgot, I received a letter from my good friend Hli in Bangkok. I'm a little worried by it and would love you to have a look at it later.'

Mrs Nomchong held Ambrose back as Charlotte left the room. She seemed distracted.

'This will be a chance for you to say farewell to Charlotte, Dr Pink. The family both in Melbourne and Bangkok have decided that she is in too much danger in Melbourne and is out of control. There also is some unfinished business we need to attend to in Siam. She and I are leaving to stay with family in the Chinese community in Bangkok. She will be gone indefinitely.'

Endings and beginnings
44 Alfred Crescent, North Fitzroy
25 November 1921, Midnight

Ambrose had sat through the sumptuous dinner in a state of shock, not sure that his conversation made any sense at all. He noticed that Charlotte surreptitiously looked his way a number of times from where she had been seated down the table, a slight frown on her face. It occurred to him that he was probably not making the best impression on his hosts, but if her aunt had spoken the truth, it seemed any impression he made on them was irrelevant in any case.

After sitting through the meal, Ambrose finally excused himself.

'What on earth is wrong?' Charlotte had whispered as she farewelled him, but he had been able to do nothing more than give her an anguished look before Mrs Nomchong, polite and serene as if she hadn't just upended his world, showed him to the door.

Now he sat in his living room, head in his hands. He had been drinking steadily through the evening and his thoughts were in a jumble. He had a bottle of scotch next to his side and hoped it would be enough to get him through the rest of the night.

Then the doorbell rang. Molly barked happily at the door—it was someone she knew. He strode to the door and opened it. Charlotte stood outside on the doorstep. She burst into tears.

'My family are banishing me to Bangkok. I'm so unhappy.'

'So am I. Charlie, please come in.'

She stepped through the door and straight into his arms.

'It will not happen. I will not let it happen,' Ambrose whispered into Charlotte's ear.

'You promise?' said Charlotte.

'I promise,' Ambrose replied.

Postscript

Port Melbourne, the docks
Saturday, 5 November 1921, 5pm

Professor Butterby walked up the gangplank of *HMS Minotaur*, followed by a small group of grunting porters struggling with all his luggage. He marched along the deck carrying a rather large travel bag made of the best leather, with a small padlock attached to the catch and strap. He had been most particular in keeping the bag separate from the others, and when one of the porters had picked it up, he had barked at him to put it down. He then quickly snatched it back. After tipping the porters, he settled into his commodious cabin and locked the door.

He went to his special bag, unlocked and opened it. After removing layers of protective cloth, he placed on his desk a heavy skull with pronounced brows and beside it a large curved tusk, at least a foot long. He stared at them for some time, finally muttering, 'You will make me the greatest anthropologist and race scientist of my age' as he placed them back in the bag.

To be continued

For the historical background to this story
https://www.rossjones.com.au

ACKNOWLEDGEMENTS

Susan Kenny, Australian Writers Centre, Lisa O'Sullivan, Kathryn Barton, Jayne Gregory, John van Handel, Cecily Hunter, Derek Jones, Paul Jones, Coralie Kenny, Virginia Lloyd, Rohan Long, Jenny Osborne, Silvio Pontonio, Emma Schwarcz, Connie Spanos, Graeme Uren, Franco Urlini, and my wonderful editors, Cerid Jones and Michelle Lovi.

www.ingramcontent.com/pod-product-compliance
Lightning Source LLC
Chambersburg PA
CBHW030620120726

47904CB00006B/1967